Images of Dorie raced into his head again. Sexy, vivid, alluring images that Shane couldn't block out.

He breathed a heavy sigh and turned his back on her, bracing his elbows against the fence. "You tempt me, Dorie. Making me think of things I got no right thinking."

"Do I?" she asked softly.

Shane felt her presence directly behind him, her flowery scent lingering in the air. He turned to find her eyes on him. "You know you do."

Dorie graced him with a slight smile. "I don't know any such thing. You continue to confuse me, Shane."

"Well, at least we have that in common."

* * *

Abducted at the Altar
Harlequin® Historical #816—September 2006

Praise for Charlene Sands

Renegade Wife

"This delightful story features two headstrong, stubborn people fighting for and against each other. The result is a tender story."
—*Romantic Times BOOKclub*

"…such a refreshing heartfelt love story to read. For a Western romance that will leave you smiling, be sure to read *Renegade Wife*."
—*Romance Reviews Today*

The Courting of Widow Shaw

"A highly romantic tale, *The Courting of Widow Shaw* delivers a satisfying ending that proves love can overcome any past."
—*Romantic Times BOOKclub*

Chase Wheeler's Woman

"This story is enticing, enchanting, totally enthralling from the first page to last. It's one of the best historical romances around. Ms. Sands has captured the human spirit, the human heart and added a sense of humor and a sense of adventure between the pages of one glorious book."
—*Old Book Barn Gazette*

CHARLENE SANDS

Abducted at the Altar

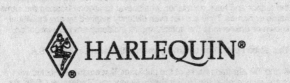

HARLEQUIN®

TORONTO • NEW YORK • LONDON
AMSTERDAM • PARIS • SYDNEY • HAMBURG
STOCKHOLM • ATHENS • TOKYO • MILAN • MADRID
PRAGUE • WARSAW • BUDAPEST • AUCKLAND

ISBN-13: 978-0-373-29416-9
ISBN-10:   0-373-29416-6

ABDUCTED AT THE ALTAR

**DON'T MISS THESE OTHER
NOVELS AVAILABLE NOW:**

Please address questions and book requests to:
Harlequin Reader Service
U.S.: 3010 Walden Ave., P.O. Box 1325, Buffalo, NY 14269
Canadian: P.O. Box 609, Fort Erie, Ont. L2A 5X3

This book is dedicated to my cul-de-sac neighbors and dear friends who have become more like family. To Deedra and Brian Williams and little Wes, Suellen and Christer Martensson, and Bea and George (aka My Honey and Me) Casparian. Thanks for your unwavering support and friendship. You are all in my heart!

Chapter One

Dorie McCabe stood at the back of the First Unity Church of God, out of sight of the invited guests, and held her breath for one moment, staring at Shane Graham up there at the altar ready to speak his vows. He was the most appealing man she'd ever laid eyes on. Handsome in his dark suit and string tie; she just couldn't allow Shane to make such a foolhardy mistake as marrying Marilee Barkley.

She reached for the gun she had holstered on her hip, then aimed it off center a bit—wouldn't serve her purpose actually shooting the groom, or the bride for that matter. She cleared her parched throat just as Reverend O'Malley opened his Bible. "Hold on," she called out. Heads turned in her direction. "Shane Graham, what in tarnation are you doing? You can't marry her."

As Shane's expression registered recognition, his eyebrows shot straight up. She had his full attention, as well as all others in attendance. Dorie couldn't miss their gasps of horror and surprise, but that didn't rightly matter. She had to do this. Shane Graham had no call marrying anyone.

Anyone, but her.

Biff Cummings, seated on the aisle nearest to her, made a move to approach. "Now, Isadora…"

She shook her head and waved the pistol in the direction of the town smithy. "Don't say it, Biff!"

He didn't. Beads of perspiration rimmed his brow when he lowered himself back down into his seat.

"Dorie?" Shane's voice, a slow, low rumble, struck her instantly and her darn silly heart sped up.

Dorie spoke from her heart and made her pronouncement loud and clear to conceal a bout of sudden and unexpected queasiness. Dorie McCabe had gumption, but she'd never broken up a wedding before. "You got no call marrying her, Shane."

With calm assurance, Shane requested, "Put the gun down, Dorie. You're not going to shoot anyone."

Shane knew her best of all. That's what she admired most about him. He'd been the only one she could count on since her mama died some three years ago. And through those years Shane had gotten to know her pretty darn well.

She held the pistol steady, her hand never wavering. Guns were one thing Dorie knew about. Her mama had taught her at a young age how to protect herself. Living alone with just her younger brother, out on the homestead, a gal could find cause for protection. "I'll put it down as soon as you walk out of this church, Shane."

He pressed his lips together and peered at her for long moments the way he usually did when measuring his options. Then he turned to Marilee to whisper something in her ear. The bride-to-be shook her head adamantly, but Shane just kept on whispering, until finally, she stopped shaking her head and only stared at him, then nodded.

Dorie had a good heart under regular circumstances, but she didn't feel sorry for Marilee Barkley today. In truth, Dorie was doing the older gal a favor in busting up the wedding. Shane and Marilee didn't belong together. No sir. They were not a good match at all.

"I'll come out to speak to you, Dorie. But you have to put down the gun."

"You coming out?" she asked, just to be sure.

"I am," he said and she knew him to be a man of his word. Shane was the most decent honest man she'd ever met. That's why she had to stop this wedding. That's why she had to convince him he'd be making a buffalo-sized mistake in hitching up with prim and proper Miss Marilee Barkley. But more important, her brother Jeremiah's future was at stake. And Shane was the only one who could help her.

Dorie holstered her gun. "Well, what are you waiting for?" She turned her back on the ceremony that wouldn't happen today, a deep sigh of relief escaping once she hit the chilly fall air.

Patience wasn't one of Dorie's virtues. If something had to get done, she did it, quick-like and without regret. Heart racing and stomach churning, she waited for Shane near the steps. Dorie McCabe never held to the rules of society, never had much call to, but she'd never done anything quite like this before. She'd never marched into a church before God, a wagonload of people and the preacher, toting a gun and making demands.

"Dorie?" Shane stood on the top step of the church, the

dark grass-green of his eyes appearing nearly black as he squinted into the sunlight. He took the rest of the steps in stride and approached her. "What's this all about?"

Dorie bolstered her resolve, her determination washing away the slim shades of fear she'd experienced for one brief moment. She was doing this for Jeremiah. "Shane Leopold Graham, you *know* what this is about. You can't marry Marilee Barkley."

Rigid lines around his eyes and mouth softened. "Apparently, I can, Dorie. I'm about to."

"Why?"

It was a plain and simple question, yet Shane appeared perplexed. He rubbed at the back of his neck. "The usual reasons, I guess."

"'Cause her daddy is rich and owns the land next to yours? 'Cause you want that land for yourself one day?"

"No!"

"Marilee's rich, Shane, and you need money for your ranch. You told me so half a dozen times how you'd like to get your hands on more land. You got a nice little spread, but you got debts and most of your cattle ain't fat enough to bring you a good price."

"No, Dorie, that's not the reason."

"Then, what is?"

He squinted into the sun, refusing to meet her eyes. "I'm ready, that's all. I want a wife."

Dorie snorted. "Humph. Like a plump chicken wants to be my next supper, you want to marry Marilee."

"Dorie, I've got to go back inside to the wedding. People are waiting." He gestured toward the church. "I'm sorry you don't much like it."

She stared into his eyes. "I don't."

He stepped closer and moved a strand of hair off her face, his finger slightly brushing her cheek. This was the man she'd known... Shane Graham, who'd look upon her with a soft gleam in his eyes. He was the only man who could help her with her brother, Jeremiah. The letter in her pocket she'd received just yesterday seemed to burn straight through her dress, reminding her what she stood to lose if she didn't bust up this wedding. "I know and I'm sorry for that," he said with genuine regret.

Darn him anyway, he had a way of getting under her skin with just a word or a look or a touch. Sweet tingles traveled the length of her spine from that slight caress. All the more reason she couldn't let him marry Marilee.

He turned to leave and panic seized her. She glanced at a stand of pine trees just a few yards away, where Jeremiah was waiting with the horses, hidden from view.

"You've been courting me for three years!" she called out.

She saw Shane's shoulders lift, heard his sigh when he turned to her with a shake of his head. "Dorie, I haven't been courting you. I come around to help out at your place. I help Jeremiah with his chores and—"

"You brought me flowers once."

He smiled softly. "When you took sick."

"You come for supper."

"You feed me sometimes, Dorie. I appreciate it and enjoy the company."

Dorie's voice became barely a whisper. "Shane, you kissed me. Did you forget that?"

Shane took a sharp breath. Hell no, he hadn't forgotten. It happened about a year ago, a stupid, unthinking move that he now regretted. But he hadn't forgotten. Dorie McCabe, for all her wild, unladylike ways, wasn't coy enough to hide her blossoming passion. She was too genuine a young woman even to know how to act demurely.

That kiss had nearly knocked him to his knees, but it had also knocked some sense into him. He hadn't meant to kiss her—it had just happened one evening after she'd cooked dinner for him. He'd been working all day out at her place, helping Jeremiah make repairs to the windmill.

The kiss, a soft quick brush of lips was meant as a thank-you of sorts, for the meal. But it hadn't ended there, as it should have, and Shane accepted the blame for allowing the kiss to escalate into something more.

He still scoffed at the notion. He'd been looking out for Dorie since she'd been orphaned at the age of fifteen. Shane had done the neighborly thing by coming around from time to time to help out. He'd worried over Dorie, a young girl living all alone on a small farm, trying to keep food on the table while caring for her younger brother. But he certainly hadn't courted her.

"Shouldn't have kissed you that day, Dorie."

Dorie's expression faltered, her mouth trembling. "You didn't like it then?"

"Oh, I liked it—" he blurted out and then felt immediate remorse in his admission. No sense giving Dorie false hope. Shane *had* to marry Marilee Barkley today. Old man Barkley had nearly blackmailed him into it. With Marilee carrying some drifter's child, she needed a husband real fast. Barkley approached him with the deal—if he agreed to give Marilee and the baby his name the wealthy rancher wouldn't call in his loans. Shane didn't much like his tactics and told him so with a six-shooter and a scowl, but Barkley hadn't backed down. He'd been desperate to save his daughter's reputation. And Shane, being the closest neighbor and a man who owed a great deal of money, was the obvious choice.

For years, Shane had struggled to earn enough to buy a parcel of land. He'd started with just a few head of cattle, doing odd jobs, hiring himself out to other ranches, anything, in order to build up his herd. And once he'd had a sizable herd, he'd worked damn hard to keep the ranch going, competing with bigger ranches for business, fighting to keep his cattle free of disease and well fed on abundant grazing land Barkley allowed him to use.

And now old man Barkley had threatened to rip all of that away without blinking an eye.

Shane had given it a great deal of thought, and had come to the conclusion that marrying Marilee wouldn't be a bad thing. He'd known Marilee for some time. She'd been under her father's watchful eye, had withstood his overbearing ways; the minute she'd gotten free from his tight control, she'd gone and done something foolish with a hired hand. Shane didn't put blame on her, but rather on a menacing father who'd tried to run the girl's life.

Now it was too late to reclaim his words to Dorie. He *had* liked kissing her, but he shouldn't have said it because now her face beamed with joy. "I liked it, too, Shane. I would go to bed at night and think and think about it. I was hoping you'd kiss me again, but you never did."

"Dorie," he began, "I had no right kissing you. I'm getting married. You and me…we're friends."

"Friends?" she repeated with a frown pulling at her lips. Hell, he was sorry to disappoint her, but he'd had no notion Dorie would react this way to his marriage.

Mr. Barkley stuck his head out of the church door. The blaze of Nevada sun put a shine on his balding head making it look like the full round of the moon. "Shane, this is utter nonsense! You gonna marry my daughter today or not? I'm giving you one minute to get yourself back in here."

Shane whirled around. "I'm marrying Marilee, Mr. Barkley. Just give me a little more time."

"One minute is all you have, boy!" He slammed the church door shut.

"Dorie, I've got to get back. This isn't fair to Marilee. It's her wedding day." He took hold of both of her hands and squeezed gently. Dorie was lovely in her own way, even though her coppery hair reminded him of wildfire in a windstorm and her clothes were worn and overly large for her petite body. "One day, you'll get married. One day, you'll know the love of a fine man."

He let go of her hands and turned to head up the steps.

"*You're* a fine man, Shane," he heard her call out, just before he felt the butt end of a pistol slam against the back of his head.

Then he felt nothing at all.

"You knocked him out, Dorie! I saw you knock Shane out!" Jeremiah reined in his horse, wearing a horrified expression.

"Hush up, Jeremiah. You want the entire congregation to come out here?" Dorie glanced at the church doors, which were thankfully still closed. "Help me get Shane up onto your horse."

Jeremiah pulled away, his stony face set. Thirteen years old, stubborn, honest and loyal to a fault, Jeremiah McCabe wasn't anybody's fool. It was one thing Dorie prided herself on. Jeremiah. "It ain't right, Dorie. You shouldn't a done this."

"I had no choice and you know it. Now, are you going to mind me? We've got to get Shane out of here so we can tend his head." She peered down, a small dose of guilt assailing her. "There's gonna be a lump the size of Sunshine Mountain developing soon."

"And you put it there!"

Regret slammed into her. Shane had always been kind and helpful to her. She wasn't proud of what she'd done to him, but still recognized the powerful need to do it. Casting aside her guilt, Dorie called out, "C'mon, Jeremiah! Hurry up."

With great reluctance, Jeremiah slid down from his horse and together they managed to lift Shane's limp body up onto the gray mare, throwing the man over like a rolled-up carpet. "Now scoot. I'll be along in a minute."

"Where am I taking him?" Jeremiah asked as he mounted the mare behind Shane's slumped body. Her brother's expression was more than a bit grim.

"You know that little shack near Cave Rock Mine?"

Jeremiah gulped. "That far?"

"Well, we can't be taking him to the homestead, Jeremiah. It's the first place anybody'd look."

The boy nodded.

"Go on." Dorie's slapped the horse's backside and

Lightning took off in a sprint heading north, up into the hills. Dorie rushed to the stand of trees and mounted her horse quickly, following closely behind.

She smiled, satisfied. Shane wasn't getting married today.

Then a frown yanked the corners of her mouth downward. She hadn't expected Shane's complete reluctance. She hadn't expected having to knock the man out, either. And she certainly hadn't expected to abduct him from his own wedding. She'd been late in getting here. If she'd been a mite earlier, she'd have spoken her piece to Shane *before* the nuptials were to take place. Heck, if things had worked out differently, she wouldn't have had to render the man unconscious.

When she thought on it, she realized exactly what she'd done.

She'd *shanghaied* the groom.

Chapter Two

Shane woke slowly, opening his eyes in stages, the ache in his head staggering. With his right hand he reached back and found the knot, a large achy lump causing him a good deal of pain. "Ow! Dammit."

Fighting off a swell of dizziness, he rose from the cot on which he'd been lying and brought himself to an upright position, bracing his boots onto the floorboards and putting his hands to his head.

A skirt, two sizes too big, covering a pair of man's boots, swished by him. "How's the head, Shane?"

The soft voice soothed, until he glanced up and saw Dorie McCabe staring down at him. Without pause, he recalled the spectacle at the church: Dorie pointing her six-shooter toward the altar, him trying to talk sense into her outside…and then the pistol butt to the head.

He gritted his teeth. "I'm gonna live, Dorie."

"Sure you are, Shane."

"But…I'm not too sure about you. If my head wasn't aching like the devil, I'd have a mind to take a paddle to your backside."

"I'm not a child and nobody paddles my backside!"

Shane rubbed his temples, making circles to ease the pain. "Don't be too sure about that," he said quietly, because speaking up only intensified the aching.

"I'm sorry for what I did."

Shane stretched back down onto the small bed and closed his eyes, the strain of sitting upright taking its toll. To Dorie's credit, she did sound contrite. For Dorie. "Sorry for busting up my wedding, or knocking me out with your gun?"

"Well, not for busting up your wedding, Shane. That's for darn certain. But I'm sorry for the bruise to your head."

"Uh-huh." Right now, he had trouble thinking straight. His head felt heavy, as though wild mustangs were stampeding straight through it.

"Why don't you sleep some more," she whispered softly, coming close to set a cool cloth to his head. "There, feel better?"

"Some," he said, waging a war with fatigue, but clearly losing.

"That's it, Shane. You need to rest." She touched his face, smooth slim fingers tracing over his jaw. "I promise you'll feel better in the morning."

"The *morning?*"

"Yes, the morning. But not to worry, I won't leave you. Jeremiah went back to the homestead but I'll be right here, watching over you."

"No," he mumbled, feeling himself fading fast. He wouldn't be able to fight it much longer. "We can't spend the night together."

Had she heard him? Shane wasn't sure if he'd spoken

the words or just thought them. Things were fuzzy in his head. But either way, he knew he had to get out of here, real quick. He couldn't spend the night with Dorie. He had to make amends with Marilee.

Ah, hell. Another thought struck him, pounding his head with throbbing pain. Mr. Barkley would have his head *and* his ranch if Shane didn't make things right with his daughter. It might appear as if he'd left Marilee at the altar, in favor of Dorie, if Shane didn't get out of here right away to explain.

Dorie's soft voice broke into his muddied thoughts. "I'll just light a little fire in the hearth and be right back." She removed her hand from his face and oddly, he missed that slight caress.

"Dorie?"

"Hmm?"

"Where am I?"

"Don't you worry about that. You just close your eyes and sleep, Shane. You'll feel better in the morning. Then I'll explain everything."

"No, not the morning," he said, attempting to lift his head, but the quick move brought piercing pain, making mush of his mind. He lowered his head back onto the cot, the soft cushion of a pillow helping ease the discomfort. His resolve, however, didn't waver. If he spent the night here, he knew disaster would ensue. "I gotta get back."

He tried lifting up again, but it was no use and soon he lost the battle to keep his eyes open. Sleep began to sound real good. "I'll just rest up a bit, then… I…gotta…get…back," he murmured, as his entire body went limp.

* * *

Shane drifted peacefully, his mind empty but for the serene hazy glow that left his head light and woozy. He rolled over onto his side, resting his head on a soft cushion and let out a deep sigh. Blissfully near sleep again, he freed himself of worry, absorbing the dark and delicate sensations surrounding him.

He thrust his arm out and sighed again at the soft cushion he found, a creamy texture that brought pleasing tingles to his fingertips. He stroked the satinlike softness, letting it sink in, pleasing him in unforeseen ways.

"Shane."

He heard his name, a sweet mysterious whisper in the shadows of his mind. His body grew tight. He sought the sound. His hand probed, skimming the silk, feeling flesh against his palms, the most delectable, satisfying sensations whirling through his clouded mind.

"Shane." The sweet plea stirred him yet again. He found the sound coming from the softest set of lips he'd ever encountered. He brushed his mouth over once, twice, and took a long drink, tasting from the sweetness. A deep guttural groan of pleasure escaped his throat. He kissed those lips again and again, the pleasure near to unbearable.

He was lost now and reeling with desire for the silk under his palms and the taste of sweet mystery that seemed to cloud his mind even more. He moved his body closer, pressing up against the cushion that arched to him, giving him comfort while making him ache.

He slipped his hands over gossamer-feeling twin mounds of flesh that peaked from his touch. The response left him breathless and wanting. He envisioned a shadowy silhouette of a woman, with fiery hair spread across the pillow and the gleaming glow of unbridled passion in her light eyes.

He was wrapped up in her now, ready to stroke her into submission, ready to claim her in the dark, ready to ease his powerful need. He thrust his tongue in her mouth, the exquisite joining bringing a whimper from her delicate throat. His hand found the juncture between her thighs, and he pressed gently, priming her for his entry, but she jolted from his touch, startling him out of this all-too-vivid dream.

He opened his eyes wide, the reality hitting him hard and fast. "Dorie?"

"Oh, Shane," she murmured breathlessly, her voice a slight shaky tremble.

Dear God. It was *Dorie*. His lusty dream had been real and the cushion of silk he'd found so pleasing had been Dorie's soft young body. He'd almost taken her, this innocent girl whom he'd tried to protect for the last three years. He'd almost seduced Dorie in her sleep.

"Dorie," he said again, rolling off of her and flopping onto his back. His hand went to his forehead, his body going cold as winter rain. "Why the devil are you in bed with me?"

"W-Where else would I sleep?" Her voice sounded breathless, throaty, so unlike the young wholesome girl he'd come to know.

The floor would have been an option, he thought, but dammit, Shane was too much of a gentleman to say that. The shanty she'd taken him to was too small for any other kind of furniture than a tiny wooden table and the bed. "You just don't climb into bed with strange men, Dorie."

"I know it, Shane. But you're not a stranger and I had to watch over you tonight. I know I can trust you."

Immediate guilt assailed him. He shook his head, ignoring the painful throbbing inside. He'd almost taken her virginity and she still trusted him. "Dorie, I almost...I mean...when you go to bed with a man...what I mean to say is...you shouldn't trust...ah, hell, Dorie. I'm sorry for touching you."

It had been the most stirring experience in Shane's life, touching Dorie. He knew for certain he'd never forget the heady sensations that tightened his body so urgently or feel anything quite so erotically mysterious ever again. He placed the blame for his actions on a sore head and a dizzy mind. It should never have happened and he was sorry for it. He'd never touch Dorie McCabe that way ever again.

"Brett Caruthers tried touching me once and I slapped his hand away."

Brett Caruthers, that little weasel who worked at the general store? "That's what you should do, Dorie. Even with me."

A stream of moonlight cast Dorie's face in a slight glow and Shane didn't like the look he witnessed on her face, all dewy-eyed and full of trust. "But, with you, the touching was...real nice. I didn't want to slap your hands away, Shane."

"Jeez, Dorie," he said, tossing the coverlet off of him and bounding up from the bed. His head still ached, but that was a far better feeling than lying next to Dorie, having her admit such things. His body still hummed from the "real nice" touching he'd done.

He planted his hands on his hips and cast her a stern

look. "You never told me why you kidnapped me from my wedding."

Dorie sat up on the bed and came to him on her knees, her scarlet hair wild and unruly. Even in the dark, Shane saw through the threadbare chemise she wore to the creamy skin underneath. He swallowed, remembering the feel of her skin, the silkiness and the soft full swell of her breasts that he'd held in his hands. "Don't be mad, Shane. I had a good reason."

Shane was almost beyond reason. One part of him wanted to throttle her for disrupting his life, the other part—the all male part—wanted to toss her down on the bed and make love to her.

Hell, he'd spent time with her, trying to help her and her brother, trying to lend his protection whenever he could. She was just a girl. He was more than ten years her senior, yet somehow, she's gotten under his skin. He couldn't have her, wouldn't make love to her, and yet she tempted him without even trying.

He'd been too long without a woman. That was it. It had been nearly three months since he'd made a trip to Virginia City to visit the ladies at the brothel. It had just been too damn long.

On impulse, Shane reached out to touch Dorie's hair. He sifted a strand of red flame through his fingers. Softly, he said, "You ought to cover up, Dorie. Get dressed. Then we'll talk."

Suddenly, the door thrust open. Big beefy hands shoved Jeremiah through. The boy lost his footing and tripped. He shot Dorie an apologetic look before slumping onto the floor.

"You left my daughter at the church for this trollop!

You're gonna pay for this, Shane Graham." Tobias Barkley barreled into the room, his ruddy face flushed with color.

"Sorry, Dorie," Jeremiah rushed out from his place on the floor. "He followed me."

"Sure as hell, I followed you," Tobias Barkley hissed, his expression filled with fury. He glared at Shane. "Damn you, Graham. Was bedding her worth your ranch? Is she that good? Why in hell didn't you wait until after the wedding? You made me a laughingstock running out on my daughter. I'll have your hide as well as your broken-down ranch!"

Shane immediately covered Dorie up with the blanket. "Now wait just a minute, Barkley. This isn't how it looks."

The older man cast Shane a dubious look. He arched a brow and Shane could only guess what was on the man's mind. He'd found them in a compromising position. "Don't play me for a fool, Graham. She's in your bed, wearing next to nothing and you were all over each other when I busted in here."

"No, I…we didn't…" Dorie fumbled with her words, then cast Shane a pleading look.

A tick worked at Shane's jaw and protective instincts surged forth. He was ready to put a fist through old man Barkley's face if he said anything further regarding Dorie's reputation. "Nothing happened here, Barkley. And nothing will. You say another word about Dorie and that'll be the last one you do say. Now, if you want to go outside, I can explain. If you don't want to hear me out, then get out, now."

"I'm not hearing your lies, Graham. We had a deal

and now it's too damn late. My daughter's gone. She took off right after you abandoned her at the church and nobody's seen her. You ruined her, and now I'm gonna ruin you. You got that, boy? As soon as I find Marilee, you're either gonna marry her like you promised, or pay for double-crossing me. And if I don't find my daughter, you'll wish you were dead."

Dorie gasped, jamming her hand to her mouth. She bounded off the bed, but Shane stopped her, placing a firm grip on her shoulders. He didn't want her anywhere near Barkley. "No," she pleaded desperately, "this isn't Shane's fault. I took him away from the wedding!"

"It's too late now." The man's wrath could have shaken down the walls of the dilapidated shanty. "I'm aiming to ruin you both."

Shane's gut clenched. Old man Barkley had the means to ruin him; there was no doubt that he wouldn't hesitate. All he had to do was call in the loans and refuse him grazing rights on his property. His herd wouldn't last long without the water and feed Barkley provided. And Shane didn't have anywhere near enough money to pay off the loans. Not yet.

But he felt even worse for Marilee. She'd done a reckless thing, but had confided in Shane that she'd fallen in love with that ranch hand. Suspiciously though, the ranch hand had vanished leaving Marilee to believe he'd run out on her. She'd been heartbroken and vulnerable, but old man Barkley hadn't cared. He'd been content forcing her into a loveless marriage with Shane, in order to save face. Shane couldn't blame Marilee for running away and escaping the clutches of her overbearing father. He couldn't blame her for wanting something better in life. "Get out, now," Shane demanded through tight lips.

"Gladly," Barkley said, heading for the door. He stopped at the threshold and turned, shooting Dorie a long scornful glare. "I hope she was worth it."

Shane let out a string of muttered curses and sat down on the bed, holding his head in his hands. Dorie swallowed hard as fierce regret stabbed at her. She'd never meant for any of this to happen. She'd never wanted to ruin Shane's life. He'd been good and kind to her and Jeremiah. He'd been the only one in Silver Hills she could count on. She'd needed him and was desperate enough to break up his wedding to Marilee to get his help.

She'd always known something suspicious was behind Shane's right quick wedding proposal to Marilee. Out of the blue, he'd begun courting her in a fashionable way. Dorie hadn't liked it then, comparing herself to Marilee and coming up short. Marilee was a lady, schooled and groomed and soft-spoken. Dorie always envied the way she had of smiling up at a man…at Shane, to get him to do her bidding. Yes, Marilee was a lady and it irked Dorie no end that Shane had decided he liked Marilee more than her. But she'd had her suspicions about the union all along and she knew for a fact that Shane didn't love Marilee—she knew it deep down in her heart.

Now, she wondered if Shane would ever forgive her.

Would he even consider helping her? She had to ask him to do her a giant-size favor. Dorie sat down on the bed next to him, fighting off tears, fighting off despair.

"Dorie, get dressed," Shane said, slanting her a look, then gestured with a nod of his head toward her younger brother. "And you'd best explain to Jeremiah what just happened here." Slowly, Shane rose from the bed. "When you're done, maybe you can explain it all to me."

Shane slammed out of the door. Dorie blinked and her heart pounded hard against her chest.

"Dorie, did you lay with him?" Jeremiah asked, his eyes far too knowing for a thirteen-year-old.

Dorie rose from the bed and threw on her clothes. "Heavens, you know better than that, Jeremiah. I had to make sure Shane was all right after that butt to the head and that's what I did. I made sure he was all right."

She nodded as if convincing herself, but memories of his lips crushing her mouth, his strong hands caressing her skin and the heat of his body surrounding her, burst forth in her mind. Tingles threaded through her body like a fine tapestry. She'd recalled it all, every sensation. She knew she'd always remember how Shane Graham made her feel for a few secret moments tonight in this shanty.

But that wasn't important now. What was important was Jeremiah. Keeping him was all Dorie had time for at the moment. She'd set her sights and had come up with a plan.

Dorie dug her teeth into her bottom lip as she peered out the grimy window. She squinted, making out Shane's form, a shadow of a man, pacing under the stars. "I'd best get this over with, Jeremiah. You wait here."

Dread pulsed in Dorie's stomach. When she'd first come up with this plan, it had all sounded so simple and easy. She'd thought and thought on it, and was sure it would work. Then Shane went and got himself hooked up with Marilee Barkley and Dorie's plan had begun to unravel like a worn-out old hook rug.

She opened the door and stepped out. Shane had his back to her, leaning on a rickety post. She sensed his underlying fury, the tight rein he kept on his control. "You ready to talk?"

She took a swallow. "First off, Shane. I couldn't be sorrier for all the trouble I've caused you. I didn't mean to ruin things."

"Breaking up a wedding has a way of *ruining* things, Dorie."

"But, you didn't want to marry Marilee. I knew that in my gut, Shane."

"I had to marry her. Barkley had me over a barrel."

"She's having your child, then?"

"No!" He turned and narrowed his eyes on her. "No. But he needed something from me and because I owe him, he called me on it."

"Marrying his daughter was payment, then?"

"Sort of. But that's all I'm saying, Dorie. Now are you gonna tell me why you jammed my head with that pistol and dragged me up here?"

Dorie braced herself for the worst. She worked up her courage, her need to protect Jeremiah stronger than her fear of Shane's anger. "I did it for Jeremiah."

Shane's face registered utter amazement. He wrinkled his nose and shot her a look of exasperation. *"Jeremiah?"*

She nodded. "I need a husband…temporarily."

Chapter Three

The words tumbled out so quickly that Dorie actually jumped from Shane's immediate reaction. He stepped back, blinked, cocked his head, then slanted her a look of bewilderment. "A husband...temporarily? What in tarnation are you talking about, Dorie? If I didn't still feel the brunt of that pistol to my head, I'd swear you were the one who'd been walloped today."

"Shane, please listen."

"I think I'm gonna be sorry for it, but go on. Say your piece."

"It all has to do with Jeremiah and, well, you see, he's not my hundred-percent, in the flesh, brother. It's complicated. We had the same mama but not the same father. Everybody knows Jeremiah's real daddy went off to fight in the war. He never came back, leaving mama to raise both of us alone."

"And then your mama died."

"Yes, Mama died," she said softly, recalling those last few days when her mama had taken real sick, but had put on a brave smile for her. Holding her hand until she

drew her last breath, Dorie had promised her mama that
she'd take care of Jeremiah. She'd never let her younger
brother down. She'd raised him up to be a fine boy. It
wasn't just her promise to her mama, but the promise
she'd made to herself that she and Jeremiah would
always be close—that they would be family, no matter
what. "And I tried real hard with Jeremiah."

"I know you did, Dorie. He's a fine boy."

Tears misted in her eyes. She closed them briefly, to
wash them away. She didn't want sympathy from Shane,
only understanding. "Thank you. But now you see, I got
this letter from the Parkers, claiming to be Jeremiah's
kin. Steven Parker, Jeremiah's daddy, may have died
while in the army, but his parents Helene and Oliver are
still alive, living in New York and they want Jeremiah.
They want my Jeremiah," she said quietly, feeling the
defeat even as she said the words.

She'd been brave for most of it, but last night as
she'd contemplated their fate Dorie had given way to
tears. She'd cried and cried, her heart pouring out once
Jeremiah had fallen asleep. Gently, as he slept, she'd
touched a hand to his cheek, gazing at him and wondering what life would be like without her brother. "They
have money, Shane. Lots of it and they wrote what a
wonderful life they could give Jeremiah if only he came
to live with them. Jeremiah is their only kin. They'd only
just now learned of him, through a Union soldier who
claimed he'd known Steven Parker at Fort Ruby."

"They didn't know about Jeremiah for thirteen years?"

"No. Jeremiah's daddy had run off when he was
young. He'd come to work the mines up by Virginia
City, lost a good deal of money investing in one and

trying to make it pay out, according to my mama. That was right before they met. Mama always said Jeremiah's daddy was an adventurer, not a man you could tie down. He hadn't been close to his folks. Hadn't cared a lick for their money, either. Mama said she always knew one day he'd take off, and he did. He'd sworn to her he'd come back, but then he took sick. Didn't even see a day of fighting, Mama said, like he'd wanted. He'd had the fever."

"And the Parkers never knew about their grandson, until just now?"

"That's right. We just kinda used the name McCabe for all of us, so they had trouble tracking down a Jeremiah Parker. But they found him anyways."

"That doesn't explain why—"

"I need a husband?"

Shane nodded and looked directly into her eyes. He had a way of getting at the truth with those piercing green eyes. Dorie drew oxygen deep into her lungs. "Because I lied, Shane. For Jeremiah. I had to. I told them I was married to a wonderful man. I told them we lived on a prosperous ranch and Jeremiah wanted for nothing. I told them Jeremiah was happy as a bumblebee in a nest of honey, Shane. Because I can't lose Jeremiah. I can't. I told those lies to make them see that they don't have to worry about Jeremiah. They don't. Jeremiah's just fine with me, Shane. But they're coming anyhow! They're coming. They want to see for themselves. And now…and now, if I don't have all those things, if they find out I lied…"

"They'll take Jeremiah." Shane finished for her. "You're afraid that if they learn the truth, they'll take

Jeremiah away from you." He nodded his head, his eyes filled with understanding.

Dorie let out her breath slowly. "I know they will." Her insides quaking now, she went on, "We don't live high, Shane. But we manage all right."

Shane scratched his head, seemingly deep in thought. A glimmer of light from the quarter moon cast Shane's face in shadows. They stood in the backwoods, high in the hills, a slight wind rustling the branches of towering pines. Chilly fall air swept clear through her as she waited for Shane's response. "It's a plum crazy idea, Dorie."

She shivered both from the cold and the reservation she heard in Shane's voice. "It's the only one I got, Shane. The way I see it, if the Parkers aren't convinced Jeremiah's living well, they'll take him from me faster than a jackrabbit stealing in a carrot patch. I don't have the means to fight them." And it would kill her to lose Jeremiah. She loved him dearly. Even when her mama was alive, Dorie had always taken it upon herself to look after her brother. Now, all they had was each other. Jeremiah didn't want to live with strangers, kin or not. He was content living in Silver Hills on their homestead.

Dorie bolstered her courage, despite her quivering lips. "W-Will you help me?"

Shane pursed his lips. She knew it was a lot to ask of him. She'd nearly ruined his life today, and now she pleaded with him to help her. She couldn't blame him if he refused, but prayed that he'd agree.

He lowered his head, stared at the ground for a long time, taking deep pulls of air. She saw his mouth twist, knew he was about to decline. Then he looked up at her, and darned if she couldn't prevent the moisture beginning to well up in her eyes. His gaze softened. "Everybody in Silver Hills knows we're not married, Dorie."

A bit encouraged now, since he hadn't responded with a flat-out no, Dorie explained, "That's why we're supposed to meet them on the fifteenth of the month in Virginia City."

Shane rubbed his nose and let out a quiet laugh. "Dorie, you do amaze me."

"We've got two weeks to get ready."

Fear entered Shane's green eyes as they grew wide with question. Dorie didn't think anything would scare Shane, not even coming up against Tobias Barkley.

"'Ready'?"

"Well, sure. We have to get to know each other better. Otherwise, we won't convince the Parkers we're well suited. We can't afford for them to have suspicions."

"Whoa!" Shane put up both hands. "Slow down. I haven't agreed to any of this yet. I've got a ranch to run, Dorie. I don't have time to…to…uh—"

"Spend time with me?"

Shane had been willing to spend his entire life with Marilee Barkley. She had all the attributes of a refined woman. She was petite and pretty, even if she was a mite stuffy. And she sure did know her manners. Dorie supposed Marilee would make a fine wife for some man, just not Shane.

Sudden panic seized her as a thought rushed into her mind. Did Shane think her a lost cause in the "woman" category? Did he think her "unfit" as a wife, even a pretend one? Dorie never had much use for womanly things like dressing up or fixing her hair just so. She'd never had cause before. But now her future and Jeremiah's depended on it.

"Am I that bad, Shane?" She'd never been one to hold back. If something needed asking, she went ahead and asked. She held her breath, waiting on his answer.

Shane closed his eyes and let out a nearly silent oath. "No, Dorie. You're just you. And you're a fine girl and all."

"You know what a man likes in a woman. You know how he expects her to behave. You courted Marilee for a time. You could teach me things, Shane. I know you could. And as I recall, you said your own mama was as refined a lady as they come. She taught you manners. If ever you take a wife, Shane…I mean, for real, you'd expect her to act a certain way, wouldn't you?"

Shane cleared his throat. Suddenly, his mouth had gone bone dry. Visions of Dorie on that bed just minutes ago played havoc in his head. Damn. A man couldn't forget someone like Dorie, and knowing how her body felt next to his, how her delicate mouth had tasted, was all he could ever "expect" in a wife. But he couldn't say that to Dorie. She wanted his help. She wanted to get close enough so that they would appear married in the real sense. Lord above, it was a tall order. "I suppose."

"That's all I'm asking, Shane. To get to know what you like." Dorie's voice softened on her plea. "There's no one else I can trust."

Dorie drew in her lip and tried darn hard to conceal her tears. Shane had to commend her for that. She wasn't trying to win him over by crying. She'd been brave so far in a situation that was out of her control and he admired her for that. Even though she'd stolen him away from his own wedding.

There was no doubt the girl was desperate. Shane would rather face a thunderstorm in the name of Tobias Barkley than spend a good deal of time with Dorie.

That was what he was afraid of mostly.

Because spending time with young Dorie would leave him wanting. He wouldn't give in to temptation. He knew that. Dorie wasn't more than a child—at least he tried to think of her that way. He had a good ten years on her, he reminded himself again. Yet, he'd felt as though he *had* to protect her. He felt as though he *had* to help her. And it finally dawned on him why. He'd pushed the images out of his head for so long, but now that he had time to think, really contemplate why he looked after Dorie after her mama died, the reason became very clear.

In a certain way Dorie reminded him of his younger sister, Lora. She'd had an innocent wildness about her, too. Some had called her spirited, but Shane just remembered her as a sweet child with big trusting eyes. She'd always looked up to Shane, always expected him to be there when she needed him. And he had, for the most part. He'd loved his younger sister dearly. But she'd wandered off one day when Shane was chopping wood on their homestead. He'd been twelve then and Lora just five. Two days later, they'd found her limp body, washed up on the riverbank. She'd always loved the water and Shane had promised to teach her how to swim one day. And although his folks shouldered the entire blame for the drowning, Shane had always felt guilty. He'd always felt that he hadn't protected Lora enough, hadn't taken proper care with her.

"Shane?" Dorie's soft voice broke into his thoughts.

He glanced down at her. She shivered in the darkness, the night wind kicking up mightily. He had an urge to wrap his arms around her to keep her warm. That was only one of the many urges he'd had tonight in regard to Dorie, but as he came to his decision, he also made himself a promise to keep his hands off. "Okay, Dorie. I'll help you."

Dorie shrieked, a joyous sound that echoed in the night. "You will? Oh, Shane, thank you. Thank you." She lifted up and brushed a soft kiss to his lips, making his mind spin in ten different directions, while his body spun in only one. He knew the girl was innocent to her tempting ways. She didn't know how she affected him and he was going to keep it that way. He wouldn't compromise her by giving in to his urges. She deserved better than that. And he couldn't forget that if Barkley did find his daughter, Shane would be honor-bound to marry her. He'd made Marilee a promise of marriage and he wouldn't go back on his word.

Shane resigned himself to spending the next two weeks helping Dorie with her charade. Then, no matter the outcome, he'd have to concentrate on getting his own life back in order.

If that were possible.

He took Dorie's hand and tugged her along. "Come on. Let's get you back inside before you catch cold."

She clung to him, her soft body pressed against his and her voice suddenly quiet and breathy. "Sure, Shane. That's a fine idea."

Lord save him from a willing woman. Shane gritted his teeth as they approached the door to the shanty and thanked heaven above that Jeremiah slept inside.

And that the sun would be rising in less than an hour.

* * *

"C'mon, Jeremiah. Climb up on Lightning. We've got lots to do today." Dorie grasped her brother's hand and helped him mount the mare behind her. The mid-morning sun beat down warm enough to take the chill out of the air. Dorie gloried in the weather, absorbing the heat, having been chilled down to the bone last night. It was cooler up here in the woods, she realized, yet this morning the pleasing scent of fresh pine layered the air. Even so, Dorie was glad to leave Cave Rock Mine and the shanty behind.

"I'm not the only one who has a bit of learning to do," she said.

"Aw, what do I have to learn?" her brother asked. Dorie could only imagine the sour face Jeremiah put on from behind her back.

"Well, manners for one. We both need lessons in that."

"You mean, like not to thump our friends on the head and drag them off."

"Jeremiah!"

"Well, that old mean Mr. Barkley didn't like what you done. And I don't suppose Miss Marilee was too happy about it, neither. The whole town knows you stole Shane away from his own wedding."

Dorie sighed deeply. Her brother had good sense, but Dorie found that, at times, when survival was at stake, one had to take more drastic measures. Good sense didn't always get you what you needed. "If Shane would have married Marilee, we'd both be in a pickle right now. Besides, Shane doesn't love her."

"And he don't love you, either."

Dorie closed her eyes briefly, hating the sting of

those truthful words. She knew Shane looked upon her as a child. He didn't have warm feelings for her. But last night in the shanty, when they'd lain close to each other, Dorie got a sense of what loving and being loved by Shane would be like. He'd kissed her gently, then more boldly, until every bone in her body nearly melted. He'd touched her in places no man ever had and she hadn't stopped him, either. She'd never felt such compelling sensations, such all-fire need deep down in her belly. "Heavens, I know Shane doesn't love me. But he is doing us a big favor."

"I told you, I wouldn't go off with those Parkers, anyhows. You didn't have to do what you did."

"I had to, Jeremiah," Dorie said firmly. She'd done her level best to explain to Jeremiah about his kin. The boy just didn't understand what money and power could attain. She had little hope of persuading the Parkers without Shane's help. She didn't have much in the way of possessions. But she and Jeremiah had a decent life on the homestead. Dorie made sure her brother had clothes on his back, food on the table and the school-ing he needed. What she gave to Jeremiah came straight from the heart.

Besides, no judge or court in the land would grant her custody of her brother, once they found out the real way Dorie earned her living. The Parkers certainly couldn't find out. But she'd done what she'd had to do. Selling eggs and butter, taking in laundry from the neighbors, didn't earn her nearly enough to see them through the winters. And if Dorie's secret talent was to be frowned upon by the townsfolk, then so be it. No one else had come to lend a hand.

No one except Shane, that is.

"Shane's gonna help us out, Jeremiah. You should be grateful for that."

"I am. But now I got to pretend you're married to him. And that we all live together on his big ranch. Shane's ranch ain't all that big and he's probably got less money than we do."

"Never mind that," Dorie said. She didn't know how much money Shane had, not that it mattered. She wasn't going to touch a penny of his cash. Dorie had money of her own. She'd saved up some. She'd been hoping to buy a buckboard wagon with her earnings, but this was far more important.

Keeping Jeremiah was all that mattered.

"And you just mind your words and think before you speak when we meet up with the Parkers. I don't like lying either, but it has to be done."

Jeremiah was honest to a fault. Dorie had raised him up that way. She'd never liked liars and had taught Jeremiah to always tell the truth. Now, she was asking him to go against her teachings, to pretend to a life that was entirely, one hundred percent, untrue. She worried more about Jeremiah's part in this than anything else. "You've got to promise me, Jeremiah."

She heard him grumbling from behind. "Well?"

"I promise, Dorie. But I sure don't like it."

He didn't have to like it, but he did have to go along with her plan. They'd only have to keep up the pretense for a day or two at the most while in Virginia City. Then the Parkers would be on their way, to finish up business they had in the West. "Fine then. So long as I've got your promise."

An hour later, Dorie reached her homestead. Home had never appeared better to her. Although the small house was in desperate need of repair, she'd done her best to make it comfortable, and it was after all... home.

"You see to Lightning, Jeremiah. Comb her down real good. I'll fix us something to eat in a while."

Dorie dismounted her horse and dashed inside the house to her bedroom, her mama's words echoing in her mind. It had been years since Dorie had thought on it, but now the vision of her mama reading by lantern light into the night forged an image in her head.

"You must always remain a lady, Isadora, in your heart and in your mind."

They'd been poor. They'd struggled, yet Dorie had always remembered her mother holding her head high. She'd been a lady, perhaps not one finely dressed with jeweled ornaments, but her mother had always kept her dignity. After losing two husbands, the fathers of her children, Rebecca McCabe Parker hadn't the time or energy to follow through with Dorie. She'd been too busy on the homestead to teach her firstborn all the proper ways of a woman. But there was a book. Dorie had recalled seeing it often, in her mother's hands, on the table by her bed, and then later—after her mother had died—Dorie remembered tucking it away underneath her mother's clothes in the chest that stood at the end of the bed.

Dorie quickly opened the knotty pine box, rifling through shawls, worn-out petticoats and a few other garments. "There you are," she said quietly, as she came up with the book she'd been searching for. She ran a hand over it, removing bits of dust and debris. "*The Lady's Guide to Perfect Gentility,* by Emily Thornwell," she recited.

Gently, with nimble fingers, Dorie opened it. The pages were worn, slightly discolored, but the book was undamaged in any other way. She read through the table of contents and smiled, gratified by the subjects it contained. This was exactly what she needed. She hugged the book to her chest, her hopes climbing. She would read through the book and follow the teachings to the letter.

With Shane's help and the knowledge she'd gain from this book, Dorie had renewed faith that her plan would most definitely work.

Shane stood at the bar at the Silver Lady Saloon and ordered a whiskey. With any luck, the liquor would ease the pain in his head. He'd had no sleep and was bone weary, yet he'd needed supplies in town that couldn't wait. He'd been in the middle of making repairs to his barn when Tobias Barkley had approached him with his plan to marry his daughter. Barkley wouldn't take no for an answer. Shane had gazed out on the ranch he'd worked so hard to build up, determined not to let *anyone* destroy his livelihood. So, with great reluctance, he'd agreed. He'd had no option.

And now, if Barkley didn't find Marilee, all would be lost.

Shane shook his head and gulped his whiskey. Now he had another problem on his hands, as well.

Dorie.

"Had a rough day yesterday?" Bart, the barkeep

asked. He kept his head down and his eyes focused on the cloth he used to wipe smudges off the mahogany bar.

"You could say that." Shane took another sip of whiskey.

"Folks here sure are saying that. They're confounded as to what happened."

Shane cast Bart a direct look. "Guess that's to be expected. Hell, I'm not sure what happened, myself."

"Old man Barkley came in here last night, talking about giving a reward to anyone who knows where Marilee had run off to. Never saw someone so blasted mad. That man ain't used to being crossed."

"Don't I know it," Shane said, pouring another drink from the bottle sitting atop the bar. "I'm sure Marilee doesn't want to be found right now."

"'Cause of what Dorie did?"

Shane shook his head. "Dorie didn't mean any harm." Even though she'd disrupted his life, Shane still felt the need to defend her actions. He was angry with her, but for some doggone reason he didn't want anyone else looking on her with ill regard.

"She sure looked fit to be tied, barging in on your wedding day and all, if you don't mind me saying."

Bart had said quite enough. But Shane figured he was just as curious as the rest of the townsfolk, wondering what exactly happened at that church yesterday. "It wasn't anything more than a misunderstanding."

"You gonna marry Marilee if Barkley finds her?"

Shane set his money down on the top of the bar. "Yep, if she'll have me." He was duty-bound to marry her. He'd offered, she'd accepted, both with reluctance, but a deal was a deal. She hadn't asked for the humiliation that ensued, and he would take full responsibility for walking out of that church yesterday. Barkley's threats had little to do with his decision. Now it was more a matter of honor.

Of course, first he had to spend two weeks with Dorie and *pretend* to be her husband.

Shane jammed his hat on his head and left the saloon.

His boots hit the sidewalk and he walked along with rapid speed. He'd never been the object of such scrutiny before. All around, people stared, some with curious looks, others shaking their heads. Darn, but it sure felt as though their piercing gazes were boring a hole right through him.

He shoved open the door at Caruthers' General Store harder than he'd meant to and entered, drawing the attention of all the customers. A woman wearing a feathered hat nearly dropped a tin of dried fruit, catching it just in time before it spilled out onto the floor. The Cantara family, all four of them, stopped shopping to gaze at him from down the aisle. And if that wasn't enough, Brett Caruthers greeted him at the counter with a crooked smile. The boy was handsome, he supposed, and about the same age as Dorie. "Hello, Mr. Graham."

Mannerly, too, when his father was looking on, but not when it came to taking advantage of an innocent girl like Dorie.

Shane grimaced, grunting a reply.

"Didn't think we'd see you in here today."

From just under the low brim of his hat, Shane eyed the boy. "That so?"

"Well, uh, Dorie sort of gave the impression that she—"

"She and I had a misunderstanding, that's all. She's a good person. Not a girl to be trifled with. It'd be best you remember that. And keep your hands to yourself where Dorie is concerned." Shane cast the boy a long hard stare.

Brett's eyes rounded and his face flushed with color. "Yessir."

The elder Caruthers came up to lay a hand on his son's shoulder. "I'll take care of Mr. Graham, Brett. You go on and sweep out the backroom."

"Okay," he said, apparently relieved, making quick strides toward the backroom. Shane was certain Brett Caruthers wouldn't be waiting on him anytime soon, but he wouldn't be messing with Dorie again, either.

"Howdy, Shane. What can I get you?" Martin asked.

"I got a list here. Let's start with tobacco and sugar, coffee, a sack of flour and toss in a handful of those gumdrops."

Martin Caruthers made fast work of gathering the supplies on Shane's list. He set the items onto the counter, wiped his hands on his striped apron, then leaned in a bit. "You know, it ain't any of my business, but Tobias Barkley was in here yesterday, ready to place a big order for some of that newfangled barbed wire. Seems he means to put up some fences."

"That's his choice," Shane said, keeping the defeat from his voice. Even so, he felt a sharp stab of anger take hold in his gut. "Most folks don't see fences as being real neighborly."

Martin shrugged. "He was just checking prices. He put the order on hold, for a time. He and some of his crew took off at dawn, searching for Marilee. Said he'll let me know about that order when he gets back. Thought you might want to know."

"Thanks. I appreciate it."

Martin scratched his head and paused, ready to say something. Shane offered the man no encouragement. He'd already had an earful today.

Finally, after a while, Martin offered, "Look, Shane. I don't know what happened between you and Marilee Barkley yesterday, but her father wasn't all too happy. It sure looked like you ran out on your intended."

"I didn't, Martin. You know me better than that."

"Yep, and most folks around here want to believe that, but it sure looked like you ran off with little Dorie McCabe."

"I know how it looked, but it ain't the truth. When Marilee comes back, I intend to marry her. That's all I can say right now."

Martin nodded his head. "Okay. You've been a good customer and a friend. I just thought to warn you what Barkley's intentions are."

"Thanks, I appreciate the concern."

A short time later, Shane climbed up onto his buckboard, his supplies weighing down the back end, and clicked the reins. Shane was only too glad to leave Silver Hills in the dust. With the sun setting, a breezy autumn wind helped to cool off his temper and clear his head.

Leaning back and heaving a wearisome sigh, he trusted his team of horses to find their way home. They were a good pair. They knew the way. Aptly, he'd named them accordingly.

Smart and Sassy.

Instantly, Dorie came to mind.

Shane cursed.

That girl was on his brain.

One minute he was thinking of his mares, then the very next, the image of wild red hair and light blue eyes entered his head. She was smart and sassy, too.

Damn.

Shane figured he just needed some sleep. His mind was addled. He was tired, drained and ready for bed. He needed to put the past two days behind him. Then tomorrow, he'd get back to work on the Bar G, feel the earth break in his hands, fix the barn, chop firewood. He'd get his perspective back.

He'd feel better in the morning.

Darkness descended as Shane made his way down the path to his ranch. After bedding down his horses, Shane entered his home, his arms filled with supplies. A strange smell strangled in his throat. He raced to the kitchen, dropped his supplies and followed the scent to the cookstove. He pulled open the door.

Burned biscuits greeted him.

He yanked them out with a cloth and tossed them onto the counter. Warily, he made a complete tour of his kitchen area. His table was set for two, with glasses and dishes thrown down haphazardly. A bottle filled with drooping wildflowers adorned the center. A broken dish and several bowls and pots sat in a wash bucket, unwashed.

Shane stepped out of the kitchen, his mind reeling. With quiet precision, he made his way to the parlor.

And found Dorie McCabe asleep on his sofa, clutching a book against her stomach with soft lantern light illuminating her form.

He stared in disbelief for a moment.

Then another sensation rushed in, as he watched the steady rise of her breasts, witnessed a soft glow streaming onto that mane of untamed fiery hair and viewed a fair amount of skin where her skirt had lifted and parted between her legs.

Shane took a hard swallow. His groin tightened.

He brought the lantern closer and called her name. "Dorie?"

She opened her eyes slowly, gazing up at him with parted lips.

"What are you doing here?" he asked with quiet regard that belied his riotous body.

"Shane," she said, arms up, stretching slowly like a sated kitten. The book on her stomach fell onto the floor. He could only make out one word that seemed to say it all. *Perfect.* "Sorry, I fell asleep."

"What are you doing here?" he repeated, a bit louder this time.

Her eyes held his. Her lips curved up. "It's time."

"Time?" he asked, backing up a step. That mouth of hers would do him in one day.

"Uh-huh." She nodded and moved her body on the sofa in ways that caused Shane's temperature to rise.

"For what?" She had the ability to confound and confuse him, time and again.

Softly, she answered, "To make me your wife."

Chapter Four

Shane's mouth dropped open. She couldn't possibly mean…no—Dorie was too doggone innocent to realize how she looked right now, draped across his sofa so provocatively, and how her softly spoken words planted lusty visions in his head.

Make me your wife.

Geesh, that sentiment alone proved how little Dorie knew of decorum. Shane had learned some in his youth, growing up with a mama who'd been raised in the East. His mother taught him manners and spoke of social graces. Shane had little use for her teachings once he'd settled on the Bar G, but those sentiments had stayed with him. Then when he'd begun his brief courtship to Marilee, he'd seen firsthand how a lady should behave.

Dorie had a long way to go in that regard. And all they had were those two weeks to make their lie believable. Shane wondered if it were even possible to pull off the charade as Dorie intended.

"Dorie, it's late."

She sat up and a curtain of untamed tresses fell across

her face, parting slightly so that her pretty blue eyes peeked out to regard him. "It's not too late to begin, Shane. I made you supper."

"Thank you, but after dinner, I'm going to bed."

"Fine, then we'll start first thing in the morning. I'll just sleep here tonight."

"No!" Shane blurted. "You can't stay here tonight or any other night, Dorie. It's not *proper*. And isn't that why you need my help? You need to know what a lady will and will not do. A lady would never sleep in a man's home, unless they were married to each other. It would ruin your reputation."

Dorie bit her lip, contemplating. She noticed the book she'd dropped on the floor then swooped down to pick it up. She studied it for a long moment. "I'm anxious to begin, Shane."

"I know you are. Let me fill my belly and then I'll take you home. Did you eat anything?"

"No, I waited for you," she answered with disappointment evident on a downcast face. At the moment, Shane thought she looked like a child who'd had her new doll taken away. It was a good reminder to keep his lusty thoughts at bay when it came to Dorie. She was an innocent who relied on him for his help. Nothing more.

Touched by her good intention, he put out his hand. "Let's get us some grub. Then I'll take you home."

Dorie took his hand and after he helped her rise, he released her immediately. "Where did you get that book?"

Dorie's eyes went bright. "It was my mama's. I remember her reading it to me when I was very young. But then, things went bad and we never had much time for reading. From time to time she'd try to remind me of things…like how to stand up proper, to always keep my shoulders back and how to walk like a lady." Dorie looked him straight in the eye. "Guess Mama wouldn't think much of how I turned out."

Shane felt a surge of emotion for Dorie. She hadn't acted coy, hoping for a compliment. No, she'd spoken in earnest, straight from her heart, not asking for sympathy or indulgence. Dorie was the most forthright female he knew. "Your mama would be proud as a peacock of you. You've managed all these years, keeping food on the table and doing right by Jeremiah, taking over the role of mother with him, as well as sister. I'd say a mother couldn't ask for anything more from a daughter."

Dorie's face transformed into something beautiful. She smiled with her eyes. "You really think so, Shane?"

He nodded. "I know so."

That's when she lifted up and kissed his cheek. It was a little peck of friendship more than anything else, but Shane felt a tingle way down to his bone-tired toes.

"I don't care if that was proper or not, Shane," she announced. "When a man makes a woman feel this good inside, it can't be wrong to show it."

Shane stared at her and sighed. "Dorie, you can't be saying things like that. And yes, it's wrong to show it. You can't go kissing a man, just because he makes you feel good."

Wasn't that what got him into this mess in the first place? Only it hadn't been Dorie, but Marilee who'd allowed a man to make her feel good inside—and look where that had gotten her. Hell, if that ranch hand hadn't said some sweet words to Marilee, none of them would be in this mess.

"Shane, don't be silly. I wouldn't kiss any ole man. *Just you.*"

Dorie's admission might have put a smile on his face if he wasn't in such a predicament. She had a way of speaking from the heart that aroused unnamed emotions in him. He knew that kind of talk from Dorie could lead to trouble. He'd always tried to be neighborly, but Dorie had taken his good intentions the wrong way. And it was up to Shane to see that she didn't come out the loser in any of this.

"Dorie, we won't be doing much kissing in front of the Parkers, so you might as well concentrate on other things right off. And remember, when Marilee comes back home, I plan to marry her. For real."

Dorie sauntered past him with her chin held high. "That's only *if* Marilee comes back home and *if* she decides she'll still marry you. Seems to me there's a whole lot of *ifs* in your future, Shane."

Shane couldn't argue her point. There *were* a lot of ifs in his life right now, the least of which was whether he and Dorie could pull off this sham and whether he could hold everything together long enough to save his ranch.

"What's the matter, Dorie?" Jeremiah asked, as he slammed the door shut behind him, waking Dorie out of her doldrums. She'd been sitting at the table all morning, reading "the book."

"It's this here book. There's so much to learn. Why, there's a multitude of chapters, Jeremiah. And I can't seem to get it all in my head. I swear I don't know how women do it."

Jeremiah laughed and took the seat beside her,

grabbing a handful of Dorie's burnt biscuits. Heavens, she couldn't cook worth a darn. But Jeremiah didn't seem to mind her offerings as long as she didn't fit him with an apron and ask him to lend a hand. "Seems that most *women* just know it, Dorie. Sort of like, knowing how to put one foot in front of the other if you want to git anywhere."

"That's what I mean. Most women don't have to read this entire book to act womanly. Of course, some might not know," she said, turning to the chapter on Choice Cosmetics for Improving and Beautifying the Skin, "that there's a way to remove warts." Dorie lifted her hands, turning them back and forth in the air, studying them. "They may not be the prettiest things, what with all the chores and all, but I don't see one wart, thank heaven. But Mrs. Caruthers sure has them. I see them every time I pick up supplies at the mercantile. And she doesn't even try to hide them. I bet she doesn't know this."

Dorie began reading slowly, enunciating each word, "To remove warts—the bark of the willow tree, burnt to ashes and mixed with strong vinegar, then applied to the parts, will remove corns as well as warts."

Dorie jammed the book closed. "There's so much to learn," she muttered. "But I'm sure glad I don't have any warts."

Jeremiah grabbed for the book. He studied the title. *"The Lady's Guide to Perfect Gent...ility."* He thumbed through the pages, his eyes growing wide. "Lots of big words in here."

"I know," Dorie said, slinking down in her chair again.

"And chapters on just about everything, Dorie. Hey,

there's a section on teeth! And on lips. And lookee here, there's a section on hair, too."

Dorie perked up. "What's it say about hair?" At least that was one subject she might understand without much help. Dorie had streaming coppery hair, thick and full with curls. She liked the look of her hair mostly, unless the wind got caught up in it, or she got drenched in a thunderstorm. Then those curls would tangle into an unholy nest and it'd be days before she could straighten it all out again.

Jeremiah took his sweet time reading silently. Then he turned to her. "It says that you should keep your hair groomed. Sorta sounds like keeping a horse, don't it?"

"Go on, Jeremiah. What else?"

"It says you got to be sure to wash it often and brush it at least three times a day."

Her shoulders slumped. "Three times?"

"Yep, that's what it says. It keeps the coat—" Jeremiah said, chuckling, "I mean, it keeps the hair shiny."

"Anything else?" she asked, thinking about how she would ever find the time to brush her long locks three times each day. Why, she barely found time to comb through her hair at night, before bed. Most times, she braided her hair, to keep it out of her face while she slept.

"One more thing. There's an instruction to cut off one inch of hair to remove any damage."

"Damage?"

"Yep," Jeremiah said, snapping the book shut. "One inch to remove damage." He reached over to lift a handful of her hair. "See here?"

Dorie looked down at the clump of hair he held in his hand. "The ends are split. That's what the book said would happen. If you don't brush and groom and cut, your hair splits."

"I guess one inch isn't so bad," Dorie offered, never realizing she had damaged hair before. "Well, let's get to it."

Jeremiah jumped up from his seat. "Get to what?"

"You're gonna cut my hair."

"No. Nope. Not me. I ain't gonna cut your hair."

Dorie rose from her seat and looked her younger brother straight in the eyes. "Yes, you're gonna cut my hair. The book says it needs cutting, right?"

"Well, uh, yeah. But I ain't good with scissors. And you'd hang my hide if I chopped off too much. You're fussy about your hair, Dorie." Jeremiah dashed to the front door and reached for the handle. "Besides, I got some logs to split. And I got to check on the chickens. Collect the eggs, you know. And then I got to fix the gate. You've been hollering that the latch is broken for days now."

"Jeremiah, get back here."

But it was too late. Her brother had run for the hills. Now Dorie was left with the task of trying to cut her own hair. She didn't much like the idea. But there wasn't anyone else.

Shane finished up his chores early. On any given day, he'd work until sundown on the Bar G, but since he'd become a temporary "husband" he had to make time for Dorie. Thankfully, he would have a few hours of peace before she'd ride over this afternoon. He prayed more than hoped she wouldn't insist on serving him dinner. He'd nearly choked down the dry chicken and biscuits she'd cooked up last night.

Shane shook his head thinking about what he'd

gotten himself into, shaking off dust from the range, as well. He was dirty, smelled of horse dung and had baked half the day in the sun. "We're heading home early, Sassy," he said, patting the trusty mare on the neck.

Shane didn't mind working hard on his land, building up the ranch and trying to keep his stock healthy, the thought of a prosperous ranch his sole ambition. Yet, his usual good humor had faded lately.

Being a part of Dorie's ruse rubbed him the wrong way. He didn't like lying, not even for a good cause. And he certainly didn't like having Dorie underfoot all the time.

Shane pulled Sassy up in front of the barn and dismounted, taking a comb and brush to her, until she was free and clear of range dust. When the mare was tucked safely into the corral she shared with Smarty, it was Shane's turn to clean up.

He walked over to the water barrel at the east end of the barn, stripped off his shirt and splashed cool liquid onto his chest. He could almost hear the sizzle, where cold water met heated skin. He soaked his shirt and used it to wash his face, arms and chest until the stubborn Nevada dust disappeared. He set his shirt out to dry on the corral fence and feeling somewhat refreshed he entered his home.

That's when he knew something was amiss.

The scent of flowers wafted in the air, a fresh delicate fragrance that conflicted with the usual earth and leather scents that followed him into his house. He heard a noise and strode to the kitchen.

"What the hell?"

"Hello, Shane."

Dorie sat on a kitchen chair, wrapped in a big rough

towel, her arms and legs bared to him, her long hair wet and dripping lemon drops of water onto the floor. She had a comb in her hand.

"Dorie, what are you doing?" Shane couldn't keep both the disbelief and the anger from his voice.

"Please don't go getting mad, Shane." Dorie's blue eyes rounded, filling with tears and she seemed truly distressed. "I've had a time of it, today. I…I need your help."

Shane stepped closer to her. A foolish mistake, because he couldn't help noticing the shape of her pretty legs, crossed delicately at the ankles, and the softness of her shoulders as her hair caressed the skin there. The flowery scent became increasingly stronger with each of his steps. "What's wrong?"

"Just…everything." A tear fell, then another and soon Shane stood helplessly by as Dorie sobbed silently in front of him.

"Ah, Dorie. Don't cry." Shane stood above her, looking down at the spirited young girl who seemed truly distraught. He'd never seen this side of her before. In the past, Dorie had always been tough in nature, willing to do battle with anyone who stood in the way of what she needed. Shane had always admired that about Dorie. And he'd worried over her less because of it. He'd never seen Dorie cry before. Not like this. "C'mon. It can't be that bad. What's wrong?"

Dorie peered up at him, stifling her sobs long enough to nod her head. "It can be, Shane. It is. I'm not good at being a woman." Dorie let go another sob.

Shane bent on his knee to look up into her eyes. He'd never seen a more appealing woman. She looked like a temptress, though unwitting, dressed in nothing but a big beat-up old towel that made her appear even more feminine, more graceful to him.

"You're a fine woman," Shane said.

"I can't do a thing right, Shane. And the book says…oh, there's so much to learn. I can't remember it all."

"You don't have to, Dorie. Not all of it. We'll pick and choose."

"Really?"

For the first time, a light of hope appeared in her eyes. "Yes, you don't have to know it all. Remember, I said I'd help."

She nodded and took a long admiring look at him. Shane had forgotten he was nearly unclothed. His shirt lay outside on the corral fence, his hat long gone. And Dorie seemed to notice all of him, all at once. Her blue gaze never wavered, the light in her eyes turning a darker shade. She reached out to touch his shoulder. His skin burned from her delicate touch. "Thank you."

"Dorie," he said in stern warning. He rose abruptly. She followed him up and the towel slipped some, exposing the top portion of her chest, where the hollow formed between her breasts.

Shane reached for the towel, before it slipped even farther. Dorie caught his hands, looking up at him with those big blue expressive eyes.

He cleared his throat. "Want to tell me why you're here, dressed like that?"

Dorie fastened the towel tighter around her and to his relief, took a step back. "I need you to cut my hair."

Shane felt his eyes grow wide. Of all the things he

might have imagined coming from Dorie's pretty saucy mouth, he'd never expected a request for a haircut. He chuckled. "You can't be serious."

Her eyes rounded and she nodded; Shane thought she might sob again. "Dead serious. Jeremiah refused. He ran out on me. And then…then I tried doing it myself. And look, Shane. Look at the mess I made of my hair."

Dorie lifted up the mass, letting it flow through her fingers onto her bare back. Shane sucked in oxygen. Her moves provocative enough to tempt a saint; he was certain she had no knowledge of the picture she posed. When he stifled his unwelcome lust, he finally saw what she'd wanted him to see. The ends of her hair were mangled, cut bluntly, so that the strands lay in an uneven mass down past her shoulders.

Holding back a smile, he asked, "Why did you cut your hair?"

"The book said that—"

"Ah, the book," he interrupted. "Say no more."

"I can't go meeting the Parkers with my hair looking like this!" She picked up a chunk of hair again. "I haven't had my hair cut since Mama died. I sorta liked it long and curly."

Shane nodded. Dorie's long coppery hair was one of her many appealing points. "It's not so bad. It's still way past your, uh, your shoulders."

"Shane, please," she said, coming close again. "You have to fix it."

"Dorie, I wish you would have asked me first, before coming into my house, taking a bath and waiting for me half-naked in my kitchen."

"The book said the hair had to be clean and wet

before cutting. I figured that's what I did wrong the first time. I just started cutting all that dry curly hair."

Shane winced, put his head down and scratched his head. Sometimes there was just no arguing with Dorie. Still and all, he liked her better this way than teary-eyed and unhappy. "Okay, sit down. And don't move. Hand me those scissors."

"Really, Shane? You'll do it?" Dorie put her hand to Shane's chest and when she stepped closer, he noticed gratitude in her eyes. A thankful expression and a near-naked Dorie was one dangerous combination. Didn't do Shane any good that his skin fairly sizzled from that innocent touch. It was all he could do to keep from flinching and backing away. Dorie didn't need to know how Shane reacted to her. He stood his ground, grinding his teeth and thinking that he'd been in worse situations in his life, but at this exact moment, he couldn't think of one.

Shane couldn't do much about Dorie's state of undress right now. She'd have to remain that way until he cut her hair, but he sure could do something about his. "I said sit down. I'll be right back."

Dorie's smile vanished. "But where are—"

Shane scoffed at himself for showing Dorie his irritation. For all intents, he should be the one setting the example. Losing his temper wasn't going to do Dorie one bit of good, even though secretly it made him feel a mite better. He softened his tone and spoke with regard. "Please excuse me for one minute."

Dorie's eyes sparkled again. She nodded, sat down and straightened in her seat. "You're excused," she said, as stately as the queen of England.

Shane shook his head and walked out of the kitchen.

He told himself to hang on to his patience. Two weeks wasn't an eternity. He'd muddle through and then he'd be out of this predicament. One of them had to be cautious and rational, maintaining sound judgment.

Shane returned to the kitchen a moment later wearing a fresh shirt, buttoned up to his collarbone, and bearing a better attitude. He'd cut her hair and she would dress back into her baggy clothes. Then they'd spend an hour or two together, going over the book.

"What, uh, do you want me to do, exactly?" he asked, holding the comb and scissors now.

"Just…fix it, Shane."

Dorie had this idea about him, that he could wave a magic wand and fix anything, including her situation. That's what got him into this pickle in the first place. She had complete trust in him. Most men would puff out their chests and drink it all in, but Shane was beyond that now. One day, Dorie would find out that he wasn't a magician. He couldn't fix everything for her. He was a simple man, with simple needs, and as ordinary as they come.

"I'll do my level best."

Shane finger-combed Dorie's locks, the moist silky strands flowing through his fingers. Her hair, like the rest of her, was all female, soft and wild at the same time. Shane began cutting, tugging gently and making sure to keep the ends even.

He'd been reduced to a barber of sorts. He shook his head at the thought, but kept working through her thick locks, cutting and evening out the strands. After several minutes and intense scrutiny, Shane looked upon his work with satisfaction.

"All done." He backed away from Dorie. "It's as good as its gonna get, Dorie. But I think you'll like it."

Dorie rose from her seat and sifted through her hair. She nodded and smiled and those pretty blue eyes of hers gleamed. She spoke quietly, almost with reverence. "You fixed it, Shane. I knew you could."

Shane turned his back on her, not wanting to linger on the incredibly soft look in her eyes. "Better get dressed now, Dorie. You can use my room, but be quick about it."

"Why?"

"Why?" He turned to her. "Why what?"

"Why be quick about it?"

"It ain't proper having you in my room, dressed like that." Shane shook his head again. Nothing about her being here today was proper, but it was going to take more than one day to make her understand that. "Never mind. We have work to do."

"Right. I'll get dressed real quick."

Shane watched her sashay away then walked out the front door. Standing on his porch, he took a deep breath. That seemed to settle him some.

Until he saw Mrs. Whitaker's buggy heading straight toward his place. She waved and smiled then reined in her horse right in front of his porch. "Afternoon, Shane."

"Afternoon, Mrs. Whitaker."

Shane's neighbor to the south had a big spread, but she and her husband, Ignatius, had pretty much dwindled down their herd, making their ranch manageable for a couple in their late fifties. They'd been real good neighbors for the most part, and though Alberta Whitaker looked crotchety with those small brown eyes and wrinkled face, she was one of the kindest, most elegant women Shane had ever met.

"I hope I'm not disturbing you. I brought you a batch of pies. Iggy just doesn't eat like he used to and, well…" she said, as Shane helped her down from her buggy, "as you can see, I have made a few too many."

Shane's mouth watered looking at three pies sitting on the floorboard of her buggy, nestled inside a crate to keep from spilling out. "Looks like I'm in luck," he said cordially. "Be sure to thank Iggy for his lack of appetite."

Alberta laughed. "I should be glad that man doesn't eat like a wolf anymore, but I do miss fussing over him. Makes me feel useful around the house. I hope you like apple. There's rhubarb and peach, too."

Shane lifted his brows. "That's a lot of pie for just one man."

"Well, I figured you might share with those boys you hired on temporarily."

Shane nodded. He'd been able to afford the help of two local boys who'd come by after their schooling on some afternoons. They'd been happy with the little pay Shane could offer and the chance for a square meal or two. And they'd helped Shane with chores that one man couldn't muster on his own.

The arrangement suited everyone, but Shane hadn't had his ranch hands come around ever since he'd made his deal with Dorie. Wouldn't do to have their tongues wagging in town about Dorie's midafternoon visits or worse yet, her late-night ones.

"I sure will. The Boyd brothers will get their fair share."

Shane knew he should offer Mrs. Whitaker a cool drink for her trouble, but that meant inviting her inside.

No telling what Dorie would be up to inside his house. So he stood there smiling at her, thanking her again.

"Shane! Shane Graham! Look at my hair. It's almost all dry now! Don't you just love—" Still clad in the towel, Dorie opened wide the front door and halted her words once she saw that Shane had company. "Oh!"

Mrs. Whitaker took a good look at her, then her eyes rounded on Shane.

Shane wanted to disappear. But the ground beneath his feet wasn't swallowing him up.

Shane rolled his eyes. "I can explain."

Mrs. Whitaker pursed her lips, but not in anger as he might have guessed. Instead, she seemed more than a little bit amused. "There's no need, Shane."

"Sure there is," he rushed out. "Dorie," he called out, then turned around to find her face flushed. At least she had the good sense to know when to be embarrassed. He put as much patience in his tone that he could manage. "Get dressed like I asked you, *before.*"

"I was just fidgeting with my hair, Shane," she said, her chin up defiantly. "Hello, Mrs. Whitaker."

"Afternoon, Dorie."

Dorie wiggled her fingers in greeting then shut the front door, finally.

"It's not what you're thinking, Alberta."

"Why, Shane. I'm not thinking at all. Just seeing is believing."

"Ah, hell." Shane was dog tired of explaining his intentions with Dorie, but it seemed he had to own up one more time. He couldn't have Mrs. Whitaker believing the worst about Dorie, even though he knew the older woman would hold her tongue.

He lifted the crate of pies from her buggy and looked into her eyes. "Please come inside. It's about time I shared this with someone, and you're about the only person I can trust with the truth. I'm going to tell you something I bet you've never heard before, over a piece of your delicious pie and a cup of my awful coffee."

Chapter Five

‹‹‹‹‹‹‹‹‹〜∞〜›››››››››

"Did I hear you correctly, Shane? You're going to Virginia City to pretend to be Dorie's husband?"

Shane sunk the fork deep into a piece of apple pie and nodded. "That's right. I'm kind of hooked into this situation. Believe me, if there were any other way, I'd be the first one to agree. But Dorie's mind is set. She thinks it's the only way to keep Jeremiah."

"By fooling his grandparents?" Alberta Whitaker was too wise a woman to place blame or judgment. She kept her tone even and devoid of accusation. "I don't know, Shane. It could backfire on you."

"It's a risk Dorie is willing to take. She's hell-bent on doing it her way. You know what happened the day of my wedding. You were there. She…shanghaied me so I could help her. And now she's spending time here, so that we can get acquainted."

Alberta's graying eyebrows rose.

"Not that way, for God's sake. I'm not taking advantage of her. She came over here because of some fool notion that cutting her hair will make her look more ladylike or some such thing. She didn't give me much choice. Dorie sort of sneaks up on you when you least expect it and then…you're in trouble."

Mrs. Whitaker smiled wistfully. "Is that so?"

"Yes, it's so. Believe me. It's not so easy trying to turn Dorie into a lady. She's young and impulsive. And she's…well…" Shane began, but couldn't finish his thought. What he wanted to say would shock Mrs. Whitaker down to her high-topped boots.

Mrs. Whitaker bobbed her head once for him to continue. "She's what, Shane?"

"Nothing. Never mind."

Mrs. Whitaker sat thoughtfully for a moment, daintily slipping a forkful of pie into her mouth. "She's a handful for you, isn't she, Shane?"

Shane grunted, watching the door. Dorie should be busting in soon, hopefully dressed in those loose-fitting garments she wore. He'd seen enough of her soft skin and wild loose hair to last him a dozen lifetimes.

"She's pretty, in her own way," Mrs. Whitaker acknowledged.

Shane grunted again.

"And I've always admired her gumption," she said. "It wasn't easy on her when her mama died. She's all but raised Jeremiah."

"That's why I'm trying to help her. She loves that boy fiercely. She'd be crushed if he was taken from her."

"I know you've done your part in trying to help those two whenever you could, Shane."

"I've been neighborly, but Dorie read more into it and now I'm afraid I'm committed to this pretense."

Mrs. Whitaker strummed her fingers, deep in

thought. "Tell me what you were going to say earlier, Shane. I'm an old woman. I think I could stand to hear it all. What is it about Dorie that worries you most?"

Shane stared down at the crumbs left on his plate.

"She's a temptation you can't afford," Mrs. Whitaker said softly. "Is that it?"

Shane closed his eyes. He wouldn't have used those words exactly, but she'd come close enough. "As I explained earlier, I'm destined to marry Marilee Barkley. Her father is certain he'll find her and bring her home. If she'll have me, I'm going to go through with that marriage. I can't be, uh…"

Alberta nodded in understanding. "Dallying with Dorie. You want to leave her reputation intact."

Shane heaved a big sigh of relief. The older woman had put into words what Shane couldn't. "That's right, Alberta," he said quietly.

"And she's here, alone with you, more than you'd like, right?"

He nodded.

"Well, then. I think I have a solution for you." She set her napkin down and smiled wide. "Since you've shared your secret with me, I think I'd like to help. Let me take over some of the teaching with Dorie. Lord knows, that girl could use a woman's guidance in such matters. I'll help her with her speech and manners and other such things."

Shane gulped down the last bit of his bitter coffee. "You'd do that?"

"I would love to help, Shane. I can spare an hour or two a day for Dorie's noble, yet deceitful cause." She chuckled. "And the time she spends with me, she *won't* be spending with you."

Shane scratched his head and grinned. "I like the way you think."

"Now, all we have to do is convince Dorie."

"Convince me of what?" Dorie entered the room and Shane couldn't take his eyes off of her. Her face framed in a fiery halo of loose tresses, she wore her hair pinned up at the sides, the shiny coppery locks in back bouncing in curls against her shoulders. And even though she wore her old wrinkled clothes, she smelled as fresh as summer rain.

"Dorie, don't you look pretty," Mrs. Whitaker said.

Dorie smiled wide and Shane realized that there probably weren't too many compliments in her life. She'd had a tough time of it and now, instead of being courted by young smitten beaus, she had to settle for a temporary pretend husband, just to keep what little family she had left. "Thank you."

"Dorie, won't you sit down and have some pie?" Mrs. Whitaker smiled graciously.

Dorie shot a curious glance at Shane before sitting down. "Looks delicious."

Alberta cut a piece of pie and placed it onto a plate. She handed the plate to Dorie. "Here we go, dear."

Shane cleared his throat. "Uh, Dorie, Mrs. Whitaker knows about our deal."

Her eyes went wide and she focused solely on Shane. "She does? How?"

"I told her."

Dorie's face twisted with accusation and betrayal. For a moment she became speechless. Then she spoke softly as if Mrs. Whitaker wasn't in the room. "Why would you do that, Shane?"

Shane took a deep breath. "Dorie, at times, you leave me no choice. You come outside dressed like you were dressed, without thought to who might see you, giving the wrong impression. I had to explain to Mrs. Whitaker so she wouldn't think the worst about you…and me."

Alberta Whitaker placed her hand over Dorie's. "I understand your dilemma, dear. And I'm willing to help."

Dorie shot Mrs. Whitaker a surprised look. "You are?"

She smiled. "Yes. I can help you make a fine impression on these folks. They will not doubt you for a moment. You know, dear, I was raised in New York myself. I married there, for the first time. My husband was a prominent doctor. We had social gatherings and celebrations every month. I know something of decorum and etiquette. Will you permit me to help you?"

"Oh, uh…" Dorie looked over to Shane for approval. He nodded.

"You don't think it's terrible, what I'm trying to do?"

Alberta chuckled, the soft sound making her seem younger and more vital. "The truth is always a better option, dear. But I won't judge you. I know how hard you've worked these past few years and I also know you're doing a fine job of raising Jeremiah. If you see this as the only way to keep Jeremiah—"

"I do. Oh, yes I do. They'd never let me keep him if they saw how we lived. Not that Jeremiah wants for anything. We have food and…and a house. And he's schooled. But they're rich, Mrs. Whitaker. They'd fight me and I'd lose my brother."

Alberta's brown eyes softened on Dorie. "Sometimes people can surprise you."

"How?" Dorie seemed truly puzzled.

"What I mean to say is that we never know how things will really turn out. Twenty years ago I'd never have believed that I'd be a ranch wife, living in Nevada with a gruff man like Iggy Whitaker. But here I am."

"You love him, right?"

"Do I love him? Why, I'd have never left the comforts of New York if I hadn't fallen head over heels with the man. A few years after my first husband died, I traveled to Kansas to visit with my cousins. Iggy was at the end of a trail drive, and I met him quite by accident on the main street of town. He nearly knocked me over. I thought he was the crudest, rudest man I'd ever met." She stopped for a moment to smile. "Two weeks later, I married the cowboy. So you see, sometimes life can surprise you."

"Oh my," Dorie said, a winsome look on her face.

"Yes, it's quite a story, but let's get back to your situation. Would you consider allowing me to help?"

"Yes, yes. I'd be honored if you'd help me. But what about Shane? I still need to—"

"You will. You'll get accustomed to each other in due time. We won't neglect that. You and Shane will spend time together."

Dorie smiled and dug into her pie. Mrs. Whitaker watched her plow into the crust then shove the fork into her mouth. She grinned at Shane and he knew a moment of great relief.

Dorie was off his hands, at least temporarily.

Two afternoons later, Shane took off on Sassy and headed toward a cluster of longhorns that the Boyd brothers had claimed had taken sick. The cattle had been infected by blowflies burrowing deep into their brand wounds, and the screwworms that hatched as a result created enough pain and illness to cause death. Shane had precious few cattle as it was; he couldn't afford to lose any.

He had a salve he hoped would cure the few in his herd that had taken sick. Shane rode hard as the Nevada sun beat down and, after riding for an hour, he finally found the infirm cattle.

Shane dismounted and grabbed for his saddlebag. He unfastened the strap and took out the round container, thick with salve. The trick of it was to get the medicine on the wound, without riling up the herd.

Shane had only done this once before and he'd had quite a time of it. Cattle didn't take to this medicine much. So he took his time, walking up slowly and looking over all ten steers that seemed to have the worst of the wounds. "Okay, we're gonna do this," he said softly. "I can't promise it's gonna feel so good, but it should help."

Shane worked on three steers gently applying the salve and all seemed to be going well. Once he headed for the fourth one, a ruckus broke out and Sassy whinnied loudly as a bald eagle swooped down, flying low enough to panic his mare. The horse bucked up, her front legs lifting high in the air. She snorted and ran straight for the herd.

Shane, stuck in the middle of a cluster of cattle now, raced to get out of the way of shuffling and confused steer. He'd almost made it, too, but for the last flustered longhorn, which lowered its head and rammed Shane's side with a horn to move him out of the way.

Shane grunted a profanity as he was lifted into the air. His hat went flying. Pain exploded inside his head. Blood spurted out of his gut. He dropped to the ground, gripping the left side of his stomach.

The earth grumbled as the small herd raced away. Shane lay alone now, but for Sassy who'd wandered over to nudge his head. "Give me a minute, girl," he huffed out, his breaths coming with great difficulty now.

Shane knew he'd bleed to death from the stab wound if he stayed out on the open range tonight. He had to get up. He had to stop the bleeding. He needed to get some help. With a grunt and all the strength he could muster, he rose to his feet and struggled out of his shirt. Wrapping his shirt around his body, he tied a knot around the deep gash to curtail the bleeding.

Sassy nudged him again and he grabbed onto the saddle horn. He stood a moment, willing himself to do this, then inhaled sharply, before putting his boot into the stirrup and using the right side of his body to lift himself up onto his mare.

That move nearly sapped all of his strength. With a click of his heels, Sassy took off. He reined her toward the one person he knew would help him. The one person whom he'd been thinking about for the past two days.

The only person he needed right now.

Dorie.

Dorie cut a pattern of the finest red raw silk and fashioned the pieces against each other, pinning the right sides together and, once the gown fit like a perfect puzzle, she lifted the needle. She'd been gifted with this talent as a youngster, her mama exclaiming her abilities were far more advanced than even her own. It was her talent with needle and thread that kept Jeremiah in clothes and food and for the most part, kept their homestead from total ruin.

Dorie sewed.

For the prostitutes of Virginia City.

She'd been commissioned by the best whores in the county. And she managed to keep her employment a secret from the fine citizens of Silver Hills. It was a firm condition of the agreement she'd made with the ladies of the night.

They'd been so taken by her expertise that they'd agreed. No one would ever know where their fine gowns were made. Or by whom.

"Ouch! Dang it!" Dorie stuck herself with the needle for the third time today. It wasn't at all like her. She never missed a stitch. Never. Except that she was overly nervous lately, worrying over the Parkers' visit coming up real soon. And she missed Shane. It surprised her how much.

She hadn't seen him since that day at his house when Mrs. Whitaker had come by to visit. Thinking of Mrs. Whitaker made her amend her last blurted out comment. "A lady doesn't use foul language. She doesn't curse, or scream out. She doesn't say 'dang it.' Dorie, when is it gonna sink into your head."

Dorie had spent two afternoons under Mrs. Whitaker's tutelage. She'd taught her the fine points of walking like a lady and talking like one. Dorie didn't have much trouble with the first, but her mouth had always run off and she had a hard time remembering what was proper language and what was not.

She knew to sit with her hands folded in her lap. That

a lady doesn't cross her legs, but may cross her ankles at times. A lady smiles coyly at a man, but never out and out laughs like a hyena. "It's a whole lot to remember," she said again, the sentiment never far from her mind.

If only she could see Shane soon. He seemed to settle her, make her feel that all would work out for the best. Dorie had faith in Shane. More faith than she had in any other person, except maybe Jeremiah.

Dorie sat at the kitchen table and sewed for hours, each stitch as perfect and as even as the next, until she got to the point were the raw silk dress was ready for its lace trim. She gazed down at her creation feeling a sense of deep satisfaction. Too bad no one but the prostitutes would ever acknowledge the work she put into each dress, but it was enough that Dorie knew. She smiled and settled back in her seat, taking a break, wiggling her cramped fingers.

Jeremiah burst in through the back door. "Dorie, come quick! It's Shane. I found him about half a mile from here. He's hurt bad, Dorie."

Dorie's gut clenched. Jeremiah was near tears. It'd been a long time since her brother had showed such raw emotion. She pushed aside the gown and jumped up. "What's wrong with him? Tell me quick!"

Breathing heavy, Jeremiah blurted. "Looks like he's been stabbed. He's bleeding all over. I didn't know what to do. He was slumped over on his horse. I pulled Sassy in with me. He's right outside, Dorie."

"Help me get him!" Dorie raced out the back door and stopped up short with a gasp. "Oh!" She found Shane slung over his saddle like a rag doll, his face ashen with blood oozing out from a crimson stained shirt tied around the side of his stomach.

"He's breathing, isn't he?" Jeremiah asked.

"Lord in heaven," Dorie said softly, placing her fingers to his throat, measuring his shallow breaths. "Yes, he's breathing." And she planned to keep him breathing. Dorie couldn't lose Shane. Not Shane.

"Help me get him inside, Jeremiah. We've got to be careful helping him down from his mare. Whoa, Sassy. Be still, girl." Dorie comforted the horse as best she could, trying to keep panic from overtaking her, as well.

"Shane, can you hear me?"

An incoherent grunt was all she heard from him.

"We're gonna bring you into the house. It might pain you some. Sorry, Shane. So sorry. Okay, Jeremiah. Grab him."

"I've got him," her brother announced, holding Shane under the arms. For thirteen, Jeremiah McCabe was as strong as an ox. Dorie felt a moment of pride seeing him take the brunt of the burden without flinching.

Dorie helped and they half pulled, half dragged Shane's body across the yard and into the house. "Let's put him in my bed. It's bigger than yours."

And once they reached her bedroom, Dorie flipped off her quilt and adjusted the pillow so that Shane would have a comfortable place to rest. "There," she said, watching Shane's face contort in pain as they lowered him down. "Now you take Sassy and go fetch the doctor. Hurry, Jeremiah. I'll do what I can for Shane."

Jeremiah stared down at the only man with whom he had ever felt kinship. "He ain't gonna die, is he, Dorie?"

"Not if I can help it. Now run. Go get Doc Renfrow."

Jeremiah nodded. "Keep him alive, Dorie."

Dorie planned on doing that very thing. She raced to

the kitchen, gathered up fresh linens, a bowl of clean water and soap then returned to Shane.

"The doc will be here soon, Shane. You hang on."

Gingerly, Dorie unwrapped the blood-soaked shirt from Shane's body. She dipped some fresh linen into a bowl of warm soapy water and cleansed his wound. The bleeding had stopped, so she thanked heaven for small miracles and continued to wash him.

Shane's eyes opened then. "Dorie," he muttered so quietly she might have imagined it.

"I'm here, Shane. You're gonna be all right."

He closed his eyes and drifted back into oblivion. Dorie figured that was a good thing. He needed his rest. With utmost care, she continued to dab his body gently, cooling his skin and sending up silent prayers to the Almighty. She stayed with Shane until Dr. Renfrow arrived, just before sundown.

"He's gonna be all right, Doc, isn't he?" Jeremiah asked, before Dorie could get to it.

The town's aging doctor took a deep breath. Standing outside Dorie's room, he nodded. "He's lost a good deal of blood, but lucky for him, the stab wound didn't pierce an organ. I think with rest and proper care, he'll be up and around in a matter of days."

"So, he's not gonna die?" Jeremiah asked.

Dorie's heart went out to her little brother. For as big and strong as he was, Jeremiah had a kind soul. He'd lost a great deal in his young life. Losing Shane would be hard for him to accept. But Shane wasn't going to die, thank goodness. She supposed Jeremiah just needed to hear it from the doctor.

"No, I wouldn't think so."

"Who stabbed him?" Dorie asked.

The doctor placed his black bowler hat on his head. "Well, my guess is that he's been gouged by one of his longhorns. I've seen it before and I'll see it again, I imagine. He's got a good-size gash there, but the stitches will close that up real quick. He's young and strong, and I suspect he'll heal just fine. Remember to apply that salve on his wound three times a day. I'll come out again day after tomorrow to check on him."

"So keep the wound clean, dress it with fresh bandages and apply the salve. Anything else?" Dorie asked.

"No, that should do it. When he rouses, make sure he gets some nourishment. He'll need to keep up his strength."

"When will that be?" she asked.

"I'd keep a close eye on him. He might sleep through the night and into tomorrow, but I suspect he'll wake up within twenty-four hours. Give him a shot of whiskey for the pain."

Dorie gulped. "Whiskey? We don't have—"

"I'll get it from Shane's place, Dorie. I know where he keeps it."

Dorie stared at Jeremiah.

"Well, I ain't never took a shot myself, but I know where the bottle is." Jeremiah lifted his chin defiantly and Dorie saw something of herself in that particular gesture.

Dr. Renfrow chuckled.

Dorie shot him a stern look, but the old doctor just kept on smiling all the way out her front door.

"I'll see he gets something for the pain."

The doctor climbed up onto his horse. "I'll be back

day after tomorrow. You send your brother if you need me before then."

"Thank you, Dr. Renfrow. I will. But I'm hoping Shane won't need any more help."

He tipped his hat and took off.

Dorie hurried back into the house and entered her bedroom. She decided she'd put the finishing touches on the gown she'd been working on right here in her own room, where she could keep a constant vigil with Shane.

"Wonder what Mrs. Whitaker would think of you sleeping with Shane tonight, Dorie?" Jeremiah cast her a solemn look.

"Oh, for goodness sake, Jeremiah, the man is out cold. And…and I don't think I'd get much sleep worrying over him all night if I wasn't in here. Besides, Mrs. Whitaker doesn't have to know the specifics of my care for Shane, does she?"

Jeremiah narrowed his eyes. "You want me to lie?"

"No, just sort of lasso around the truth a bit. We don't have to mention me sleeping next to Shane."

"I could take turns with you, Dorie. I could watch over Shane."

Dorie chose her words wisely, not wanting to rile her brother any more than he seemed to be. Suddenly, her thirteen-year-old brother had become both her conscience and her judge. "You need your sleep, Jeremiah. Shane's gonna need your help in the morning. You're gonna have to ride out, fetch the Boyds and work his ranch tomorrow, at least for part of the day. His horses need tending and he'd appreciate you checking on his herd." She didn't add that Jeremiah was too sound a sleeper for her to trust him with Shane's care. He'd probably wind up fast asleep next to the man within minutes. No, Dorie couldn't trust anyone with Shane's care but herself.

"I'll do that for Shane, for sure."

"He'll be thankful. Now you go on. Get to sleep. I'll see you in the morning."

Jeremiah cast a final worried glance at a still and pale Shane, then bid her good-night.

Dorie had finished the gown she'd been working on an hour ago. Satisfied with her accomplishment, she'd folded the gown neatly and hid the garment, where she hid all the gowns she sewed, in a large cedar trunk just under the bedroom window.

She yawned, feeling tired and ready for bed. She pulled out her nightdress from her mother's old armoire and turned her back on Shane. He'd been asleep most the day so she'd be assured her privacy, undressing in the far corner of the room.

Once done, she climbed in next to Shane, taking a cool cloth to his forehead. Moping his brow, she noticed his skin moist from perspiration. She prayed he wouldn't become feverish through the night.

Finally she dozed, sleeping lightly enough to wake and check on Shane every hour or so. It was past midnight when she heard Shane groan, a deep guttural cry of pain. He squirmed and made slight movements on the bed, his face contorted with discomfort.

Dorie didn't hesitate. She spoke to Shane quietly. "Open your mouth, Shane. I have something for the pain."

Shane kept his eyes closed, but gave her an almost imperceptible nod. He opened his mouth slightly and

Dorie put the whiskey bottle to his lips. She poured the liquor in slowly, drop by drop, gently commanding him to drink up.

Dorie kept up this cycle throughout the night. Each time Shane grunted in pain, she poured more whiskey down him, hoping to ease the sting of his injury. Finally, after several hours of mopping his brow, making him comfortable on the bed and dosing him with alcohol to relieve his pain, Shane slept.

And so did Dorie.

Shane opened his eyes to darkness. His head swam with fuzziness, and it took a moment for him to recall the pain on his side that nearly crippled him. That nagging ache seemed better now. His mind, however, was muddled, and as he turned his head to one side a glimmer of predawn light shone on a woman lying by his side.

An angel with coppery red-gold hair, wild about the pillow, and a lovely peaceful face slept beside him.

Dorie.

Shane glanced about the room, too confused to figure where they were. He'd never seen this room before, or so it seemed. Then his gaze wandered over to the night table, where he noticed an inch of whiskey left in a bottle. Suddenly he knew why his side felt better while his head jumbled like jumping beans.

He was drunk.

And lying in bed with Dorie.

Shane felt a stirring below his waist.

He looked at Dorie's sleeping form and, unable to resist, he reached out to touch her cheek.

She opened her eyes. "Shane," she breathed out. "You're awake."

"Just barely, honey."

"That's good, Shane. Real good."

"Why are you in bed with me?"

"I've been caring for your, uh, injury."

"Plying me with whiskey?"

"That, too," she whispered. "Dr. Renfrow said to give you whiskey for the pain."

Shane cracked his lips apart in the smallest smile. "I'm feeling no pain now."

"I'm glad." Dorie's sky-blue eyes danced.

"God, you're pretty," he said, his addled brain shutting down. He really felt no pain now and all his inhibitions took flight. The sweet stirrings in his body intensified and, ignoring the warnings at the back of his mind, he whispered, "Come closer, Dorie."

Dorie didn't hesitate. She scooted closer to him. Her female scent invaded his senses and he gazed down as early light cast a glow on a nightdress that silhouetted Dorie's womanly body. "What is it, Shane?"

"This," he said, bringing his mouth to hers. He claimed her lips with gentle firm pressure and her generous response nearly rolled him from the bed. She made soft sounds and wiggled closer. Shane continued to ignore the fuzzy warnings in his head.

He drove his fingers into her hair, threading through the silky texture at the same time he drove his tongue into her mouth. They kissed that way for long moments, openmouthed and frenzied. The ache to his side didn't compare to the growing ache below his waist.

Heady sensations washed over him. He couldn't

remember a time he felt so damn good, so glad to be a man and so damn happy to be alive and in bed with a beautiful woman. Shane slipped the nightdress off Dorie's shoulders. He kissed her there and moved his lips lower, until he found the soft creamy texture of her breasts.

She cooed, "Oh, Shane."

"Tell me to stop, Dorie," Shane said, his mind not wrapping around the idea, but a muddled sense of decency coming through.

Dorie didn't want Shane to stop. She recalled the night in that shanty when she'd kidnapped him and the wonderful way he'd made her feel then. She'd dreamed of him so many nights after that and daydreamed of being with Shane this way. She'd never given her body to another man and doubted that she ever would. It would always be Shane Graham. "Don't…stop, Shane."

He tugged harder on her nightdress and it fell to her waist, exposing her chest to him. "Damn beautiful," he said, reaching out to touch her.

His fingers grazed the tips of her breasts, and her belly tightened. Heat surged and she tingled all over. "Oh, Shane."

Shane caressed her lovingly, his hands sure and gentle on her skin, but when he bent his head and kissed her, moistening her globes with his tongue, sweeping white-hot sensations spiraled down past her belly. She ached in secret places and found she needed to touch Shane in response.

She caressed his chest, stroking her fingers through fine curling hairs, feeling his strength and learning the texture of his body. She'd touched him earlier, when she cared for his wounds, but this was different. This was powerful and potent and all-consuming.

He kissed her hard on the mouth this time, and his whiskey breath tasted heady, filling her with need. "Shane, is this what it's like when a man claims a woman?"

She spoke the words straight from her heart, eager to know it all now—eager to find satisfaction and completion in Shane's embrace.

Shane stopped kissing her. He blinked then blinked again. Pain contorted his face and Dorie thought his wound might have ruptured again. She feared the bleeding had begun anew.

"What is it, Shane? Your wound?" She reached out for him, but he held her arm away.

"It's not the wound on my side, Dorie. Damn it, it's the hole in my brain." Shane flopped his head down onto his pillow, his eyes wide-open and clear now as new morning light filtered in.

"I don't understand. You were kissing me, Shane. And I didn't mind. I liked it and—"

"Quiet, Dorie! Don't say another word. I'm sorry, damn it. So sorry for touching you."

"Don't be sorry," she implored. "Just don't be!"

Shane spared her a glance. He shook his head and helped lift the nightdress up, adjusting it into its proper place on her shoulders. "Pain and whiskey weaken a man, Dorie. But my head's clear now and I'm as sorry as a man can be."

Dorie was beside herself. She didn't want Shane's apology. She wanted him. All of him and she didn't care if it wasn't proper or fitting or ladylike. She glanced down his body to where the proof of his desire was obvious from beneath his long johns. Dorie had never seen a man in this state, but her instincts told her what it meant.

Shane wanted her, too.

Dorie drew in a breath. She bit down on her lower lip, then opened her mouth to speak.

"It'd be wrong, Dorie. Real wrong. I'm gonna marry Marilee. And where would that leave you?"

"You shouldn't have to marry Marilee."

Shane grunted. "A man does what he has to do to survive."

"Do you get…this way when you kiss her?"

Shane let out a belabored sigh. "Dorie."

"Well?"

"No, okay? I don't get *this* way with Marilee, but it doesn't matter. Now, you'd best get out of this bed. Jeremiah's bound to walk in on us now that the sun's up."

Dorie nodded. "You're right. He'd have a conniption seeing us like this." Dorie rose from the bed and straightened her nightdress. She'd never understand Shane but she was sure glad he wasn't more injured. Even if he'd just broken a piece of her heart, she wanted to see him healthy, just like before.

"I can't say I'm sorry enough, Dorie."

"There's no need," she said, her face downcast.

"But there is a need to thank you for caring for me. That longhorn got the best of me and I'm mighty sure you saved my life."

"It was Jeremiah who found you."

"Then, I'll be sure to thank him, too."

Dorie walked toward the door. "I'll be back later, with some broth."

"I'm not hungry."

She turned to Shane. "Dr. Renfrow said you needed nourishment."

"Dorie, about the only nourishment I need right now is at the bottom of that bottle." He pointed to the bottle of whiskey. "Hand it to me, please."

Dorie nodded and handed the bottle to Shane. She had a feeling he'd drink himself into oblivion with what remained of the liquor. And it wouldn't necessarily be a bad thing.

She wished she could do the same.

Dorie simmered broth on her cookstove. She added a few onions and carrots for flavor, but figured if Shane woke up, his stomach would rebel if she tried anything fancy. It'd be enough if she could get him to drink the broth for now.

"Is he awake yet?" Jeremiah asked, entering the kitchen, putting his hat onto a hook and taking a place next to Dorie by the stove.

"He was awake for a time this morning. He's sleeping now."

"It's a good thing that he woke up, right?" Jeremiah spoke with nonchalance, but Dorie knew how worried he'd been about Shane.

"It's a *very* good thing. Shane's going to be fine in a day or two."

Dorie didn't know if the same held true for herself. She'd been the object of Shane's desire for a brief moment and her heart and her body would never be the same. Shane had kissed her like he'd meant it, and touched her most private places. He'd made her feel womanly and desirable and she refused to believe it was the whiskey and pain that caused him to behave so. She wouldn't believe it. Not for a minute.

Shane had wanted her and no amount of apologizing would change that fact. Shane Leopold Graham, for all his denials to the contrary, for all his claims of drunkenness and injury, had indeed wanted Dorie McCabe. She'd hold on to that fact for the time being.

If only he hadn't committed himself to wedding Marilee Barkley. Or rather, committed himself to her father. Tobias Barkley had the means to ruin Shane. And he'd do it, too. He had money and power to spare.

Just like the Parkers. They had the ability to ruin Dorie's life. They would take Jeremiah away, if her plan to fool them into believing she and Jeremiah had a fine life didn't work. Dorie let out a deep sigh.

If only she and Shane were truly married, instead of just pretending. They'd spend their time raising Jeremiah, a herd of cattle and maybe a baby or two of their own.

If only…

"You're burning the broth," Jeremiah said, grabbing the wooden spoon from her hand. He stirred the soup and narrowed his eyes. "What's got you all dreamy-eyed, anyways?"

Dorie wiped her hands on her apron and turned away from her brother. "Just, uh, thinking how things should be."

"You mean you're daydreaming about Shane again?"

She whipped around. "I don't daydream about Shane."

"Sometimes at night, I hear you in your sleep. You say his name."

"I do not. And why are you spying on me anyway?"

"Not spying, really. Just checking on you."

Dorie's eyes softened on her brother. "You check on me?"

Jeremiah took a swallow and stirred the soup faster. "Well, I hear you talking up a storm. I got to make sure you're all right, don't I?"

Dorie smiled and walked over to Jeremiah. She put her arms around him and squeezed. "I don't know what I'd do without you, Jeremiah," she whispered.

Jeremiah's eyes misted and he turned away so Dorie wouldn't see. "I don't want to find out, Dorie."

"You won't. I promise." Then she smiled with newfound enthusiasm and determination enough to see her plan through. "It's all gonna work out."

She ladled the broth into a bowl and picked out a large spoon from the cupboard, then draped a kitchen linen over her shoulder. "After I check on Shane, why don't you pay him a visit. You can tell him how his livestock is doing. I'm sure he'd appreciate knowing you're looking after things for him."

"I will. I'll come by to see him later."

Dorie nodded and headed for Shane's room.

Perhaps a real lady would find shame in what she and Shane had almost done this morning. Perhaps she should feel disgrace over their encounter. And maybe, too, she should experience mortification at having to face Shane again. But Dorie didn't feel any of those things.

She couldn't wait to see him, awake and alert.

She couldn't wait to see him healthy.

She couldn't wait to continue on with their lessons.

Dorie entered his room with a tray in her hands. "Oh!" She gasped and nearly tripped over her own feet when she saw what Shane was up to.

Chapter Six

"Shane, you take your pants off straightaway. And get yourself back in bed!"

Dorie rushed over to set the tray on the night table, infuriated at the scene before her. Shane had one leg inside his pant leg, while he balanced on the other. He struggled and she witnessed the twisted contortion on his pale face. She caught up to him just in time before he lost his balance and toppled over. She took the brunt of his weight, but the impact was far too much for her and they both tumbled down onto the bed.

Shane cursed up a storm as Dorie lay there, breathing hard, staring up at the ceiling. "What in heaven are you trying to do?"

"That'd be obvious."

"Okay, forget that question. *Why* are you doing it?"

"I can't lie around here all day. I've got a ranch to run, livestock that need feeding."

Dorie raised herself up from the bed to face Shane. She glared down at his stubbornly set face. "You almost died out there on that range yesterday, Shane

Graham. And now it looks as if you're bleeding again."

Shane touched his bandage, coming up with blood on his fingers. "Damn it."

"And I'll thank you to watch your language around a lady." She lifted a haughty chin at him. If she'd learned anything from Mrs. Whitaker's instruction, it was that a man should always show a lady respect.

Shane remained silent, his frustration visible on his pained face.

"Now hold still a minute. I'm gonna pull your pants off and sit you upright, then I'll have to sop up this blood and redress your wound."

Dorie did exactly that. With utmost care she removed Shane's pants, pulling them off carefully, but making sure to keep his long johns in place. Then she helped him sit up on the bed. "I'll be right back."

Within minutes, she had fresh dressing for his wound, a bowl of water and the salve that Dr. Renfrow had given her. She unwrapped his newly soaked bandage and applied enough pressure to stop the rest of the bleeding. Then she applied the salve and redressed his wound with a fresh bandage. She wasn't too gentle, either. Shaking her head, her anger escalated. "Would you just look at this, Shane? You were doing so well. The wound was healing fine. Lucky for you the stitches didn't pull out. I stopped the bleeding and put the salve on again. You'd better not try another fool thing like getting up on your own and dressing yourself. Dang it, Shane, what's Dr. Renfrow gonna think when he sees you haven't made any much progress. Why, he's gonna think that Dorie McCabe is a fool woman who doesn't know how to care for an injured man, that's what.

"Do you think that Jeremiah and me weren't planning on looking out for your ranch? What kind of fool notion is that? After all you've done for us, don't you think Jeremiah is smart enough to get himself over there and feed your livestock and look after your cattle? Just this morning he gathered up the Boyds and they worked your ranch. So, you see, there's no sense in working yourself into a tizzy about things. I've got everything under control."

Dorie took a sharp breath, needing the oxygen to fill her lungs back up after her long tirade. She stared at Shane.

"You through?" he asked, his lips tight.

She nodded.

"Fine. I'll be sure to thank Jeremiah. As for you, Doc Renfrow better not come to any wrong conclusions. You saved my life and I'll be sure to tell him. You're taking good care of me, Dorie, and I appreciate it."

She nodded again, hearing the frustration in Shane's voice. He was a man used to doing things for himself. He didn't like taking a helping hand.

"But I have to return to my ranch."

"Why, Shane? You're not healed and, heavens, you haven't even had a meal yet. I brought you broth. It's probably colder than Lake Washoe by now, but it's nourishment that you need. Lean back and let me feed it to you."

"I can feed myself, Dorie."

"No, I don't think you can. You're weak, Shane, and your fool intentions sapped what was left of your strength. I see it in your eyes, and the way your body is slumping. Don't fight me. Lay your head on the pillow and let me feed you."

Shane sucked in oxygen and stared at Dorie for a long moment, making up his mind. Finally, he leaned back, straightened on the bed, and placed his head against the pillow. "This doesn't set right with me. I can do for myself."

"And you will, once you're healed." Dorie found a place on the bed next to Shane. She took up the tray, placed it on her lap and began to feed Shane.

Once he'd finished without any further complaint, Dorie set the tray on the night table. "I'll fix you a proper meal later, if you feel you can eat something more substantial."

"Thanks," he said through gritted teeth.

"I know this isn't easy on you, Shane."

He grunted.

"It's just for a few days."

He grunted again. Then he looked her square in the eyes. "Do me one favor, Dorie."

"Sure, Shane. What is it?"

"Don't sleep in this bed with me tonight."

Dorie gasped. "Oh." She hadn't expected that. And suddenly their early-morning encounter rushed forth into her mind. Shane kissing her. Shane touching her. Shane wanting her. The vivid images brought color to her cheeks. She blushed full out.

But how could she sleep without knowing he was all right? What if he needed her during the night? "What if your wound opens up? What if you start bleeding again during the night?"

"I'll call for you."

"But what if you lose consciousness again? I won't know. I won't be there."

"Dorie, I'll be fine. I'm feeling better now."

Dorie saw the lie in that. He looked weak and tired and he surely didn't look *better*.

"I won't sleep much from worrying over you."

"No need to worry."

"But why, Shane? When it's so much easier for me to be in here with you."

Shane's green eyes focused solely on hers. Then his gaze traveled over her body, the heat of his attention creating warm tingles wherever his eyes touched. "You know why."

"It's because of what happened this morning. You said it yourself, it was the whiskey."

Shane pursed his lips.

"If that's the case, then you won't have that worry. The bottle is empty."

Shane appeared dubious.

"I'll be here in case you need me, Shane. And you won't have to concern yourself with doing anything inappropriate." Not that she thought they'd done anything to feel shamed, but it was obvious Shane had admonished himself countless times over it today.

"It doesn't exactly work that way, Dorie." Shane's voice held more than a note of frustration.

She could only come up with one conclusion from his arguments. "Then it's because you don't trust me."

Shane sighed and shook his head slowly. "No, honey. It's not that at all. It's because...I don't trust *myself*."

"I made fried chicken and potatoes," Mrs. Whitaker declared as she walked up the steps of Dorie's house, carrying a big straw basket in one hand. "Jeremiah told me what happened to Shane and I thought I'd fix you all some supper. You must have your hands full here, dear."

Dorie stood on the porch, noting the elegant way Mrs. Whitaker held her head, the ladylike sway of her gait and the soft charm in her voice. The clothes she wore were a bit nicer than one would call ranch clothes, with softer colors and finer fabric, but Dorie figured it wouldn't matter if the woman wore a sack. She just had a way about her.

Dorie found herself admiring the older woman, while finding herself completely lacking. If only Mrs. Whitaker could transform her into a refined, graceful woman, half of Dorie's battle would be won.

"It's nice of you to come by, Mrs. Whitaker. And I'm grateful for the food. I plan to try to feed Shane a meal a little later on."

"How is he?" she asked. "May I?" She gestured to a wooden bench on the porch and when Dorie nodded, she took a seat. Dorie sat down next to her.

"Stubborn as a mule," Dorie blurted.

Mrs. Whitaker chuckled. "Most injured men are. They don't like being tied down to the bed."

"That's for sure. Shane is resting now. He's been asleep most of the day."

"It's probably the best thing for him. Jeremiah says he was stabbed by a longhorn?"

"Yes, he found him slumped over his horse out on the range. It looked as if he was heading here for help. There was a wagonload of blood, but Dr. Renfrow says he'll be fine."

"There was a *great deal* of blood."

"That's what I said."

"No, you said there was a wagonload of blood." Mrs. Whitaker winked and cast her a quick smile. "You must always remember your speech, Dorie. Even when your guard is down."

"I'm trying to, but it ain't...I mean, it isn't easy."

"There, you see. If you think first, then speak, you'll remember the finer points we've discussed. It's not difficult speaking correctly if you take your time."

Dorie nodded. "I guess I just don't know how to slow down. I say whatever jumps into my head."

"You'll get it in time, dear. When you think, consider the words in your head first, before you open your mouth to speak."

"I suppose I can do that," Dorie said, without much enthusiasm. She wanted her plan to work so badly, but at times, she wondered if she could accomplish her goals in less than two weeks' time.

"I suppose Shane will be here a little longer?" she asked.

"Maybe just one more day. He wants to leave now, but he ain't...I mean, he isn't healed enough. Why, I caught the fool man trying to get dressed today. He could barely stand on his own. The wound opened up and started bleeding again. He worried me to death. I had to pull his pants off and tell him he wasn't going anywhere. He wasn't all too happy about it."

Mrs. Whitaker's brows rose and Dorie once again wondered if she'd said something wrong. "No, I don't suppose he would be. But as long as he's here, you could take advantage of the situation."

Dorie's mind spun in a dozen different directions. She honestly didn't know what Mrs. Whitaker meant, but if she'd been privy to their early-morning encounter, she might not have said it quite that way. "What do you mean?"

"Well, while he's here, it'd be a good chance for you to get to know each other."

Dorie mentally counted to ten, curtailing the rush of blood to her face. She had experienced a rare chance to know Shane by the power of his kisses, the strength of his body, the desire he could barely contain. Oh, Dorie would relive those intimate moments for years to come. And his last words to her had caught her quite by surprise. She'd never have believed that Shane had trouble trusting himself while he was around her. He'd always given the impression he thought of her as little more than a child—one that needed his protection. His admission had opened her eyes and she realized that maybe he hadn't only wanted her while plied with whiskey, but at other times, as well.

The revelation warmed her heart considerably.

"How?" she asked softly. "How should we get to know each other better?"

"Well, a wife has to know things about her husband. For instance, do you know his favorite meal? Do you know how he likes his coffee? Or whether he prefers his chicken fried or baked?"

"Fried, right? That's why you brought him fried chicken."

"I'm only guessing. But, *you* should know these things if you want anyone to believe you're married. There are a whole variety of things you should find out. Now's the time. Shane can't very well refuse. He's got nothing else to do, right?"

"Right." Dorie smiled, the idea sinking into her head. "But he won't like it."

Mrs. Whitaker patted her arm. "Maybe, or maybe not, but you'll find a way. I have every confidence in you, dear."

"Really? You do?" Dorie felt ten times better now. If Mrs. Whitaker had faith in her, maybe she could pull this whole thing off.

"Yes, I really do. And…Shane should know your likes and dislikes, as well. A husband needs to know your favorite flower, color, time of day. Why, my Iggy knows me like a book. Sometimes I think that man knows me better than I know myself. That's what you need to convey to the Parkers. That's how they'll believe you're truly happy and in love."

"Okay, I'll try it. After I feed Shane your delicious meal, I'm sure he'll be in a better mood."

"Good. Then it's settled."

"Yes. Would you care to come inside for a glass of iced tea?"

"Yes, I would, dear. Thank you."

"It's my pleasure," Dorie said, quite elegantly. "Please join me."

Dorie opened the door for Mrs. Whitaker and they entered her house, her mood suddenly lighter.

"It's downright bribery, Dorie, that's what it is," Shane grumbled, folding his arms across his middle, not entirely sure whether making that move was smart or not. The sudden thrust from that particular gesture stung his side with fresh pain. He shifted into a more comfortable position on the bed, sitting up against the headboard, with his back braced by a pillow. Dorie sat dangerously close, her bottom planted beside his thigh, lucky for him the sheet and blanket separated them.

"It's not a bribe, Shane. But since you're being so stubborn about this, I thought it best to make a deal."

Shane stared at Dorie, willing himself to forget the muffled images in his head of kissing her this morning, and touching her soft skin, caressing her perfect breasts. Images that hadn't been far enough from his mind all day. Hell, he'd even had a dream about her today and he'd not been pleased with his body's reaction to that dream. He'd woken up stiff and miserable. "I've already made one deal too many with you."

Dorie's eyes widened and Shane noted the anguish he'd just caused her. "If it weren't for Jeremiah, I wouldn't have asked you for help."

Shane softened his tone. "I know you were pretty desperate."

"I never thought to break up your wedding, Shane. Even though you shouldn't be marrying Marilee, I wouldn't have barged in like that."

Shane didn't want to rehash this. He'd made a promise to Dorie and he'd find a way to fulfill his vow. But her last little tactic rubbed him the wrong way. "It's in the past, so forget what I said. Now, about your latest bit of blackmail, you promise to stay out of this bed tonight, if I do what?"

"All you have to do is tell me some personal things about yourself. And I'll share the same with you. That's all."

Shane narrowed his eyes. "What kind of personal things?"

Dorie shrugged. "You know, things only a wife might know."

Shane scrubbed his jaw. He took a swallow of air. He was a private man and liked to keep it that way. How the hell would he know what a wife would know about him? He'd never been married before. "And you'll let me alone to sleep in peace?"

"Was I *that* disturbing to your peace, Shane?" she asked softly.

Ah, hell. Dorie spoke with a winsome, hopeful tone in her voice as if it pleased her no end knowing she could addle his brain and create havoc with his body. He'd practically admitted to her that she tempted him with or without the benefit of alcohol. "More like a distraction. I like sleeping alone."

"I promise I won't disturb you, unless you need me. So, we can start with easy things. What's your favorite meal?"

"Anything that doesn't smell like horse dung and/or chew like leather is fine with me."

Dorie folded her arms across her middle, and the move that meant to show her frustration, only added to his. Her breasts lifted and the material of her blouse hugged the soft globes underneath more tightly. "That doesn't help, Shane."

Shane prayed for patience. "Okay, let me think. I guess, I like beef stew best of all."

Dorie smiled. "Beef stew. Want to know what mine is?"

"Sure, why not," he said, giving up the battle.

"I like roasted turkey with all the fixings, potatoes with gravy and candied carrots. Oh, and I like cranberries. My mama used to make a cranberry and walnut dessert that I loved. So, how do you like your coffee?"

"My coffee? Black without grounds at the bottom."

Dorie chuckled, the sound of her laughter almost as distracting as her pretty blue eyes and shiny coppery hair. Shane had been bedridden too long. His well-honed willpower had almost disappeared. "I don't like coffee much, but if I do, I take it sweet and creamy."

Sweet and creamy? Again, Shane prayed for patience.

"So, I know you drink whiskey. Do you drink any other kind of liquor?"

"Why?" he asked, glancing around the room. "Do you have any?"

"Lord, no. I don't drink liquor, Shane. And it wouldn't do to have it in the house. Jeremiah is just a boy."

"Right," he said, his hopes dashed. "I drink anything the barkeep shoves my way. But only if I'm so inclined. I don't usually drink anything at all when I'm home. If I'm in town and a mite thirsty, I'll have a drink. The alcohol at home is for medicinal purposes only."

Dorie nodded as if she thought to file it all inside her head. "I understand."

Shane smiled for the first time in two days. Dorie took this very seriously. He had to commend her for her diligence. When she wanted something, she went after it with unrivaled determination.

Dorie tapped her foot on the floorboards. "What else should I know about you?"

Shane hadn't a clue.

"Was I your first love?"

Shane cleared his throat. "Excuse me?"

"The Parkers might want to know how we met? Was it love at first sight?"

Shane scoffed. "No such thing."

"There is, too, Shane. My mama said my papa fell in love with her the moment they met."

Shane held his tongue. He wouldn't add that that marriage hadn't ended well, with Dorie's papa taking off to trap beaver. He'd never returned and then her mother discovered that he'd taken an Indian wife and a year later, died. It only proved his point. He didn't much believe in love at first sight, and had a hard time believing in love at all. Shane had no experience in that regard.

Dorie appeared pensive. "We should have our story straight. They might ask."

"If they do, then I'd say they're pretty nosy."

"But they're coming here to make sure Jeremiah is well cared for and loved. They're bound to have all kinds of questions." Dorie tapped her foot again. "Let me think."

After a minute, Dorie's eyes lit. "We met at a church social. You asked me to dance and…and well, you sort of swept me off my feet."

Shane pursed his lips. "A church social?"

Dorie nodded with a smile.

"Okay, a church social."

"And we got married about five years ago."

"That'd make you thirteen, Dorie."

She bit down on her lip. "Oh, right. We got married two years ago."

Shane lowered his lids, thinking the Parkers wouldn't hold him in too high regard figuring he'd wedded and bedded a young girl. "If you say so."

"And we're madly in love."

"Right."

"Well, you can pretend, can't you?"

Shane scratched at his beard, the stubble itchy and uncomfortable. He'd need a shave soon.

"Well?" Dorie asked again.

Shane yawned. He'd had enough of this for now. He'd agreed to Dorie's plan but he hadn't figured to spend all of his waking hours readying for the day when the Parkers would come. He didn't care for lying, and this scheme of Dorie's required more than a king's ransom of lies. "I'm getting tired, Dorie. You promised to let me sleep. Be sure to thank Mrs. Whitaker for supper. It was delicious."

"Are we through?" Dorie asked, her voice laced with disappointment.

"Yep."

"We'll have to finish this another time."

"Yep," Shane agreed, slinking down into the bed and covering himself. "Another time. Good night, Dorie."

"Good night, then. Remember, call if you need anything."

"Uh-huh."

Once Dorie slipped out the door, Shane breathed a sigh of relief.

He couldn't have a repeat of what happened this morning. Their little "marriage" story reminded him how young Dorie truly was. She was just a girl. With a woman's body.

But he wouldn't think about that.

Tonight, he vowed he wouldn't dream about Dorie McCabe and her sweetly innocent charms.

Tonight, Shane planned on sleeping the sleep of the dead.

And tomorrow, after Doc Renfrow gave him the okay, he'd head back to the Bar G.

Where it was safe.

Chapter Seven

Dorie put away her sewing for the day and headed to the kitchen. She'd gotten up extra early to complete chores she'd neglected while she'd tended Shane. She'd baked biscuits, and churned butter to barter with Mr. Caruthers at his general store, then she'd done the wash, making sure Jeremiah had clean clothes to wear and they had fresh linens for their beds.

Dorie smiled thinking how Jeremiah had kicked up a fuss when she'd climbed into bed with him the last night Shane had slept here; the two of them squeezing into the small confines of his bed. Jeremiah slapped her in the face with a wayward arm and then kicked her in the shins when he turned his body. And Dorie had realized something that night that hadn't yet occurred to her. Her brother, though young in years, had grown into a strapping young man. It didn't seem fitting to share a bed any longer, so she'd climbed out and had fallen asleep on the parlor horsehair sofa.

Not that she slept too well. She'd worried over Shane and had peeked in on him at least three times that night.

He'd slept soundly and she'd thanked the Almighty that he seemed on the path to recovery.

Dorie cut up a flank of beef and added it to the pot, tossing in carrots and celery and small potatoes. She simmered the stew, stirring with care, wanting this meal to turn out perfectly.

Jeremiah startled her when he slammed the back door. "You back from Shane's place?"

"Yep, just got back."

"How's he doing today?" she asked.

"Just fine, Dorie."

"But I mean, is he healing up good, or is he working himself into an early grave?"

Jeremiah stole a biscuit from a basket Dorie had set out and before she could swipe at his hand, he grabbed another one. He took big bites out of both, a trick he'd learned when their mama was alive, so that she couldn't possibly ask him to put one back into the basket. "Like I said, he's fine. Just like he was yesterday and the day before that."

"Well, I haven't seen him in three days and it's time I found that out for myself. I'm making stew and when it's done, I'm heading over there. Want to come along?"

"Nope, I just got back. Don't plan on going again."

"Okay, then," Dorie said, stirring the stew and hoping her biscuits were soft and flaky enough for Shane's taste. "I'll bring him supper, but I'll be home before you go to bed."

"As long as you leave me a portion of stew—a big portion. I worked up an appetite riding with Shane today."

Dorie stopped stirring to smile at Jeremiah. "And when have I ever left you without a meal, little brother?"

Jeremiah shrugged and stole another biscuit from the basket. "Jeremiah!"

He raced out the door before Dorie could catch him, but she wasn't really angry with him. He was a good boy and she loved him with everything in her heart.

While the stew simmered, Dorie entered her bedroom and faced the cheval mirror. Since her meetings each day with Mrs. Whitaker, she'd been painfully aware of her own lack of style. Dressing up hadn't been a priority in her life. It'd been all she could do to put food on the table and make a good home life for her brother. But now, things had changed.

Dorie had changed.

She wanted more. She wanted to be a real lady. To dress like one and act like one. She wanted Shane to stand up and take notice. But the image reflected in the mirror didn't give her much hope. She wore her clothes loose, for comfort and practicality. She often just knotted her curly locks up atop her head in bird nest fashion and most times her face needed a good washing. "Dorie, it's time for you to grow up."

She shuffled through the bottom drawer of her armoire, pushing aside winter sweaters, to find a few of her mama's old things. Dorie lifted out a pink-and-yellow calico dress that she remembered her mama wearing on special occasions. It wasn't exactly fancy, but it was fashionable and clean, with puff sleeves and a bit of lace. Dorie took a good hard look at it, working up a few details that needed changing. Then, with her mind set, she pulled out her sewing needle to make a few minor adjustments to the bodice. Her mama wasn't a large woman, but she certainly was bigger boned than Dorie.

A short time later and after a quick washing, she combed her hair until it shone, then fitted a ribbon around the tresses to keep them off her face. She donned her mama's calico dress, with a few newly added touches, and gazed at herself in the mirror.

"Better," she said quietly, liking the way the soft colors made her complexion glow. The dress fit her hips perfectly, and the puff of material at the top of her shoulders, flaring down tighter to her wrists, made her feel more feminine than she had since…well, since her mama would dress her up for Sunday services as a young girl.

In the kitchen, she covered the pot of stew with its lid and placed it inside a small crate, topped with the red-checkered lined basket of biscuits. She stuck her head out the back door. "I'm leaving now," she announced to Jeremiah, who was whittling on a piece of wood on the back porch. "I'm walking to Shane's house. Your stew's sitting on the cookstove."

"See you later," he said, never taking his eyes from his task.

And then Dorie made the trek to Shane's house, hoping to surprise him.

Dorie walked up the path to Shane's house, just as she viewed a buggy pulling away. She craned her neck to see the driver's face, and was struck by a jolting shock. Her stomach clenched when she noticed Shane standing on his front porch, smiling warmly, waving farewell to Mrs. Roberta McPherson. The young and newly widowed milliner returned his smile.

Dorie came to a dead halt and held her breath as unfettered jealousy swept through her. What was Roberta doing here putting a smile on Shane's face? she wondered. Why, her husband wasn't dead a year yet. Dorie knew there were more than a few men waiting in line for her, Roberta being so pretty and all, so why'd she showed up at Shane's place?

Dorie stood frozen, her mind spinning. The crate of food in her arms weighing her down, she decided to find out what was going on before she dropped the darn thing. She marched straight ahead, catching Shane before he entered his front door.

"Shane? Shane Graham, wait up!"

Shane turned just as she climbed up the steps. "Dorie?"

Well, she'd surprised him all right, but his face lost all the warmth he'd held for Roberta just seconds ago. "What are you doing here?"

She'd hoped for a friendlier greeting. Dorie shifted the crate in her arms and when he finally noticed her burden, he relieved her of it. "Here, let me take that."

"It's supper. I made you your favorite, beef stew and, well, you can see I brought a basket of biscuits, too."

Shane looked down at the crate. "Biscuits?"

"Yes, I hope you like them. I made the whole meal for us to share tonight. There's more to do."

"I thought you were taking lessons from Mrs. Whitaker?"

"I am. She's been such a help to me. I see her for an hour or two every day. But you and I have more to learn about each other."

Shane nodded. "Okay, come in and thank you kindly for the meal."

"Are you hungry, Shane?" she asked as she strode

into Shane's house, when all she really wanted to know was why Roberta McPherson had come calling. Mrs. Whitaker had warned her about blurting out the first thing that popped into her head; Dorie took heed and commended herself for the restraint.

Shane patted his stomach and cast her a look of regret. "Not really."

With the sun fading on the horizon, Dorie realized that she might have dallied too long at home. She glanced around the parlor, catching a quick glimpse of Shane's small dining room. Dishes lay atop the table— a table that had been set for two with a cluster of fresh day lilies in a vase between the plates. "Shane, why was Roberta McPherson here?" Dorie asked, ignoring Mrs. Whitaker's instruction in favor of easing her curiosity.

Shane scratched his head. He hesitated long enough to make Dorie's nerves go raw, and when he answered there was a hint of guilt in his voice. "Roberta found out about my injury. She brought over supper."

"You ate supper with *her?*" Dorie asked, unable to disguise the accusation in her tone.

"She's just being neighborly, Dorie. Nothing wrong in that."

Dorie looked over at the crate of food she'd brought that wouldn't get eaten now. Then she remembered she'd dressed up special for Shane tonight and he hadn't even noticed. Not when he'd just had supper with someone like Roberta. Dorie couldn't compete with her natural beauty and refinement. She wore the most fashionable clothes and designed the most colorful hats. Her shop was the envy of all the young girls who couldn't afford to buy such things.

Dorie included.

"I see," she said, looking down at her boots, holding back anger and disappointment. She'd wanted to surprise Shane with his favorite meal and, instead, she'd been the one surprised.

"I didn't know she was coming over," he said. "But if I had, I wouldn't have encouraged it."

Dorie's head shot up with renewed hope. "You wouldn't?"

Shane shook his head. "No, Roberta is nice enough, but I let her know I still planned on marrying Marilee Barkley. Roberta is a friend and that's all. She understood."

"Well, she might have understood, but I sure don't."

Shane sighed and set the crate onto the kitchen table. "Let's not go through that again, Dorie." He lifted the cover from the pot. "You know, this stew looks good. Have you eaten?"

Dorie followed him inside his kitchen, shaking her head. "No. I thought to eat with you."

Shane took in her appearance, his gaze traveling down the length of her from her new style of hair, stopping at her cinched-in waist, then on to the tip of her booted toes. He glanced once again at the stew. "Sit down and join me. I think I've got room enough to try some of this."

Dorie sat while Shane picked up two plates and forks and set them down on the table. Then he ladled out a portion of stew for each of them. Dorie didn't mind eating with Shane in his kitchen, while Roberta had set a fancy table for him in his small dining room. At least he was willing to try the meal she'd cooked especially for him.

"I appreciate you cooking for me, Dorie, honest I

do." He took up his fork and dug into the food. "I also appreciate you saving my life." He took a moment to chew his food then glanced over at her. "It's delicious."

Dorie beamed with delight. "It is?"

"Best stew I've had in a long time."

Dorie's heart soared. "Thank you."

"As I was saying, I realized when I got back home that I wasn't a very good patient."

"No, you were fine."

"I was bad-tempered and grouchy and I didn't treat you right."

Dorie smiled and lifted the fork to her mouth. "You treated me just fine, Shane."

Shane stared at her lips for a long moment, then blinked away whatever thought had entered his mind. "So, you admit I was grouchy?"

Dorie chewed on her food slowly. "I didn't say that."

"You didn't have to. I'm saying it for you. Fact is, without your help and Jeremiah finding me, then coming here to help out this week, I doubt I'd be sitting here eating a meal with you." He took hold of her hand and squeezed. "What I'm saying is, thank you."

A lump formed in Dorie's throat. She looked deep into Shane's grass-green eyes, her heart tumbling over itself. "You're welcome."

Shane nodded and continued to eat until he'd emptied his plate. Dorie knew a measure of complete joy and didn't even mind that Shane hadn't touched one of her biscuits.

"You're looking well," she said. "Are you healing?"

Shane touched his side, pushing aside the material of his plaid shirt a bit. "I'm healing better than I thought. The stitches come out tomorrow. There'll be a scar but that doesn't matter as long as I have my full strength back."

"That's good news. Not about the scar," she said, thinking of his manly body, all muscle and firm skin. She hated to think he'd be marred in any way, but he was right. As long as he felt healthy and strong, that should be all that mattered. "I mean to say that scars don't bother me. I have one myself."

"You?" Shane scanned her body from top to bottom, looking for one. Then he came to his own conclusion. "No, you don't."

"I sure do," she said with a knowing smile. "I was eight years old and fell about ten feet out of a tree. I landed right smack on a bundle of pinecones. One stuck me—" she lifted her hip slightly and pointed with arrowlike precision just beyond her hip, to her derriere "—right here."

Shane glanced to where she pointed and took a big swallow.

"It bled like a son-of-a-gun." Her hand flew to her mouth. "Oops, I mean to say, it bled quite heavily, and when Mama finally stopped the bleeding, there was a hole the size of…well, a big hole on my cheek."

Shane didn't say one thing.

"It's healed now but there's a scar that goes clear down to my—"

"I think I'll try a biscuit," he interrupted, reaching over to grab a biscuit. He stuffed it into his mouth and began to chew. And chew. And chew. Once he swallowed, he took a look at the basket of biscuits as if trying to puzzle something out. "The sun's almost down, Dorie. I'll have to drive you home soon."

"But I thought we could spend some more time together. We need to finish—"

"Shh!" Shane interrupted. "Listen." He sat up straighter in the chair, then stood abruptly. "Did you hear that? I think it's my heifer. She's ready to drop her calf."

Dorie sat quietly, listening. She heard a loud sound, not quite a mooing but definitely an animal in pain. "Yes, I hear it. We'd best check on her."

But Shane had already dashed out the back door. She found him outside in a corral on bended knees checking the heifer.

"Is she okay?"

Shane shook his head. "Don't think so. The calf's wedged up inside her and she'll never get her out without help. Dorie, run to the barn and get my gloves."

Dorie returned with two pairs of gloves. She handed Shane a pair and then slid her hands into the other. "What do you think you're doing?" he asked.

"I'm helping."

"You ever pull a calf before?"

"No, have you?"

Shane nodded. "About a dozen times. Now, step back. I can get this."

Dorie stepped back and watched, while Shane struggled, the heifer struggled and nothing much happened. The heifer made another anguished sound. "Damn, the calf's wedged in there real good, coming hoof first."

Shane broke out in a sweat and he breathed in, putting a hand to his side. He winced in pain and Dorie realized he hadn't fully recovered. He'd used all his strength and at that awkward angle, he still couldn't pull out the calf.

There was just enough room for Dorie to put her hands on the calf's legs, while Shane grabbed the hoofs. "Let me help," she said. "Together, we'll get it out."

Shane balked for half a second, until the heifer cried out again. "We can try. Okay, on three. One, two, three."

Dorie pulled from the side, while Shane grabbed hold of the hoofs from the cow's back end. They yanked hard, both making grunting sounds. Dorie lost her balance, bumped into Shane and they both fell into hard packed mud.

"Sorry!" Quickly, they righted themselves and grabbed hold again. When they tugged again, they felt some give and Shane shot her a look of triumph. "Here we go."

The heifer made her last final grunt, the calf slid out and both Shane and Dorie wound up in the mud again, this time, successful; the newly delivered calf squirming beside them.

Dorie sat full out in the mud, staring at the calf. "Is she going to live?"

"She sure is." Shane stood and reached down to help Dorie. "And so is her mama."

Dorie righted herself and turned her attention to the baby calf she helped deliver, then glanced at the new mother. "What's wrong with her?"

The cow's back end had dropped down to the ground and she seemed unable to move. "Sometimes new mamas get paralyzed from the delivery. She'll be up and around soon as the shock wears off."

"And her calf?"

Shane bent down to lift her up in his arms. "She'll be fine, too." He carried her away from the muddy area and set her down in a batch of clean straw. "There you go, little one. Your mama will be paying you a visit soon."

Shane turned to Dorie, taking in her appearance. "Darn it, you got your pretty new dress all muddy. Even got some in your hair."

Dorie rejoiced that Shane *had* noticed her dress. "Doesn't matter. It'll wash and it wasn't new, just something of my mama's I fixed up."

Shane glanced down at the new calf, watching her breathe. "Even still, you looked pretty in it. And I liked the way you put up your hair. Now, you're all a mess."

Looking at Shane, Dorie thought he looked a mess, too, but never more handsome and appealing.

"What do we do now?"

"Now?" Shane looked up at her. "Now, we clean up a little and I'll take you home."

Inside the kitchen, Shane handed Dorie a cloth he'd soaked with fresh warm water. "Here, it's the best I could do."

Dorie accepted the cloth and began wiping down her dress.

"Uh, you might want to start with your face first, before you dirty that all up."

Dorie let out a gasp and ran her hand down her face. "My face." She began mopping furiously at her cheeks. "How on earth—"

"You've got that right. The earth. It seems to be all over us." Shane chuckled and regarded Dorie's smudged face. She laughed, too, and his mood lightened considerably. In fact, he'd been bored silly with Roberta earlier, but he never felt the least bit bored with Dorie.

She kept him on his toes. And, oddly, life wasn't dull when she was around. She'd even managed to help him deliver a new calf and probably saved two lives by doing so. Now here she was, wearing the prettiest dress he'd ever seen on her, and hadn't given one complaint that it was all but ruined. "Sorry about the dress."

"It was worth it," she said, and Shane knew she meant every word. Dorie wasn't pretentious, unless of course, she was trying to pull the wool over the Parkers' eyes; but when all was said and done, she had an earnest, generous nature.

"I'll make it up to you," he said, without the foggiest idea how.

"How?" she asked.

"You'll just have to wait and see."

Dorie smiled and said softly, "I think I'll like any surprise you have for me."

Shane glanced at her lips, then at a face scrubbed clean, glowing like a soft ripe peach. Catching himself weakening to Dorie's innocent charms, he snatched the cloth from her hands and began swatting at the front of the dress, trying to undo the damage. Drying clumps of mud fell to the floor.

Dorie turned her backside to him. "Most of the mud landed here when I fell."

Shane cleared his throat. "You don't want me to, uh—"

She smiled and nodded.

Shane cursed silently. Then he began to direct his quick swipes with extreme caution, most of his scrubbing beginning at the knee and ending at the hem of her dress.

Dorie watched from over her shoulder and when he

stood to face her, she shook her head. "You didn't get much mud off."

"Here, I think you'd better do the rest." He handed off the cloth. "I'll clean up outside by the water barrel, then hitch up the team and take you home."

Dorie swatted her backside quickly, leaving a trail of mud on his floor. "Shane, can we check on the heifer and her calf before I go?"

Shane grinned. "That's what I'd planned on doing first. Ready?"

Dorie nodded and followed him out the back door to the corral where they'd left the animals. "Oh, look! Mama found her little one."

"Yep, didn't take her long." Shane waited while Dorie sunk down on the fresh straw, her face filled with awe and sheer joy as she watched the new calf suckle at her mother's teats.

"Birthing is such a miracle."

Shane agreed. Each time he helped bring a calf or new foal into the world, he felt the same way, awed by the grace of God and struck by the miracle of nature. He wondered if he'd ever be fortunate enough to father a child, and, instantly, Dorie's face flashed in his mind along with the image of mother and baby. He shook off that thought quickly, wondering where it had come from.

Then he walked over to Dorie and reached for her hand. "C'mon. It's getting late. I don't want Jeremiah to worry."

Dorie laced her fingers with his and they walked hand in hand around the corner of the house, stopping at the water barrel. Shane splashed cool water on his face then moistened his hair attempting to remove as much grime as possible. He shook his head and droplets scattered about.

Dorie stepped back from him and giggled. "I had a dog that did that."

Shane narrowed his eyes. "You don't say?"

"Yep, he wasn't much to look at, but he sure was entertaining."

"You teasing with me, Dorie?"

She lifted her chin. "Maybe."

Shane smiled. He liked Dorie McCabe. Too much.

And just when he decided he'd really better get her home, she reached up to touch his face. "You missed a spot." Her finger brushed his jaw, then she flicked a piece of mud off his chin. She appeared so engaged in her task that she didn't notice the slight tremor that coursed through his body.

"Any more?"

Dorie looked her fill, searching his face for mud smudges and Shane couldn't keep from staring into her pretty blue eyes.

"You're staring at me," she said quietly.

"Yep, I guess I am."

"Why?"

"I guess I'm realizing how pretty you are."

"Oh, Shane."

Shane reached his hands to her hips and gently nudged her toward him as he bent his head. He didn't much care that his hard length was pressed against her, or that she seemed pleased about it. He hated admitting it, but he'd missed Dorie and her wild antics. He'd missed her fussing over him and even missed her tougher than granite biscuits. Itching to kiss her again, he lowered his mouth closer to hers when a harrumphing sound stopped him cold.

"She must be better'n three whores on a single bed."

Shane whipped around to find Tobias Barkley approaching. The man had appeared out of nowhere. "Barkley, what the hell are you doing here?"

"I'm checking on my investment." Then he glanced at Dorie, her muddied dress and her coppery hair spilling from its pins, and his ruddy face turned even redder. "You don't listen well, boy. Are you forgetting I loaned you money, cash the bank wouldn't credit you, and you're using my grazing land for your meager herd."

"I haven't forgotten a thing."

"Good, I thought maybe the trollop's got you thinking of backing out of our deal. Now, that wouldn't be smart at all."

Shane held his temper. "Say what you came here to say, Barkley."

"One of my men has a lead on Marilee. Apparently, she'd gotten farther than I thought. But I'm going after her first thing tomorrow. And when I bring her back, you're going to marry her."

"I said I would."

He shot a look at Dorie and narrowed his beady eyes. "And you'll be faithful to my daughter."

Shane didn't like his insinuation one damn bit. "Wait a minute, here. Don't you go thinking anything bad about Dorie. Or me. Once I take my marriage vows, I'll stick to them."

Tobias Barkley didn't seem convinced. "You'd better. You dally with the girl for right now, but once you marry my daughter I'll expect nothing but complete loyalty."

Shane trembled with fury. "Get off my land, Barkley."

"I'm going. Don't you worry. You've got two weeks. Two, hear me, and when I bring Marilee back, you'll marry her."

"If she'll have me."

"You'd better make sure that she does. And you'd better lose the trollop by then, or there'll be hell to pay."

"Stop calling her that," Shane warned through gritted teeth. "Now, get off my property."

Tobias Barkley laughed at the warning and headed back to his horse. Shane wasn't satisfied until the man rode down the path and out his gate.

Dorie put a hand on his arm. "I'm so sorry, Shane."

He stared in Barkley's direction, almost wishing him back so he could put a fist through his smug face. "If he says one more nasty thing about you, I'll kill him."

"No, you won't. You're no killer. But thank you for sticking up for me. Shane, I'm so sorry for the mess I've made."

"It's my mess. I'll clean it up."

"By marrying Marilee?"

Shane had no choice. If Marilee came back and would have him, he was bound to marry her. He'd given his word to Barkley, but to Marilee, as well. And he wouldn't go back on his word. Damn it, being honorable meant losing a part of himself to gain what he desperately needed for his ranch to survive.

But in a small way, Shane had to feel grateful to Barkley for showing up here tonight. He'd stopped Shane cold, from doing something with Dorie he'd been dreaming about. Kissing her again. Holding her and, in truth, his mind ventured further down that path before he could catch himself. The things he wanted to do with Dorie wouldn't be considered honorable.

Barkley reminded him of all the reasons Shane couldn't hold Dorie or kiss her or make love to her. In his own crude unknowing way, he'd been the one to clear Shane's mind of any notion of being with Dorie.

Except, of course, to pretend to be her husband in one week's time.

Shane had to give Dorie the answer that she didn't want to hear. "Yes, I'm going to marry Marilee."

"But before Mr. Barkley showed up, you were about to—"

"To make a big mistake. I'm a fool, Dorie. I have no other explanation. Listen to me," he said quietly but with firm resolve, "no matter what I say or do in the next few weeks, don't go thinking I'll go back on my word. If Barkley returns home with Marilee, I *will* marry her."

Dorie closed her eyes slowly, and he hoped she wouldn't cry. The last thing he wanted to do was hurt Dorie. He'd only wanted to protect her.

"Dorie?"

"Take me home, Shane."

"All right." He headed for the corral to fetch the horses. But Dorie's next words stopped him in his tracks.

"Well, at least you're right about one thing."

He turned to her in puzzlement. "Only one?"

She snapped her head up. "You are a fool, Shane Graham."

Shane had to agree.

Chapter Eight

"Dorie, dear. You're doing so well. Why do I find you pouting as if you've lost your very best friend?" Mrs. Whitaker asked, as afternoon sunlight streamed into her kitchen window.

Dorie shrugged her shoulders. "Maybe I have."

"And whom would that be, might I ask?"

"It'd be Shane, of course. He's bound and determined to marry Marilee. Mr. Barkley's found her and he's bringing her home. I'll have just enough time to meet with the Parkers before Shane has to marry a woman he doesn't want."

Mrs. Whitaker set a piece of pecan pie in front of her. Dorie didn't have the heart to eat a thing. She thanked her for the offer but shoved the plate away.

"And how do you know that he doesn't want to marry Marilee?"

"Because he doesn't like being with her the way he likes being with me."

"Has he told you that?"

Dorie thought back to the early morning when she'd

tended to Shane's wounds. His body told her what he couldn't say, then finally she'd managed to get him to admit he didn't react the same to Marilee. Dorie only understood it because she'd felt the same warm throbbing in her lower regions every time Shane kissed her, every time he'd touched her. "He tells me with his body—" she blurted. "Oh, I didn't mean that exactly how it came out. He and I, uh, we haven't done anything wrong. Honest."

Mrs. Whitaker smiled. "I think I understand. It hasn't been so long ago that I don't recall how it feels to be falling in love."

"Love?" Dorie shook her head. "No, I don't *love* Shane. I loved my mama and I love Jeremiah, but, well…I don't know. I've never been in love before. As for Shane, he certainly doesn't love me. Half the time, he seems unhappy to see me. And lately, well, I haven't seen him at all since mean old Mr. Barkley came by Shane's place threatening him."

"Dorie, Shane has a lot to consider. He's worked hard to build up his spread. He's a man of honor. And he made Marilee a promise not too long ago. He made you a promise, too. And as much as it might be hurting him, he's trying to do the right thing for both of you. You wouldn't want him to back out of his promise to you any more than Marilee wants him to break his promise to her."

Dorie took a minute to let it all sink in. She hadn't thought of the situation exactly that way. "He's in a pickle, isn't he?"

"Yes, I'd say so. So, why don't you concentrate on the situation with the Parkers instead. We still have work to do. As I said, you're coming along, Dorie. You're making tremendous progress."

"Really? I don't feel like I am, and every time I read the book I get more confused. Heavens, I barely understood the chapter on 'Gentility and Refinement of Manners in All the Relations of Home and Society.' I don't even understand what the title means. Sometimes, I think I'll never convince the Parkers of anything."

Mrs. Whitaker slid the plate of pie her way again. "Eat up, Dorie. I think I have the solution to this."

"Really," she said, encouraged by the hopeful tone in Mrs. Whitaker's voice. She picked up the fork and took a bite of pie. "How?"

"Well, for one. Forget the book. We don't need it anymore. We're going to do a real-life rehearsal."

"A rehearsal? What kind of rehearsal?" Dorie asked, setting down her fork to look intently at her mentor.

"Well, I'm inviting you and Shane over to dinner tomorrow night. You're to come as a real couple, husband and wife. Iggy and I will pretend that we don't know the situation. You and Shane need to convince us that you're married. You'll be able to see your strengths and weaknesses this way. Afterward, we'll discuss your success."

"Or failure?"

"Yes, that, too. Oh, this will be fun. We'll see how far both of you have come along."

"Do you think Shane will agree?"

Mrs. Whitaker patted her arm. "I'll see that he does. Don't worry about him. Just present yourself as Shane's wife. I'll have him pick you up at six o'clock tomorrow evening. You just be ready."

Dorie's spirits lifted. Mrs. Whitaker made it all seem

so possible. And this way they'd know for sure if they were convincing as a couple. If only Shane would go along with the ruse. A dozen thoughts streamed through Dorie's mind and excitement stirred deep down in her belly. She'd find out now what it would be like being Shane's wife.

If only for an evening.

"Did you write to Henry in Virginia City?" Dorie asked Jeremiah the minute he woke from sleep the next day. Still in his brown-and-white-striped nightshirt, he'd moseyed into the kitchen and grabbed a biscuit.

Squinting from dawning sunlight, he answered, "I told you I did. Right when you asked me to."

"And?"

"And he wrote back, Dorie. I just forgot to tell you. He invited me to stay with him while the three of us are in Virginia City. His mama says I'm welcome anytime. Just like always."

"That's good, Jeremiah. I just can't afford spending money on two hotel rooms while we're there. And I know you'd like to see Henry. You and he would play for hours and hours when you were little ones. I'm glad you stayed friends even though he moved away."

Jeremiah shrugged and rubbed his eyes with two fists just as he did when he was a child, which made Dorie smile and feel a jolt of sadness at the same time. She loved her brother so much. She couldn't imagine her life without him. And now, everything would be over in just a few days. The Parkers were due to arrive in Virginia City on Saturday. This being Tuesday, Dorie had only three more days before she and Shane ventured to town.

She figured to get there a day ahead of the Parkers, to settle in and get accustomed to the surroundings.

Besides, Dorie had other business to conduct in Virginia City, and she had to find a way to get some private time while there. Going to Virginia City had always excited her before, and she'd always come home with enough cash to see her through the bad times. The only part she didn't like was when she had to sneak around. Keeping secrets hadn't been one of Dorie's best qualities, but in this case she had to. She'd been keeping this secret for three years.

"Sit down, Jeremiah. I made you hot oatmeal."

"Oatmeal again?" he complained, taking a seat at the wooden table.

"I thought you liked oatmeal."

"I do. It's just that I'm tired of it. I have it every day, practically."

Dorie let out a deep slow sigh of regret. At times like these, she wondered if she shouldn't just let Jeremiah go home with the Parkers. They'd have more than oatmeal to offer him in the morning. Probably he'd fill his belly stuffing down thick bacon strips and juicy ham slices, fluffy eggs and fancy pastries and all. He'd probably have the finest clothes and go to the best schools. "I'll fix you a better breakfast tomorrow," she offered softly.

Jeremiah looked up and she couldn't hide her crestfallen face from him. "I don't mind oatmeal, Dorie."

"I wish I could provide better for you, Jeremiah. Maybe it'd be best for you to go with the Parkers."

Jeremiah stood so abruptly the chair squeaked noisily against the wooden floor. His eyes gleamed with indignation. "I won't go, Dorie. You can't make me. I'd eat a thousand pounds of oatmeal and I still won't want to leave here. Gosh," he said, tears misting in his eyes. "All I said was that I get tired of oatmeal once in a while."

His face red, his hands trembling, Dorie reached for him and hugged him tight. "I'm sorry for saying that. You won't have to go with the Parkers, Jeremiah. I promise. I can't bear to think of living here without you. It's you and me, always. Right?"

He nodded and Dorie figured he couldn't get the words out from the choked up feeling and tears falling down his cheeks. "I'm doing all I can, little brother, to keep you with me."

"I…know."

"I think everybody's nerves are jumbled lately," she said, giving him one last squeeze before she let him go. "But it'll be over soon. The Parkers will see what a fine life we live. They'll see that you're happy living in Silver Hills with me and…with Shane."

Jeremiah wiped his eyes and cast her a dubious glance. "Shane and I are going to Mrs. Whitaker's tonight for a rehearsal of sorts. We're going to pretend to be married. And hopefully we'll be so convincing that the Parkers won't have any doubts in their heads about it."

"I guess that's good. Right?"

"I'm hoping it goes all right."

"What about me? Shouldn't I know what you're planning?"

"You? Why, I hadn't thought about you, Jeremiah." And Dorie realized how true that was. She'd been so absorbed in learning how to be a lady and Shane's wife that she hadn't thought of what Jeremiah might need to know. "That's right, you're going to have to learn about us, our…marriage," she said with a lifting of her lips, "and our life at Shane's ranch. Maybe you should come with us to Mrs. Whitaker's."

Jeremiah shook his head. "No. You go with Shane. You're pretending to be his wife, so go do it. You can teach me what I need to learn another time."

"Tomorrow. I'll sit down with you tomorrow. It'll be better this way. Because whatever problems we find tonight, we'll correct and then I'll have all the information you'll need to know. But I'm warning you, Jeremiah. It's necessary to stretch the truth. I know you don't like doing that."

"You mean…lie, don't you, Dorie?"

Dorie bit down on her lip. There was no fooling her brother. She nodded. "Yes, but for the greater good."

"Whatever that means. I'll do it to stay here with you. I'll do and say whatever I have to."

Dorie heard regret in his words and felt it in her heart, as well. She didn't like putting him through this. Lord knows, she wasn't being entirely fair to Shane either, and she herself wasn't much for deception. Unless absolutely necessary.

Dorie was one hundred percent certain this was necessary.

"What are your plans today?"

"I'm riding over to Shane's."

"Aren't the Boyds going over there today?"

"Yep, but Shane's going into town. He's on some sort of mission and he asked if I could spend a few hours helping out."

Dorie wondered what kind of mission would take

him off to town today. She only hoped Mrs. Whitaker had convinced him to come over for the rehearsal. Dorie cringed thinking of Shane's expression when the older woman explained her plans for the evening. "Okay then, finish your meal and I'll clean up the kitchen. Then I've got some chores to do myself. There's so much to do before meeting up with the Parkers on Saturday."

Dorie picked up plates and began washing, listening to the sound of Jeremiah scraping two bowls of oatmeal, clean.

She smiled.

And felt more hopeful than she had in days.

Later that afternoon, Dorie looked over the dress she'd worn to Shane's the other day when she'd helped deliver the calf. She'd washed it twice since then, darned a rip near the hem, but still the dress didn't look clean enough to wear tonight. Wrinkled and with some mud stains still visible, the once pretty pink-and-yellow calico wasn't fit for wearing in public.

Dorie rifled through her drawers, pulling out her options and placing them on the bed. She had a cream-colored lace blouse with a high collar that buttoned down the back that she'd considered appropriate enough for church. But all of her skirts were loose-fitting in tones of drab grays and browns. She'd never had occasion to wear anything nice, not since she was a little girl when her mama would fix her up so pretty and take her to Sunday services. No, her clothes these days were only practical enough to wear while milking the cow, making tallow and churning butter. She'd never had call for anything else.

She'd wear the cream blouse and the cheeriest of her gray skirts to Mrs. Whitaker's house tonight. In her mind she counted away the hours before her rendezvous with Helene and Oliver Parker. Dorie knew now what she had to do, and began to set her plan in motion. She'd work into the wee hours of the night if necessary.

With her plan set firmly in her mind, she boiled water over the cookstove and set about taking a lavender-scented bath. The book had full instructions on how to make oneself presentable and, though Mrs. Whitaker had said they didn't need the book's advice any longer, Dorie liked the idea of soaking in scented water and scrubbing her hair clean before meeting with Shane tonight.

Dorie brought the oval-shaped steel tub in from outside and set it into the kitchen. One day, she hoped to have a nice porcelain tub long enough to stretch full out and relax in. Shane had a tub like that and she'd soaked in his tub the other day, but he hadn't been all too happy about it.

"Forget about Shane," she scolded herself. "Just concentrate on what you have to do, Isadora McCabe."

Dorie filled the tub with one bucket of cold water, then three more buckets of water she'd heated up real good. She watched as steam wafted up before dropping in a small amount of lavender oil. Mrs. Whitaker had given her both the lavender oil and an egg-shaped fancy soap that smelled like someplace far away, some-place…exotic. At least that's what Mrs. Whitaker had said. The flowery scent drifted up inside the room and Dorie removed all of her clothes and sunk down deep into the tub. She closed her eyes, enjoying the peace and got as comfortable as possible in the steaming hot tub.

She began to wash her body clean using the scented soap. The fragrant lather slid down her body, softening up her skin. When she was finished with her body, she leaned way back and let the water bathe her hair. She sudsed the wet tresses all the way down to the ends, then put a dollop of lavender oil in her hand and worked it through, lightly wondering if the oil would make her hair glisten like sunshine.

Dorie rested back in the tub, too relaxed now to think. She enjoyed the hot water caressing her neck, and though her knees weren't immersed, she could just about fit the rest her body in the water. She soaked with eyes closed and drifted off.

Shane brought the buckboard up to Dorie's house an hour earlier than he'd been instructed. He'd dressed in his Sunday best, but his heart wasn't in this dinner that Mrs. Whitaker had proposed. He'd been doing just fine lately, keeping his distance from Dorie. And that's exactly what he'd intended to do, until they made their trip to Virginia City. Soon their unholy ruse would begin and, he hoped, end in a matter of days. But the invitation wasn't one Alberta would allow him to refuse, and if this dress rehearsal helped send the Parkers packing then it would be worth it. He'd be free of his obligation to help Dorie any further.

He took the steps to her front door and was about to knock when Jeremiah sauntered by, holding a lead rope on Lightning. "Hey, Shane. You coming for Dorie?"

He nodded. "I'm a little early."

"S'okay. Go on in. Dorie won't mind. She's probably

in there fixing supper for me or fussing with her hair, getting ready."

"You sure?"

Jeremiah squinted into the late-afternoon sunlight. "I'm sure. I've got to groom Lightning. She needs a real good rubdown for all the riding I've been doing lately, then I'll be in."

"Okay, thanks."

Jeremiah nodded, his dark blue eyes fixed on what Shane held in his hand. Shane held the package to his side, trying not to bring attention to it.

"What you got there?"

"Uh, something for Dorie is all."

Jeremiah's dark russet hair fell into his eyes as he cocked his head, trying to get a better look from his spot near the barn. "It's not her birthday or nothing, is it?"

Shane didn't know when Dorie's birthday was, though he did remember an invitation for cake one year. "Don't think so."

Then the young boy's eyes lit. "You brought her a gift. Oh, she's gonna go on and on about it. Nobody brings Dorie gifts."

Shane realized too late that that was probably true. He hoped Dorie wouldn't read more into the gesture than was fitting and proper. He wasn't a gentleman caller, bearing gifts in order to gain a woman's affections. No, this was simply a token of…repayment. Yes, that's what it was.

"It's not that kind—"

But Jeremiah had already lost interest and had entered the barn. Shane spun around and opened Dorie's front door. "Dorie!" he called out. "You in here?"

When she didn't answer, he headed for the kitchen. Jeremiah had said she was most likely cooking him supper. He approached the door and a flowery fragrance, light, airy and completely female, teased his senses. How odd for that scent to be coming from the kitchen. He popped his head inside the door and peered inside.

And witnessed a sleeping Dorie, buck naked, lying inside an oval basin bathtub.

All the air rushed out of Shane's chest. He swallowed hard, unable to tear his gaze away from the most serene and beautiful sight he'd ever encountered. With her nearly dry coppery locks draped over the tub, Dorie was exposed to him, her face peaceful, her breasts, full and ripe and peeking out from the still water, her shapely legs drawn up at the knee. Shane knew he shouldn't look. He should tear his gaze away and back out of the room, but his feet stayed planted. He watched the gentle easing of her chest, viewed the creamiest skin a man could ask for and gazed upon liquid-veiled auburn curls that concealed her womanhood.

Shane took a calming breath and continued watching her, his manhood fully alert. He wanted nothing more than to forget about this dinner with the Whitakers, remove all his clothes and join Dorie in that tub. He ached to touch her again, to kiss her lips and weigh the twin rosy-tipped globes in hand. Something began to snap within, but he pulled hard with all his might to rein in lusty thoughts of making love to Dorie, driving his body deep into hers and pleasuring them both.

Shane shuddered at his own thoughts, hating himself for not having more control. He understood the moment for what it was, realizing that he would never again witness Dorie in such a state. He reminded himself of her youth and inexperience. She was vulnerable to him because he agreed to help her. He couldn't take advantage of her. He wouldn't.

With one last look, Shane finally did back away, entering the parlor. Then he thought better of being inside the house with Dorie, opting for the porch, where the cool air might hasten to bring him some relief. He exited the house through the front door and waited.

But the image of Dorie swamped his body with heat, and no amount of cool afternoon air would ebb the tide that flowed within him.

He cursed himself for not heeding his own dire warnings to stay away from Dorie. He cursed himself for his lack of willpower. He cursed himself for wanting her the way a man wants a woman. His mind told him no, but his body begged to differ. His body begged…for her.

Shane shook off that ill notion and scratched his forehead so hard he drew blood. He winced and cursed aloud this time.

"Shane?" Dorie stood just inside her doorway, wearing an overly large robe, wrapped together with tie strings, looking at him curiously. But all he could think about was what she probably didn't have on underneath that robe. He cursed again.

"Shane, did you cut your head?"

"No—yes. It's nothing." He stared at her, his mind flashing images of her sleeping naked in that tub.

"Come in. I'll tend to it."

"No. Don't worry about it."

She narrowed her eyes, ready to argue, but he shook his head and, for once, Dorie didn't argue. "O-kay."

He followed her inside, the package weighing heavily in his arms. Suddenly, he felt like a fool.

"Am I late?" she asked. "I must have fallen asleep in the tub."

Shane closed his eyes and prayed for mercy. "No, I came a little bit early."

She smiled and cast him another puzzled look. "Why?"

"I, uh…" He shoved the package at her. "Here. This is for you."

Surprise registered on Dorie's face as she stared down at the package. "For me?"

He nodded. "Just open it."

Dorie sat on the parlor sofa and rested the package in her lap. She made a fuss over the ribbon ties, carefully unwinding them, then removing the paper. She lifted out the light blue dress and stood to gain a better look at it fully. "Oh, this is…it's so pretty, Shane."

Shane had hoped she would think so. It wasn't fancy by any measure—a simple dress from the general store—but the color suited her eyes and he judged the fit would be right. "You ruined your dress in the mud the other day and don't say you didn't. I know it was damaged beyond repair."

"But you didn't have to do this."

"I, uh—" he began and swallowed hard. "I wanted to." And that was the truth. Shane had more critical things to spend his money on, but something compelled him to gift Dorie with something she really needed. She'd helped tend him when he was injured, then helped save his heifer and the calf, doing so without qualm; purchasing her a new dress seemed the least he might do.

"It's too much," she whispered. Apparently, Mrs.

Whitaker's instruction was taking, because the old Dorie would have said what she'd really meant. That he couldn't afford it.

"It's just a simple dress," he said, feeling awkward.

"Oh, Shane. It's very thoughtful of you." She set down the dress and walked over to him. "Thank you. I'll wear it tonight."

"Fine. I thought you might need, uh…might want to wear it tonight."

She smiled and reached for the dress. Then, on an impulse he clearly witnessed by the light in her eyes, she pressed a kiss to his lips.

Shane closed his eyes, breathing in the sweetly feminine scent of exotic flowers, and imagining untying that robe to press his hands inside and caress her soft skin.

He jammed his hands in the pockets of his trousers, willing himself to keep from doing all those things. Willing himself from disrobing Dorie, picking her up in his arms and marching straight into her bedroom.

Lucky for him, Dorie broke off the kiss quickly. Then she smiled into his eyes. "I love the dress. You're the most honorable man I know, Shane Graham."

And once again Shane was reminded of all the reasons he shouldn't touch Dorie McCabe ever again.

Chapter Nine

Dorie didn't have much experience with courting. Actually none at all if she thought on it hard enough, but tonight she sure felt as if Shane was courting her. He'd come over looking handsome in a pair of dark trousers and his Sunday best white shirt. He wore a string tie and, from the looks of it, might have made a trip to see the town barber today, as well.

He'd brought her a gift, a pretty blue dress that matched the color of her eyes. She glanced once more in the mirror, still surprised that he'd picked a dress that fit her so well, cinching in at the waist and flaring out slightly. She lifted her hair up, pinning the curls in place and allowing a few soft tendrils to touch the rounded scoop of her collar. Floss fringe edged her wrists and the hem of her dress, making a plain frock something more stylish.

Dorie filled her lungs and picked up her reticule, ready for her first and only dress rehearsal at being Mrs. Shane Graham, dutiful wife and doting sister. She hoped she'd pass muster, because in fewer than three days, she and Shane would be doing this for real in Virginia City.

Dorie recounted all of the lessons she'd had with Mrs. Whitaker about composure, grace, manners and proper speech. Heavens, she sure hoped she'd remember it all.

"You're ready, Dorie. Now just be yourself." She repeated to herself Mrs. Whitaker's final words of advice. "And the Parkers will love you.

"That's if you can fool them into believing you've been living with Shane for the past two years as his wife," Dorie added.

Dorie hesitated no longer. She strode into the parlor, then remembered her lesson on proper gait and slowed her pace, then raised her chin in the same manner as Mrs. Whitaker and sashayed into the room with what she hoped was poise.

Shane waited by the window, his profile visible to her as he stared out to view the shadows in the yard as the sun began to set on the horizon. "I'm ready," she announced.

Shane spun around. With sober eyes and an expression less than encouraging, he swept his gaze up and down her body before nodding.

Nervously, Dorie walked forward, remembering Mrs. Whitaker's words of caution not to blurt out the first thing that popped into her mind. She wanted to scream at Shane for his lack of enthusiasm. Why hadn't he commented on the dress he'd brought her? Why, being a seamstress of sorts, she knew this dress fit her better than most she owned and, at the very least, the soft sapphire color did complement her eyes.

"Shall we go?" she suggested most elegantly, holding back her anger and concentrating on the night ahead.

Shane nodded. He opened the door for her and they

walked to his buckboard. Dorie didn't climb right up, but waited by the side of the wagon for Shane.

He stopped, blinked his eyes then came up behind her, placing his hands lightly on her waist to help her up to the seat. "Thank you," she said, remembering her manners.

She fussed a bit with her dress then waved a farewell to Jeremiah, who had poked his head out the barn door as the wagon lurched forward. Shane hadn't said one word to her since she'd kissed him. Maybe her boldness had him riled; she couldn't be sure. No matter, she wouldn't have taken back that kiss. It was her way of thanking him for the thoughtful gesture of buying her a dress, and if he didn't like kissing her, well, he sure hadn't shown it. He'd kissed her back fully and she knew he had enjoyed it just as much as she had.

They sat side by side in the moving wagon for a full five minutes in complete silence. When she'd finally had enough, Dorie shot him a glance. "It's a nice night."

Shane grunted.

Dorie pursed her lips and drew a breath. "I want to thank you again for the dress."

He nodded.

She tried again. "You look handsome tonight, Shane. I've never seen you in your Sunday best."

Shane slipped a dubious glance her way.

Then she remembered Shane's "almost" wedding to Marilee. He'd been dressed in his best then, too. "Oh, I guess I have. But that doesn't count."

He bunched up his brows as if trying to puzzle something out, but didn't say one word. Not one *darn* word.

Dorie's well-intentioned patience was at an end. She couldn't hold her tongue and speak pleasantries any longer. "Shane Graham, what's gotten into you? You haven't said a thing to me since we left my house!"

Shane pulled the horses to a halt, stopping the wagon just yards from the Whitakers' ranch gate. He closed his eyes as if praying for peace or some such thing, then turned to look at her.

A coyote howled, the distant eerie cry familiar but, oh, so unnatural. Soft breezes blew by, lifting the curls off her shoulders. Dorie sat ramrod still under the setting sun and waited for Shane's response. And waited. Finally, when he spoke, his words were slow and deliberate. "I am not your savior, Dorie. I am not your white knight coming to rescue you. I am not a hero. And I'm certainly not the most honorable man you know. Far from it."

Dumbstruck, she uttered a soft, "Oh."

"I am not courting you."

Dorie took a swallow.

"I brought you that dress today because you helped me with the heifer. It's repayment for the dress that was ruined."

"Repayment?" Dorie felt as if she'd been punched in the gut.

"I'm doing this to help you keep Jeremiah. Once it's done, I'm through. I have my life to live, Dorie, and so do you."

Dorie's heart ached from Shane's softly spoken but hurtful words. "I know, Shane. That's why I'm grateful to you. You're kind and honorable. You're the only man I trust."

"Damn it. Don't trust me, Dorie. I'm not honorable."

"Yes, you are, Shane."

Shane shook his head briskly. "No."

"Why, Shane? Why are you saying these things to me?"

Shane turned in his seat to look her squarely in the eyes. "I walked in on you, Dorie, taking your bath. You were asleep in that tub. An honorable man would have closed his eyes and backed out of the room. But not me. No, I looked my fill. I couldn't keep from looking at you, *all* of you. And you know what I wanted to do? Hell, I wanted to strip off all my clothes and join you in that tub. It was all I could do to leave that kitchen. You're young and innocent and I've nearly taken from you something you should only give to the man you marry."

"What if that man is you, Shane," Dorie said, holding back tears. It wasn't enough that Shane wanted her; she wanted to know he *wanted* to want her. The notion barely made sense in her head, but that's how she felt.

"It can't be me, Dorie. That's what I'm saying. It could never be me. I'm bound to marry—"

Dorie shushed him by pressing her fingers against his lips. "Don't say her name." She closed her eyes. "Not again, Shane."

She pressed his lips hard, not wanting to hear his declaration. He'd told her over and over how he would marry Marilee when the time came, but with each day they'd spent together Dorie was sure he'd be throwing his life away with a woman who didn't want him, a woman he didn't want.

Shane plucked her fingers from his mouth. "It's going to happen—my marriage. You need to concentrate on Jeremiah and what's happening in the next few days. Once that's settled, you can move on with your life. And one day, maybe sooner than you think, you'll meet someone who is just right for you. You'll fall in love and marry. You'll have the family you crave, Dorie."

Dorie didn't want any man. She wanted Shane, but her pride had taken a terrible blow and she wouldn't let him see how his harsh words had hurt her. "The man I marry would have to see me as a woman, not as a child in constant need of protection. He'd be a man not afraid to climb into that tub. He'd be a man who would bring me gifts because he cared for me, not because he owed me something. He'd be someone I could *trust* with my heart."

Shane appeared shocked by her calmly spoken tirade.

"He'd be a man who would want me, regardless of my age or my inexperience. He'd teach me all I needed to know. So, I guess you're right, Shane. When I find *that* man, I'll marry him."

Shane gritted his teeth. His face twisted in anger. "You do that."

She folded her arms across her middle. "I will."

He nodded and raised his voice. "Good."

"Let's get going."

Shane lifted the reins and spoke to the horses. Within minutes, they arrived at the Whitakers' ranch house. His face flaming, he set the brake. "Now, how are we going to pretend to be a happily married couple?"

Dorie fumed silently. Shane was better at pretending things than he thought because he wasn't honest with himself half the time. But he refused to see it. He didn't think himself honorable. Dorie wished it so. The sad fact remained that Shane Graham had always done the honorable thing when it came to Dorie. "Shane, you shouldn't have any trouble. You're good at faking how you really feel."

Dorie didn't wait for his assistance. She climbed down from the buckboard on her own and smoothed the wrinkles from her dress.

She'd call on all her pretenses once inside the house.

Standing next to Dorie and ready to knock on the Whitakers' front door, Shane controlled his anger the best he could. He'd made a devil's bargain and now he'd have to go through with it. He wondered how one little gal could tempt and irritate him so darn much, looking like an *angel* in shades of soft blue, rather than his one true tormenter.

Still, he'd told her the honest truth. He'd laid out his feelings, the way things had to be, with all honesty. So Dorie would have no cause to think anything different. For that, Shane commended himself. But for hurting her the way he had, he'd never forgive himself.

He knocked and, shortly after, Iggy Whitaker opened the door to greet them. "Well, look who we have here," he said with a rich smile. "It's Mr. and Mrs. Graham. Come in, please. My wife's still fussing in the kitchen, but she'll be joining us soon enough."

"Thank you," Shane said, placing a gentle hand on Dorie's lower back. "Shall we?"

There was the slightest hitch in Dorie's back when he touched her, but she smiled warmly at Mr. Whitaker and nodded politely.

They entered the parlor and Mr. Whitaker offered them a seat on their tufted green velvet sofa. Shane took note of the home, his gaze scanning the house for all its finery. A tall polished walnut grandfather clock stood in one corner announcing the hour, photos and paintings in gilded frames hung on the wall, and crystal vases and such caught the light, twinkling on the mantel. The Whitakers had a large spread, with twice the cattle and land that Shane had. Ranching had been good to them over the years, and Shane thought that he only wanted a small portion of their success. He didn't need all the finery, just a life free of complications, where a man could hold his head high in town, where he could enjoy a bit of comfort without constant worry over the fate of his ranch.

Shane waited for Dorie to sit then took his place beside her.

"It's nice of you both to have us to dinner," she said.

Mr. Whitaker glanced at Shane before responding. "Wouldn't have it any other way. You two need a bit of help, I understand."

"No, they don't," Mrs. Whitaker said, entering the room with a tray of drinks. "Hello, Shane and Dorie. Nice of you to come." Then she turned her attention to Iggy. "The Grahams are a happily married couple, dear. They need no help."

"Oh, right," Iggy said, handing Dorie a glass of lemonade with a wink. Then he bent to hand Shane a drink, speaking quietly into his ear, "It's amazing what we're willing to do for the women we love."

Shane balked at that notion, but didn't argue. Iggy might have agreed to this ruse out of love for his endearing wife, but Shane only agreed out of his sense of obligation. Besides, he'd have to listen to another tirade from Dorie if he hadn't granted her this one night of rehearsal.

"So tell me, how is Jeremiah?" Mrs. Whitaker asked, taking a seat at a smaller opposing sofa, next to her husband.

Dorie's blue eyes took on a bright gleam. "He's doing

fine, thank you. He's a big strapping young boy. Sometimes, when I look at him, I can't believe he's the same little boy who used to follow me around like a puppy. I'm proud of the way he's turned out. He's good and honest and—" She cleared her throat and moisture reached her eyes. "He's thirteen now. And a big help on the ranch. Isn't that right, Shane?"

Shane nodded, noting Dorie's genuine pride in her brother. "He's a quick learner that's for sure. He does what he's told and when he comes over—"

Dorie nudged his side and bunched her brows.

"Oh—I mean, when he's not attending school, he's outside helping me with chores. He rides fences and is getting pretty good at pulling a cow out of the mud."

"Jeremiah loves ranching, doesn't he, Shane?" Dorie asked with an encouraging smile.

"As much as I do, I think. He'll make a fine rancher one day, all on his own."

Dorie settled back in her seat, apparently satisfied with the way things were going. Shane thought it wasn't going too badly, either. He sipped lemonade, relaxed back against the sofa, as well, but when his thigh brushed against Dorie's an unbidden flash of her lying naked and serene in that bathtub plagued his thoughts. She smelled like heaven right now, her fragrance a mixture of flowers and fresh air.

"Dorie did a great job in raising him."

Dorie fixed her gaze on him, her expression thoughtful. "Thank you," she said softly. "And Shane, he's like a father to Jeremiah."

Shane blinked back his surprise and took note of the pride in Dorie's tone. Did she really think of him that way—as a father figure for Jeremiah? On second thought, he supposed it would be good for the Parkers to think that Shane had acted like a father to Jeremiah. That would make sense enough.

"Shane loves him like a son," Dorie added, squaring her gaze on the Whitakers. Shane did the same, still wondering if there was truth in what she claimed. He certainly cared for the boy, enjoyed his company and looked after him when necessary.

Mrs. Whitaker sipped her lemonade and smiled. "I suppose he's going to school in Silver Hills?"

"Well, yes. He's in school, whenever he's not busy helping me at the—helping Shane, I mean, with his ranching duties."

"I see. Well, he certainly wouldn't have chores if he lived in New York. He'd go to the best schools and get a fine education. I suppose he wouldn't be opposed to that—no chores?"

Dorie's face flamed. "He doesn't much mind his chores. And he's had good schooling here. He can read. He can write. He's a bright boy."

"Ah, but there's more to learn about life than reading and writing. There's a whole world of things he could learn. Why, he could be anyone he wanted to be, do anything he wanted if he lived in New York."

Dorie held her breath and tried for composure, but Shane saw the indecision on her face. He intervened, "Jeremiah is happy with us. He's quite a young man."

"That's why the Parkers would love to get to know him better," Iggy said. "I suspect they'd be extremely eager to become acquainted with their only living kin."

"Yes, I think so, too." Alberta nodded and stood up.

"Let's finish this conversation in the dining room. Supper is ready."

Dorie stood quickly. "May I help you?"

"Oh, that would be nice, Dorie. Yes, let's have the gentlemen take their seats. You and I can bring in the meal."

Dorie seemed eager to leave the room and Shane had to admit he'd been tense watching her struggle to say the right things. He followed Iggy into the dining room and took the seat offered.

"Well now, you're really in a pickle, aren't you?" he asked.

Shane chuckled. "You know it. I hate all this deception."

Iggy rubbed his jaw. "Can't say as I blame you. But sometimes it's necessary. When I first met Alberta, she couldn't stand the sight of me. She thought I was the crudest man living on earth. So it took some deception on my part to finally convince her she loved me just the way I was."

"How's that? What did you do to deceive her?"

Iggy took a deep breath and shook his head. "I'm not proud of this, but after trying to court her, hitting her with all the charm I possessed—which wasn't much back then—I was pretty desperate. She'd been visiting family and was due to head back East shortly. There'd been a bank robbery the day before she was to leave. I hated doing it, 'cause it meant losing time with her, but I joined up with the sheriff and deputies to trail the bank robbers. We found them out a ways, ten miles from town, holed up in a little shanty. There was a shoot-out and a bullet grazed my shoulder. It was a slight wound. Actually, I'd bled more running into a tree branch once, but Alberta didn't know that.

"I stayed in that shanty, and sent word back to her that I'd been shot."

"And she came running, right?"

"She came all right. But there wasn't anything tender about the reunion. Once she saw that I wasn't dying, she told me off but good for scaring her like that. Then, when I pointed out that she'd been worried about me and that she cared more than she wanted to admit, well, she came around. I wasted no time, proposed on the spot in that very shanty. We were married the next day."

"That's one hell of a story, Iggy."

"I know. Neither of us lived to regret it, either."

Shane nodded, thinking that Iggy had a purpose for telling this tale. "Dorie and I, we're not…"

Iggy pursed his lips. His face, just showing signs of wrinkles, held a dubious expression. "Not in love?"

"Not by a long shot. She's young and—"

"Good-natured."

"Impetuous," Shane countered.

"And pretty as a picture."

Shane couldn't argue. It wasn't that Dorie wasn't pretty in her own way but she just wasn't the woman for him.

And those thoughts gave way to an image of her naked in her bath, all creamy skin and soft curls.

"I can't disagree that she's appealing, but—"

"Alberta didn't think she'd ever fall in love with me, but I wore her down. Sometimes, love sneaks up on you. You can't fight it."

Hell, Shane had been fighting the lust he felt for Dorie ever since this whole dishonest sham had begun, but that's all he felt. Not love. Never love. He wouldn't allow himself to think on that any further. He had Tobias and Marilee Barkley to think about, not to mention what was best for Dorie. She'd find someone she could love. It stung Shane when she'd suggested that he wasn't man enough for her. That he'd been lacking in some way because he thought of her as a child rather than a woman. That she hadn't thought him a man she could trust.

Her words struck a chord. But he couldn't ponder his predicament further. Mrs. Whitaker entered and he looked up with a smile. She brought in a tray of seared gravy-topped steaks, and Dorie followed carrying a dish of creamed potatoes and carrots and a platter of warmed bread.

Shane couldn't take his eyes off of Dorie, playing the role of his wife so well. She looked every inch the lady tonight, as well, and hadn't done one impetuous thing yet. She seemed to follow suit in whatever Alberta was doing.

"Thank you for the help, Dorie dear. Now let's all take a seat. Let's see, I think we'll have…Shane say grace tonight."

Startled, Shane looked up. Alberta nodded. "You do say grace every night, don't you?"

"Not since I was a young boy."

"Do you remember?"

Shane hesitated as all eyes in the room waited for his answer. "I can put something together. Just give me a minute." Images and words filtered into his mind as he thought back to those times when his mother and father would take turns saying grace each evening, including Shane in the ritual at least twice a week. Shane wasn't comfortable speaking aloud what was inside his head, but he'd learned something of thanking the Almighty for the good things in his life from those early times sitting at the table, bending his head in prayer. "We thank you, Lord, for the abundance of good food presented here today, and for the kindness of our neighbors and friends. We thank you for sunshine and rain and good health for those sitting at this table today. Amen."

A quiet chorus of "amen" went around the table and, when Shane looked up, Alberta smiled and nodded. "Nicely done, Shane."

"I, uh, should have said something about thanking the Lord for my wife and for Jeremiah, but somehow lying through my teeth while sending up a prayer to the Almighty didn't set right. I don't think I'll be able to do that with the Parkers, either."

"That's all right. Just ask that Mr. Parker say grace when you're dining with them. Then you don't have to worry about it."

Dorie glanced at Alberta. "That's a good idea, Mrs. Whitaker. You are a gem."

"A gem? Why, Dorie, I don't think I've ever heard such a nice compliment before. I'm glad to help, but now, um, let's see, while we're passing around the dishes, why don't you tell us how you and Shane met."

Iggy began to pass the platter of steaks around the table. Shane forked a steak, the juice spurting out of the center as he slid it onto Dorie's china plate. "Here you go, honey. I'll fill your plate while you tell Mrs. Whitaker how we met."

Dorie cocked her head to one side and cast him a mischievous look. "You tell the story much better, sweetheart. Why don't you tell the Whitakers how we met?"

Shane spooned creamed potatoes off another platter and plopped them down onto Dorie's plate, none too gently. "No, I insist. You go on, now. They're waiting."

"Oh, well, all right, *sweetheart.* It was love at first sight," she began. "Shane took one look at me, and that was it. I met him at our church's yearly bake sale and social. He asked me to dance and we did. We danced and danced and danced." Fully immersed in her story now, Dorie's blue eyes beamed excitedly. "We were having a grand time, until another man tried to cut in. I'm afraid Shane caused a ruckus when the man wouldn't back down. Shane bloodied the man's nose. Poor fellow, he had to be rushed to the doctor."

Iggy Whitaker chuckled. Alberta simply grinned.

Shane's temper flared. "I didn't cause a ruckus, *dear.* Not over some silly dance."

Dorie placed a calming hand on Shane's arm. "Yes, you did. The whole town practically witnessed your outburst. Why, you couldn't stand the thought of another man taking me into his arms. Of course," Dorie continued with a gleam in her eyes, "later you were repentant. But at that moment, you knew you wanted me for your wife. It was truly the sweetest and most frightening thing I've ever experienced."

"Why is that?" Iggy asked, his gaze fastened intently on Dorie, no doubt waiting to see what she'd come up with next.

"Why, because Shane was so much older than me."

The glass of lemonade missed Iggy's mouth. He spilled a measure of liquid onto the table, but that didn't stop Dorie. She continued, "That frightened me. Here I was just sixteen and Shane, well, he was a *mite* older than that. I wasn't all too sure that bloodying a man's nose while trying to impress a lady would be considered proper at all. But he was so sweet and, aside from drawing blood on that dance floor, he'd been a perfect gentleman. After that, he courted me for a time, bringing me flowers and gifts. He was most attentive. I couldn't help falling in love with him. And now, we're happily married. With a baby on the way." Dorie patted her flat belly. "Of course, Jeremiah is thrilled at becoming an uncle. Isn't that right, my love?"

Shocked and stupefied, Shane couldn't respond. If he'd had food in his mouth, he would have surely choked. He simply stared at Dorie, thinking she'd lost her mind.

Dorie kissed his cheek. "Shane still gets a bit tongue-tied when I speak of the baby. But he's as excited as I am. And Jeremiah is simply overjoyed at the thought of having a little one in the house."

The Whitakers held back their amusement the best they could, but Shane caught them both smirking and stifling chuckles they seemingly couldn't quite contain.

They ate in silence after that, Shane suddenly losing his appetite. He chewed his food as if it were sawdust, too dumbfounded to enjoy the meal.

Dorie hadn't missed a beat. She'd come on full force with a story that baffled him. She'd never discussed with him any of this, except that they'd met at a church social. She'd painted him out to be some sort of ruffian who, once married to her, became fully civilized. And that bit about her being with child muddied up his brain. The thought of Dorie carrying his child scared the living daylights out of him.

But it appeared that Dorie had the whole story planned out in her mind, ahead of time. To her credit, the tale explained in just a few words what might have taken hours to discover. Their age difference, for one. And how happy a marriage they had now. After all, a baby would prove that the two of them had a future together, and she'd brilliantly included Jeremiah in the whole picture. With a new family member, a baby coming, how could the Parkers even fathom tearing him away from his home?

Yes, Dorie was determined to make this work. That's what scared him most. When Dorie set her mind to something, there was no telling what might happen.

Shane chewed on his food a little longer then shoved away his near empty plate. "Delicious meal, Alberta."

"Yes, it was delicious. Why I ate everything up. Eating for two sure brings out one's appetite," Dorie said.

Shane set his glass down with a gentle thud.

Dorie jumped slightly in her seat but refused to spare him another glance.

"Yes, I remember," Alberta said, playing along. "Of course it's been years, but I can recall having an enormous appetite."

"Wish I'd have been there then," Iggy said, looking at his wife with love in his eyes. He'd met Alberta later in life, after she'd been widowed and a mother of two. They didn't have any children of their own.

Alberta covered her hand over his and patted gently. "You've been the best father to my children, Iggy. They think of you with warmth and fondness."

Shane watched Dorie's expression as she, too, witnessed the loving scene between the Whitakers. The sense of longing and yearning for a love like theirs was clearly evident on her face. Shane wondered at the effect Dorie constantly had on him. One moment he was ready to strangle her and the next, he wanted to cradle her in his arms to give her words of reassurance and encouragement. Which only angered him further.

Alberta stood and announced, "Why don't you and Dorie go outside for a breath of air while Iggy helps me clear the dishes and make coffee."

Shane secretly thanked Alberta for her perception. Shane needed some time alone with Dorie. He'd just about had enough of her antics and tall tales. "I think that's a fine idea."

"Oh," Dorie said, glancing first at Shane before pleading with Alberta, "let me help. The men can go outside, for a smoke." She bobbed her head up and down hoping to gain agreement.

"I gave it up years ago," Iggy said. "And I don't mind helping. You two, go on outside. We'll have coffee ready in no time at all."

"Yes, go on," Alberta insisted.

Shane stood and waited for Dorie to rise. Then he grabbed her hand. "Come on, *honey.* We have a few things to discuss."

Shane let go of Dorie's hand the minute fresh air hit his face. He bounded down the steps then walked down the path leading to the front gate. He turned and waited. Dorie stood on the front porch, watching him closely. "You coming?" he called out.

Dorie cocked up her chin, lifted her skirts and climbed down the steps like royalty. "I'm coming."

She wasn't three feet from him before his let go his anger. "What's gotten into your head, Dorie? We've never discussed me sending some poor smitten man to the doctor, like a ruffian who can't hold his temper. And we certainly never discussed me getting you…I mean you being…" He shoved his hand in his hair then pointed at her belly. "With child!"

"I seem to recall you not being interested much in discussing our plan. You didn't care at all, Shane. So I made up what I thought was fitting."

"Fitting?" Shane spoke through gritted teeth. "It's too big a lie, Dorie. It's sacrilegious!"

"No, it's not, Shane. It's perfect. Don't you see, once the Parkers realize that Jeremiah has a family here, a true abiding family, they couldn't possibly think of taking him away from me."

Shane shook his head and continued to shake it while Dorie continued.

"It's part of the ruse, Shane."

"And what of Jeremiah? It's bad enough to make him lie about all this, but to pretend he's going to be an uncle? I'm not sure he'll even do it. That boy is honest to a fault. He doesn't like lying any more than I do."

Dorie placed her hands on her hips and defended her actions. "You can thank me for Jeremiah's honesty. I taught him right and I'm proud of him, but this can't be helped. I don't enjoy lying either, Shane. It's necessary and I'm desperate."

"It's too much, Dorie," Shane said, trying to reason with her.

"What's got you so upset, Shane? The lying, or having to think of me carrying your child?"

Shane shuddered. "You carrying my child?" Shane let out a derisive chuckle. "That frightens me to death."

"It shouldn't," she said quietly. "The thought just came to me today and, well, I wouldn't mind, Shane. Having your baby—"

"It's never going to happen."

"No, not unless you're willing to jump into the tub with me, Shane. You wanted to. You admitted that much to me."

Images of Dorie raced into his head again. Sexy, vivid, alluring images that Shane had trouble blocking out. He breathed a heavy sigh and turned his back on her, bracing his elbows against the fence. "You tempt me, Dorie. Making me think of things I got no right thinking."

"Do I?" she asked softly.

Shane felt her presence directly behind him, her flowery scent lingering in the air. He turned to find her eyes on him. "You know you do."

Dorie graced him with a slight smile. "I don't know any such thing. You continue to confuse me, Shane."

"Well, at least we have that in common."

Shane studied her eyes, so clear and earnest and blue at the moment. His gaze traveled down the length of her, the contours of the dress fitting her snugly. And then he looked a bit lower and lingered on her belly, flat and smooth. Shane realized why he'd been so unsettled by the notion of Dorie carrying his child.

Dorie would make a wonderful mother.

He envisioned her mothering his children, the baby at her breast, the softness in her eyes, the sweet contented face of a new wife and mother.

"We can't have a baby," he blurted out.

"Not even a pretend one?"

"It wouldn't be right, Dorie."

"Anything that keeps Jeremiah by my side is right, Shane. Can't you see that?"

Shane cleared his throat. "Sometimes...you go too far."

Dorie smiled with warmth in her eyes and stepped closer. "Or not far enough." With that, she reached up on tiptoes and wrapped her arms around his neck. She didn't give Shane time to protest or back away. Not that he would have found the willpower to push her away, because the moment her sweet giving lips brushed his, all of Shane's defenses crumbled.

Chapter Ten

Shane braced his hands on her tiny waist, his fingers splayed wide, and while his mind told him to back away, his body needed her closer. She kissed him softly and Shane kissed her back, unable to resist her generous mouth and warm nature. She smelled like heaven, her subtle lavender scent invading his nostrils, the softest coppery tresses brushing his cheek.

A little sound escaped her throat, evidence of pleasure and desire stirring within her, and Shane felt the same way. He held her close, his body fully alive with pulsing need. With the next little moan she uttered, Shane mated their tongues and the kiss deepened. He stroked her backside and she wiggled in closer to him until there was no doubt to the extent of his desire for her.

Shane gently broke off their kiss and rested his forehead against Dorie's silken hair. Holding her tight, he whispered, "What am I going to do with you, Isadora McCabe?"

"I could think of a few things," she breathed out.

"You shouldn't go tempting a man by saying those things."

"I'm not trying to," she countered softly, "and I wouldn't say these things to any man. Just you."

"Ah, Dorie."

She pulled back enough to search his eyes, her lips trembling and her voice a mere whisper in the night. "Is it so wrong to speak from my heart, Shane?"

Yes, Shane wanted to say, but now wasn't the time for a lecture, besides which Dorie didn't much listen to him. She had her own mind and did what she believed right. He had no control over her, which could only mean trouble at the end of the day. Still, Shane couldn't resist the earnest expression on her face, parted lips and words spoken with such innocence. "No, Dorie, it's not wrong, but you need to think before you say things that might…cause you harm."

"You wouldn't hurt me, Shane."

"Not intentionally."

"I know." Dorie lifted her lips to his once again, the kiss a sweet gentle coupling compared to the lusty encounter from before.

"Hummmph." The loud interruption startled them both. They turned their heads to find Iggy and Alberta standing on the porch wearing smug expressions. Shane had the feeling they'd been out there a while, watching. "Dessert is ready, unless you've had…enough?" Iggy asked in a tone that implied they'd already had their share of sweets. Alberta elbowed him in the gut. "Uh, coffee's ready, too."

Shane ran his hand through his hair. "Thank you. We're coming in right now."

Shane placed his hand on Dorie's back, gently urging her forward. She climbed the steps first, while Iggy held the door. But Alberta grabbed at Shane's sleeve before he could follow Dorie inside.

"A word with you, please."

"Of course."

Iggy shot Alberta a warning look that she readily ignored. He entered the house behind Dorie, leaving the two of them alone on the front porch. Alberta walked to the end of the porch and leaned against a post, facing him. Shane took the steps necessary to look her in the eye.

"You two remind me of Iggy and me when we first met."

"How so?"

"One minute you're fighting as if you can't stand each other, and the next you're kissing and making up."

Shane backed up a step. "Wait a minute here. We're not doing that. What you saw—well, it's Dorie's impetuous nature again."

"Shane, she may not realize it, but she's in love with you."

Shane blinked back his surprise. Dorie had a sweet nature and naturally she'd be beholden to him for helping her, but he didn't think Dorie knew about love yet. To tell the truth, after more than thirty years, Shane hadn't any experience, either. He'd never met a woman he'd wanted to settle down with. He'd always thought there'd be time enough for that, later, once his ranch got going strong. "No, you're mistaken."

Alberta arched her brows and smiled. "I don't think I am, Shane. I've spent some time with Dorie lately and I think I know her a bit now."

"I hope you're wrong, Alberta."

"Why, would that be so bad?"

"Hell, yes, it'd be bad. I don't want to hurt her."

Alberta turned to stare at the front gate, where he and Dorie had been locked in an embrace moments ago. "From where I stood, looked to me that neither of you were hurting. In fact, you both looked happy. Content. For a minute there."

"Yeah, a minute. But that's all it was. I've been trying to explain to Dorie why I have to marry Marilee. She just doesn't understand."

Alberta raised her voice slightly, turning to face him fully now. "Now, *I* don't understand. Seems to me when a man takes a woman into his arms and kisses her like there's a fire that needs putting out, I guess that would confuse even the most intelligent of women."

"What are you saying? You think I'm confusing Dorie?"

"I don't know. Are you?"

Shane hesitated and wondered if he'd been doing that very thing—saying all the right things trying hard to push her away, but having trouble thinking straight when she was near. "She's so damn innocent. She tempts me without even knowing it. And then she infuriates me."

"Ha! Just like my Iggy. He said the same about me. And we've been happily married for all these years. It's…love, Shane."

"No…it can't be."

Shane paced the wood decking up and back several times while Alberta remained silent. Then finally she asked softly, "What if it is?"

"Then I'm a dead man."

Alberta chuckled. "It's not that bad."

"You're right. It's worse. I can't get involved with Dorie. Aside from her being too young for me, I gave my word to marry Marilee. You know what Tobias Barkley is holding over my head. There's too many reasons why Dorie and I—"

"You want her. And don't deny it, Shane. I saw the way you were kissing her."

Shane closed his eyes briefly. Then he stared at Alberta and neither denied nor agreed with her.

"She's young and pretty and she's just about conquered her tomboyish ways, Shane. If not you, then some other smitten man is bound to court her. Is that what you want?"

"Yes, damn it. Nothing would make me happier." Shane heard the lie in his words the moment he uttered them. Picturing Dorie with another man didn't sit well. He couldn't fathom seeing her on another man's arm, kissing or bedding someone else. He wanted to be free of her; then again, he didn't.

For the past three years he'd looked after Dorie and her younger brother. He thought of himself as their protector. But somewhere along the line he'd stopped likening Dorie to the sister he'd lost when he was a child. In the beginning, he thought he could make up for not saving Lora by helping Dorie. He'd had noble ambitions in that regard. Now, Shane felt anything but noble. No matter what his feelings were for Dorie, his fate was sealed. Shane had no choice in the matter.

Alberta walked over to him, patting his arm. She spoke in a gentle caring tone. "If that's truly what you want," she began, "then you need to let Dorie go. Completely. Don't encourage her. You have to be the strong one. If I'm right and she's in love with you, then she'll be crushed when you marry Marilee. Don't give her false hope, Shane. She's had a tough life and, frankly, I admire her for her courage. Don't make it any harder on her than it already is."

"I don't want to, Alberta. But Dorie isn't easy...to set aside."

Alberta smiled sadly. "I know. You're a good man, Shane Graham."

Shane let go a frustrated sigh. "I'm trying to be. I'm truly trying."

"You're quiet again, Shane," Dorie said as they reached her homestead. Shane pulled the wagon brake and set the reins aside, watching Smart and Sassy halt up in front of the house.

"I'm thinking."

"You're angry with me again, aren't you?"

Shane shook his head. "No, not so much angry as..."

"Irritated."

Shane took a breath then scoffed. "Doesn't do any good being irritated with you. You're gonna do what you want, no matter what I say."

"That's not true. I value what you say to me."

"Do you? Could have fooled me."

Dorie sat ramrod straight in the wagon seat, recalling Mrs. Whitaker's words to her tonight, once they'd gotten a moment of privacy. And she had to admit, though reluctantly, that her mentor had been right. "Are you talking about our baby?"

Shane lifted wide silver-dollar-size eyes her way. "There is no baby."

Dorie smiled. "I know that, silly. I just sort of liked the way that sounded."

When Shane began to protest again, Dorie stopped him. "No, it's fine, Shane. I won't pretend to be carrying your child if you'd rather I didn't."

Shane removed his hat and ran his hand through his dark brown hair. "I'd rather you didn't. But what's got you changing your mind?"

"I had a change of heart, that's all." Dorie wouldn't admit to him that Mrs. Whitaker had made some rather good points tonight when they'd had their talk. Shane didn't want her pretending to be with child. It would only cause tension between them, as it had tonight. The Parkers wouldn't see a loving couple, but rather a man very uncomfortable with the idea of fathering a child. Shane wasn't a man to take deception lightly. It would be difficult for him to feign happiness at becoming a father when the idea disturbed him so much.

Dorie wouldn't dwell on why the thought of her having his child caused him such distress, but it had ruffled her feathers. And the more she pressed, the more Shane rebelled at the notion. Mrs. Whitaker pointed out that the friction the idea inspired would only add to the problem, rather than make her situation easier. Dorie couldn't disagree. She wouldn't do anything to jeopardize her chances with the Parkers.

Shane narrowed his eyes and his wary expression caused her a moment of injury. "Why?"

"Because it upsets you so much, Shane. That's why. You're doing me a big favor and I…well, I don't want you angry with me."

"Really?"

His skeptical tone caused her a measure of uncertainty. "You don't believe me?"

"It's just that...I *know* you. You backed down from the notion awfully quick. When you want something, you go after it, Dorie."

She shrugged and said softly, "It's more important that we get along these next few days."

Shane nodded. "That's true. Maybe you're growing up, after all."

Dorie's ire ignited. She lashed out, refusing to hold back her temper. "I'm a woman, Shane! Not that you've noticed. You think of me as a child. But I've had to grow up mighty fast these last few years. It's time you recognized that."

Shane surprised her when he agreed. "You're right. I'm not giving you enough credit." Then he smiled, his green eyes flashing bright. "I'm glad you've changed your mind tonight. It's the right thing to do."

Dorie's temper eroded seeing Shane's mood lighten. But she still wasn't entirely convinced. She'd hold that as her ace card, in case things didn't go well with the Parkers. She could always pretend that she'd found out from the doctor in Virginia City that she was with child. She wouldn't share that with Shane, though. He wouldn't take her backup plan well. "We'll see."

Dorie climbed down from the wagon unaided, then lifted her gaze to look at Shane one last time. "Thank you for coming with me tonight. I do appreciate your help. Mrs. Whitaker said we were convincing enough. And I didn't make any mistakes with what fork to lift when. So, I think we're ready. Oh, and Shane, I'm sticking with my story of how we met."

Shane nodded, without argument. She figured he'd been too happy about winning one battle to worry over the other. "Fair enough."

"I guess I'll see you day after tomorrow then."

"I'll pick you and Jeremiah up first thing Friday morning."

"Fine. I plan to spend tomorrow morning preparing my brother as to what to say. I think Jeremiah will do fine." She sent him a shaky smile, as sudden fear and apprehension curled her stomach. "Well, good night, Shane"

"Night, Dorie."

Shane lifted the reins and Dorie turned to go back inside, but she couldn't take another step. *This was it.* The next time she saw Shane, they'd be pretending to be married for real and deceiving Jeremiah's grandparents. She spun around quickly before Shane maneuvered the wagon out of her yard. "Shane!"

He stopped to look at her.

"This is going to work, right?"

Shane studied her for a moment. "We'll do our best, Dorie."

She nodded and smiled, watching him prompt the horses with soft words. The wagon ambled onto the road leading to the Bar G Ranch.

Butterflies winged their way through her stomach.

Her bravado all but gone, Dorie sent up a prayer to the Almighty. "Let our best be good enough."

"You boys know what to do now, while I'm gone?" Shane asked his two part-time ranch hands as they stood by the pen that housed the new calf and her mama.

Casey Boyd, the older of the two brothers, answered quickly, "Sure, we know, Mr. Graham. We'll water the horses and feed them, check on your herd each day."

"That's right. Check on the corral gates, too, and make sure they're locked each night. I'll have Smart and Sassy with me, but you'll need to keep an eye on the other horses and the milk cows."

"And the new calf," Logan Boyd said, his eyes trained on the baby calf, following her mama around the small pen. When Shane returned, he'd set them both free to wander the range. "Mind if go into the pen and see her sometime?"

Shane warned the boy not much older than Jeremiah. "You can go in there, but if the mama gets riled, hightail it out of there real fast, okay?"

"Sure, Mr. Graham, but the mama isn't one to get riled. She knows Casey and me by now."

"Just in case, you be careful." Shane had enough to worry about without thinking that one of these young boys might get hurt on his property. They were good boys and hard workers and he was lucky he'd found them. They worked when Shane needed them, when it came to rounding up and branding, and now he couldn't do without their help. Or Jeremiah's. He'd been a big help lately, as well.

Once again Shane wondered if Jeremiah looked upon him as a father. He was fond of the boy, but he'd never thought of him in those particular terms before. Not until Dorie had planted that notion in his head.

"I'll be heading to Virginia City for a few days. I won't be long."

"We know," Casey said. "You're going to take Jeremiah and Dorie into the city."

Shane's lips twisted into a slight frown. He hadn't told anyone about his plans other than Alberta and Iggy Whitaker. He'd wanted to keep it that way, but it appeared someone spoke out of turn.

"Who told you? Was it Jeremiah?"

"No sir."

Casey shuffled his feet and stared down at the ground.

"Well then, how did you boys find out?"

Logan shot Casey a quick glance. "Mama says we ain't supposed to…gossip."

"It's not gossip, Logan. I'm just curious. I'd planned on telling you my plans this morning anyway."

But he hadn't planned on announcing that he intended to take the McCabes with him. The three of them going into Virginia City together would certainly set some tongues to wagging. Shane silently cursed, wishing the next three days over already, so he could get his life back. At least until Tobias Barkley returned home with his runaway daughter.

"Uh, well, Miss Dorie went into the millinery yesterday and told Mrs. McPherson all about your trip together, then Mrs. McPherson told Mrs. Caruthers and then Mrs. Caruthers told our mama. That's why we knew to come out here extra early this morning. We figured you'd need our help, boss."

Dorie spoke with Roberta McPherson about their plans to travel to Virginia City? Shane didn't usually have a suspicious mind, but he figured Dorie had been up to something. She hadn't much liked seeing Roberta the other day when she'd stopped by to check on him.

Shane could only shake his head. Trying to figure any woman out was task enough, but figuring Dorie's motives for anything was downright impossible.

At least she'd given up the fool idea of claiming to be newly pregnant. Shane had won that battle, but he feared the next few days would test his patience and his resolve. At least he had Jeremiah as a chaperone. He'd be a sound and reliable buffer between them. Dorie would be extra careful around the Parkers, too. Maybe Shane worried for no real reason.

"Thanks again for coming out early. I'll be back soon as my business in Virginia City is over."

Logan looked up from viewing the baby calf. "You getting married, boss?"

Stunned at the question, Shane let out a derisive chuckle. "Not if I can help it. Why? Is that what Dorie said?"

"Nope," Casey interjected. "Not Miss Dorie, but, uh, well—"

"Mama said it's going around town that you're spending too much time with Miss Dorie and it's about time you married her," Logan, the younger less cautious brother announced.

"Mama didn't say it," Casey said. "She likes you, boss. It's the other ladies. They're the ones saying—"

"Boys, it's okay. Miss Dorie and I both have business in Virginia City and we decided to make the trip together, that's all. I'm not getting married. Not to Dorie McCabe, anyway."

Logan pushed his hat up further on his head. "If you was to marry, Miss Dorie is real nice. She bakes us cookies and biscuits when we're visiting Jeremiah."

"Biscuits?" Shane thought that was a real good reason not to marry Dorie McCabe, but didn't voice his opinion. "Well, rest assured, I'll be back in a few days and I won't be married to anyone."

"Yes, sir," they chorused.

Shane left the boys in the yard after giving them one last set of instructions, hitched up the horses and loaded the wagon, then headed down the road toward Dorie's homestead.

The morning sun beat down unusually hard for the season, the air thick already, and Shane figured their drive wouldn't be at all pleasant. Good thing Virginia City wasn't too far a ride, but the long struggle up the mountain surely would tire out his horses, the mining town being at the uppermost crest of the Nevada hills.

When Shane pulled his wagon up to Dorie's house, he found the two siblings waiting outside in the front yard. Jeremiah held a couple of valises and Dorie sat upon a rather large brown leather trunk.

"We're all packed and ready," she said, her blue eyes twinkling.

Shane set the wagon brake and stared down at the chest. "We're only going for three days, Dorie. What've you got in that trunk?"

"Oh, uh…"

"She's bringing the—"

Dorie stepped on Jeremiah's booted foot. "Ouch! Dorie, why'd you go and do that?"

"I'll explain to Shane, in my own way," she whispered.

"Explain what?" Shane got that gnawing feeling in his gut again. No telling what Dorie was up to.

"The trunk is a necessity. It's got *female* things in it."

Female things? Whatever that was supposed to mean. But somehow Shane got the idea that he didn't want to know.

"Load it up, Jeremiah," she said, and when her brother frowned and stood his ground, she added, "I'm sorry about stomping on your foot. I apologize. *Please,* load the chest in the wagon."

"Okay," he said, none too pleased.

Shane jumped down to help Jeremiah with the trunk and set the valises in. Jeremiah hopped into the backseat while Shane helped Dorie up onto her seat in front.

"Are we ready for this?" he asked.

"As ready as we'll ever be," Dorie responded.

And an hour later, Shane chuckled at the two McCabes as the wagon made a slow ascent up the hills to Virginia City.

"Geesh, Dorie, how many times are you going to ask me? We've gone over this four times already this morning and I lost count of how many times yesterday."

"It's important, Jeremiah. Don't sass me. Just repeat what you know about Shane and me. How'd we meet?"

Jeremiah grumbled, his words spoken in a flat tone. "You met at a church social. It was love at first sight. Shane didn't like giving you up as his dance partner, so he bloodied some man's nose. After that, he courted you with flowers and gifts."

"That's right. And how long have we been married?"

"Two years."

"And?"

"And," Jeremiah continued in a mocking manner, "you're happy. The happiest couple on earth. And I'm happy, too. I love school and working on Shane's ranch. Excuse me, our ranch."

Dorie glanced at Shane with dismay. "He doesn't realize how important this is."

Shane whispered so that Jeremiah wouldn't hear. "Sure he does. He's a smart boy. He'll say the right things. I think it's time you let up on him."

For once, Dorie took his advice, albeit grudgingly. "If you think so."

"I do. We'll be there soon enough. Sit back and relax the best you can."

"Hmmm," Dorie did as she was told, resting back and closing her eyes. "Good thing, the Parkers won't arrive until tomorrow. I need a good night's sleep."

"We all do."

Shane was eternally grateful that Jeremiah would be sharing their room at the hotel. No temptation there. Shane wouldn't have to worry about making another mistake with Dorie. Lord knew that he'd made enough of them to send him to hell and back. With Jeremiah there, Shane could sleep in peace. They all would. The events of the past two weeks had taken a toll on everyone. Yes, Shane looked forward to a long restful slumber tonight.

As the wagon continued on, Shane viewed a patch of flat ground up ahead, where the mountain leveled off and the streets tiered into several layers. The unique design of the town created by man, rather than by nature, gave the city a status all its own. Mining had surged upon the scene a few years back and silver had become the mainstay of Virginia City's growth and wealth. The town bustled with the kind of energy that Shane had yet to see equaled. Tinkers, miners, clergymen, shopkeepers and the like walked the sidewalks with hurried strides, and horses and wagons nearly collided into each other on the crowded streets.

Shane only came to Virginia City out of necessity. He had no use for such masses. He'd found most of what he needed within the confines of the smaller, less busy town of Silver Hills.

"Dorie!" Jeremiah exclaimed, tapping her on the shoulder. "Isn't that the turnoff for Henry's house?"

Dorie shot up straight in her seat and glanced at a fork in the road on the outskirts of town. "Why, yes. I believe it is." She put her hand on his arm and Shane turned to rest his gaze on her. "Shane, you'll need to turn off here."

Puzzled, Shane reined the horses to a stop. "What?"

"My friend Henry lives down that path. It isn't far, just up ahead," Jeremiah explained.

"Are we going there for a visit?" he asked, still a bit confused.

"No, we're not. Jeremiah is. He's to spend his nights there with his good friend, Henry. It's really very generous of Henry's folks to offer to take him in. The boys will have a nice visit."

Shane blinked as dawning knowledge crept over his mind. "Are you saying that Jeremiah is *not* staying at the hotel with us?"

Dorie nodded. "That's right. He'll spend some time with Henry when he's not with us and the Parkers."

Shane glanced at Jeremiah and held his tongue. "Dorie, step down from the wagon. We need to have a discussion."

"But, Shane—"

Shane jumped down from the wagon and gave Dorie no time to protest. He reached her side and took hold of her hands. "Now, Dorie. We talk or I turn this wagon around." He helped her down while she spouted her indignation.

"Oh, all right! I surely don't know what's got you so upset."

Shane turned and stomped his way down the road some distance from the wagon taking Dorie with him. He released his hold on her the minute they were out of earshot of Jeremiah.

"What are you up to now, Dorie?"

"Nothing, Shane. What's wrong? Is the altitude getting to you? You don't look so good right now." She truly appeared concerned and puzzled.

"It's not the altitude, damn it."

Dorie glanced toward Jeremiah. "Keep your voice down. Jeremiah is skittish as it is."

Shane spoke through tight lips and lowered his voice some. "I thought all three of us would share that hotel room, Dorie. That was the plan."

"No, Shane. Don't be silly. It never was the plan. Wouldn't look right for the three of us to rent one room. The hotel room only has one bed. And I, well...I couldn't afford two hotel rooms with the cost and all."

"That's the problem, Dorie. You said it. The hotel room has only *one* bed."

"It's all right, Shane. Truly it is. I've slept on the floor before. I don't mind."

"Dorie, damn it! You're putting us together in that room for two whole nights, without...without—"

"Jeremiah? Yes, I know."

"A chaperone, woman! You and I will be alone in that room."

"But, Shane, we've slept in the same room before. More than once."

Shane didn't need any reminders. He'd had a tough time forgetting touching Dorie's soft skin and caressing her in places he had no right to touch. He'd been fighting his lust for her, knowing full well they'd both be sorry if he succumbed to her charms. He'd had his fill of wishful nights, thinking about Dorie lying beside him.

"That's when I was injured. Both times. You clocked me on the head the first time, and the second time a longhorn beat you to it."

Dorie looked at him with amazement. Then she chuckled, her bright blue eyes gleaming. "Shane, you do surprise me at times."

"This isn't funny, Dorie. If anyone back home gets wind of it, your reputation will be ruined."

Dorie waved off that notion. "I'm trying to keep my brother by my side. I don't much care what others think."

"You should. A girl like you—you'll want to marry one day and raise a family."

"I'm trying to *keep* what family I have. Don't worry about me, Shane. I know what I'm doing."

"Like spouting off to Roberta McPherson about you and me taking this trip together?"

"Oh." Dorie blinked a few times then got busy straightening out the wrinkles in her skirt. "That wasn't intentional. I went to Roberta's shop and, well, the conversation sort of got, uh, out of control."

Shane folded his arms. "I'm listening."

"Well, she was so smug about you and all, saying

what close friends you two were. She said you confided some private things to her and she'd keep them close to her heart. I didn't much like hearing that, so I blurted out about our trip."

Shane exhaled heavily. "And?"

"Well, that stopped her in her tracks. She didn't have much cause to gloat after that."

"Dorie, the whole town knows that we're going away together."

"With Jeremiah. I made that very clear, Shane. And I don't really care what—"

"Hey, you through yet?" Jeremiah called out impatiently. "What's the big ol' secret anyways? Are you two arguing again?"

"We're not arguing," Dorie called out, then hooked her arm into his. "We're just discussing our plans. Right, Shane?"

Shane began walking with Dorie latched onto him. "Right," he muttered. "But if anyone is sleeping on the floor, it's going to me, Dorie."

"Seems silly that any of us have to sleep on the floor. I'm sure the bed's big enough for two."

"Dorie," Shane warned, "I mean it. I'll turn the wagon around and we'll part ways real quick."

Dorie smiled, reminding him of a satisfied cat. "If you insist."

"I do."

Shane wondered after a moment if he'd just won the battle or lost it. Either way, he'd be hugging the floor tonight.

Chapter Eleven

"This room is beautiful, Shane." Dorie took it all in, from the colorful floral wallpaper to the lacy deep gold velvet curtains. She spun around glancing at the furnishings and Shane figured she'd never been around such finery in her life.

"It should be, for what it cost," Shane muttered, dropping the valises down, then tossing his hat onto the marble-topped mahogany armoire. He'd wrestled Dorie's big trunk up the stairs right after he'd signed in with the desk clerk as Mr. and Mrs. Shane Graham. It still made him jumpy thinking of all the deception yet to come.

"Well, it couldn't be helped. The Parkers are staying here at the Silver Rose Hotel and it wouldn't look right if we took a room in a different part of town."

"Especially since most parts of this town aren't fit for decent folk."

Dorie let his comment drop while she busied herself with unpacking her valise. Shane did the same, and it seemed strange sharing space with her in the six-drawer armoire. He'd hung most of his things from the fancy brass hooks provided, and the rest he placed in the lower drawers, leaving the upper drawers for Dorie.

"You've got those drawers filled up almost and you haven't yet opened your trunk." He pointed to the massive trunk that nearly buckled his knees while carrying it up the stairs. "You gonna tell me what's in there now?"

Dorie glanced at the trunk. She nibbled on her lower lip. "Uh, not yet."

"What's the big secret?" Shane asked, approaching the trunk. He looked down at it with curiosity. "You got a dead body in there or something?"

"Shane!" Dorie chuckled nervously. "How about I *show* you what's in the trunk after dinner?"

"Why? Is it gonna ruin my appetite?"

"No, silly. It's just…I'm not ready to show you yet."

Shane shrugged, refusing to think on it any further. His stomach grumbled and he realized that evening approached and they hadn't had supper yet. They'd wasted away most of the afternoon with Henry Randolph and his folks. The Randolphs insisted they stay for a visit and, while Dorie seemed anxious to leave, Shane figured the more time they'd spend with company, the less time he and Dorie would have to spend alone.

Wasn't a bad idea using a measure of prudence.

"I'll just clean up a bit and then we'll go downstairs," Dorie said. Shane sat on a wing chair, the only place to sit his bones other than the fancy bed. Shane figured he'd never feel the softness of that lavish quilt-covered mattress and that was just fine with him. Maybe he'd sleep in the chair tonight, propping his legs up on Dorie's mysterious leather trunk.

Shane watched Dorie dip a small towel into a porcelain bowl of water she'd just poured. She used the corner edge of that towel to wash her face, scrubbing road dust from her cheeks, before lifting her chin and stroking her throat with the moistened washcloth. Water droplets ran a path down her throat and into the bodice of her modest dress, the act so feminine and appealing Shane shifted uncomfortably in his chair.

Her cheeks rosy now and her lips moist and just as pink, her whole face glowed. "Your turn," she said, offering him a dry washcloth. "That's if you like."

Shane rose and cleared his throat. "I suppose."

Dorie stood by his side, watching as he scrubbed his face and neck, none too delicately. Her eyes took on a gleam once he'd finished. "What?"

"Nothing," Dorie said with a smile. "Except this feels right. Like what a normal married couple would do, watching each other clean up."

Shane couldn't deny the scene was domestic, but he wasn't enjoying it, not one bit. Being this close to Dorie made him jittery, and nothing irked him more than acting like a nervous schoolboy around a woman.

He tossed down his towel, noting how Dorie then took both towels and folded them neatly—next to each other on the dresser top. "You ready?"

"Sure, let's go downstairs."

Shane locked the door behind him as they exited their room. Dorie immediately laced her arm through his and, instead of dining at the hotel, they strolled down the street until they found a café.

"We can save some money until the Parkers arrive," Dorie said, but Shane had no intention of having her pay for their meal anyway.

The café was small and crowded but they managed to find a place to sit down. They ordered the same items from the menu and Shane found it intriguing that he and Dorie liked similar dishes—chicken and dumplings with creamed corn, and apple cobbler for dessert.

They ate in silence, the boisterous little eating establishment too loud for any kind of conversation. Once they had their fill they took another stroll to stretch their legs. Shane led Dorie through the part of town that he deemed safe, although no part of Virginia City would ever be completely safe for a woman alone. The city's male population outnumbered the female by at least ten to one and a young pretty girl strolling the streets by herself only meant trouble.

If anyone could find trouble, it'd be Dorie McCabe.

"Shane, we should go up to our room now," Dorie announced, as they approached the hotel.

They'd been walking the streets of town now for forty minutes, engaging in polite conversation. Shane had hoped to stay out of that hotel room until both were too exhausted to do anything but sleep. He didn't want any undue temptation. And he figured a tuckered out Dorie would fall asleep on that comfortable bed the second her head hit the pillow.

It's what he'd been hoping, at least.

"So soon? It's early yet. Do you want to see the opera house? Or how about the—"

"I imagine we'll be doing some of that tomorrow with the Parkers, Shane."

Dorie had a point.

"How about I buy you a sasparilla?"

"You've already bought my supper, Shane. I don't

expect you to pay for things. I got you into this, remember?"

Shane smiled grudgingly. "I won't be forgetting that anytime soon."

"Besides, I thought you wanted to see what I had in my trunk."

"I do." He'd been curious ever since laying eyes on that brown leather trunk early this morning, and with Dorie being so mysterious about it's contents, Shane figured he should know what she had in there.

"Well, I'm getting too tired to walk anymore and if we don't go up now, I'll just flop into bed."

That's what Shane had hoped, but Dorie appeared truly worn out tonight and he couldn't push her any more. "Okay you first," he said, gesturing with a wide sweep of his arms. They entered the hotel lobby and Shane followed her upstairs. She waited while he opened the door and, once inside, the room seemed to have shrunk in size. Only the glow of one lantern light illuminated the hallway, and once Dorie lit the lamp inside, Shane closed the door completely, locking them in.

"Have a seat, Shane. I figure it's time to show you how I've been surviving all these years."

Shane sat down on the wing chair.

"It's a secret only Jeremiah knows about. Now, I'm sharing it with you. Promise not to think unkindly of me after I show you."

Shane's heart raced with uncertain dread. Dorie wasn't much for keeping secrets. Up until the time when Mrs. Whitaker schooled her on manners and such, she'd usually blurt out exactly what was on her mind. So Shane figured this wasn't something that made Dorie proud. Now he cursed his own curiosity, but it was too late. He'd asked, and she seemed overly determined to show him. "I'll try, Dorie, but I can't promise."

"Okay, close your eyes."

"Close my eyes?"

"Yes, that's what I said. Please."

"They're shut good and tight."

Shane heard Dorie open the trunk, followed by muffled swishing sounds. After a minute with his eyes closed, he felt Dorie's close presence, breathed in her flowery scent and heard her clear her throat. "Okay, you can open them now."

Shane opened his eyes to find Dorie standing before him. He blinked once then stared.

"This is how I make a living, Shane. And I'm not ashamed of it."

With her hair falling from it's pins, her face rosy, wearing an elaborate gown of crimson silk and white lace, fitted to her body like a sleek glove, Shane sucked in a lungful of oxygen and came to one instant conclusion. Dorie had never looked more beautiful…or flashy. She looked as if she was ready to…entertain a man.

This is how I make a living.

Her breasts strained the confines of the material holding her in. Twin mounds rose up and out, and only the teasing of thin elaborate lace hid the very tips of her breasts. The gown accentuated her tiny waist, flaring out at the hips, creating a vision that was all female, all alluring.

Shane rose from his seat, his groin tight, his heart beating hard. But while he admired her beauty, he condemned her wholly for her lack of decency.

And I'm not ashamed of it.

Her prideful words pounded in his head.

"*This* is how you make your living?" he asked, wanting clarification.

"Yes, I sell my wares. And I'm good at what I do."

Shane slammed his eyes shut. Rage filled his heart for thinking Dorie the innocent in all this. For believing he'd been protecting and helping a young girl who had no one else. He'd denied himself her charms, thinking to hold her reputation intact when all the while she'd been taunting and tempting him. He spoke through gritted teeth, anger seething forth. "You played me for a fool, Dorie McCabe."

"No, Shane. I couldn't tell anyone my secret. I was afraid no one would understand. I was desperate after mama died. And I have this talent for—"

Shane grabbed her waist, pulling her forward, meshing their bodies together. Through the thin silk he felt her breasts crush against him. "You owe me, Dorie."

"I know I do. I was planning on paying you. I'll have some money soon. Just don't be angry."

Shane's mind shut out all rational thought. "Oh, I'm angry and you will pay me, but I don't want your money, Dorie." Shane reached around and cupped her derriere, pressing her more firmly into his arousal. She gasped then sighed against him. "Shane," she said softly, her startled eyes softening to his.

He had no more words. He'd had his fill of Dorie's lies and deception. He'd wanted her for a long time, and now that he knew he could have her, nothing would stop him. He crushed his lips against hers, thrusting his tongue into her mouth. Their tongues danced and fire erupted inside him. He'd been tempted too long. Now, he'd be given his due.

He stroked her tongue in openmouthed frenzy, her little throaty moans spurring his desire. He wove his fingers deep into her hair, pulling her head back to kiss her throat, lick her lips and continue on with kisses that made him ache.

Then he pushed away the material from her bodice, feeling the soft lace against his hand. But the lace didn't compare to the feel of Dorie's soft flesh in his palm. He slid his hand in to cup her breast, flicking his thumb over her nipple, making her nearly swoon with cries of delight. He pushed harder against the material, bending down now to taste the sweetness there, to moisten and tease the tight peak until Dorie cried out even louder. He stretched the material of her gown aside as far as he could to gain further access, his mouth greedy for more of her.

"Be careful…" she breathed out. "Please, don't rip the gown."

Shane didn't care about ripping the gown. He'd split the material down to her toes to take it off her if need be. He lifted her then, deciding to enjoy the comfort of the bed, and they both went down together, Shane toppling over her.

"Shane," she whispered between kisses. "I mean it. We can't rip the gown."

Shane pulled at the material of her gown again bearing her creamy soft shoulders. Planting hungry kisses there he ignored Dorie's pleas. He'd never force himself upon a woman; but from Dorie's soft sighs and moans of pleasure she'd given him every reason to believe she enjoyed this as much as he did. He didn't give a damn about her gown. "I'll buy you another one."

He pulled at the fabric even more and the gown

slipped down further, her breasts popping out from their confinement. With hungry eyes, he looked his fill without regret or guilt. "You're perfect," he whispered, bending down to kiss each rosy tip, his manhood growing harder with each passing moment.

"Oh, Shane," she breathed, running her fingers through his hair and arching her body to him. "So are you."

Shane didn't believe her now. She was schooled to say pleasing words and so he shoved aside thoughts of her doing this with other men from his mind. He couldn't think right now, his body had taken over. He wanted her.

Shane yanked at the dress again, wanting more of her, but when a bit of lace tore the sound startled Dorie. She pushed at Shane, shoving him off of her and raising herself up on the bed. "Oh no!"

"Let me take the damn thing off you then."

Dorie's face fell inspecting the damage. "Yes, take it off me," she agreed and Shane moved to unfasten the buttons that ran a path down from her bustline to her waist. "I'm sorry." She smiled at him. "But I can't afford to ruin this. I haven't sold it yet."

"Why sell it?" Shane asked, busy with the buttons now, ready to claim Dorie once and for all.

"Because, that's what I do. I sell the gowns I create."

Shane stopped unbuttoning her, his fingers freezing up, his mind working hard to comprehend. "You sell the *gowns?*"

Dorie's eyes fluttered a moment, distracted by the tiny tear in her lace. "Yes, I told you. I sell them to the brothels. These gowns are for prostitutes. That's how I make my living, Shane. Like I said, I sew."

Shane's arousal crumbled. His heart beat with dread. He began shaking his head. "You never said you sewed. You said you sold your 'wares'."

"My wares are my gowns," she said puzzled. "I sew them at home and sell them here. I have a standing order with Mrs. Miniver's House. I do what I have to, Shane. I'm not ashamed of it, but I can't let my secret out to too many. At least, I'm smart enough to know that."

Stunned, Shane still couldn't believe the wealth of feelings Dorie evoked in him. Lust, anger, regret, relief and disdain. "So, you and I, you let me…I mean…we almost…" He winced. "You've never done this before?"

Dorie shook her head. "No. I told you. I never let anyone touch me, except you."

Shane gulped down hard. The realization of what he'd done, the mistake he'd made, was more than he could bear.

"I have to get out of here," he said, his head ready to combust. He pointed his finger, ignoring the sexy picture she made, standing there with a confused expression, half in, half out of the gown she'd created for a whore. "I want you to get into bed and be asleep by the time I get back. Do you understand?"

"But, Shane—"

"No! This was a mistake."

"Where are you—"

"I don't want discuss this. Just go to bed, Dorie. I'll be back later. Much later. Don't you dare wait up. Got that?"

He didn't wait for Dorie to agree, he simply grabbed his hat and exited the room.

And headed for the nearest saloon.

* * *

Dorie woke to a room filled with sunlight. She stretched her arms above her head and yawned before she realized where she was and what had happened last night.

Shane still managed to confound and confuse her. One minute he'd been kissing her senseless, the next he'd been so angry he couldn't bear to stay in the same room with her. Dorie hadn't quite been sure exactly why he'd been angry. Was it that she'd lied about her craft? She'd explained herself and had trusted him with the truth. Or was it because he'd misunderstood her meaning? He couldn't possibly think she would actually sell *herself*... But that would explain his sudden ardor last night. Dorie hadn't been sure exactly why he'd suddenly pulled her into his arms, she'd only been glad that he had.

She'd hoped he had come to his senses, realizing he couldn't marry Marilee, not when he wanted her so badly. And he had. Last night he'd told her with his body how much he wanted her. Then he'd stopped, claiming it a mistake, much to Dorie's dismay. She feared Shane would never see things her way, not when he felt honor bound to marry a woman he didn't care for. Not when Tobias Barkley held the future of the Bar G Ranch in the palm of his hand.

Dorie looked over to where Shane slept on the wing chair, slouched with a half-empty bottle of whiskey braced against his thigh. He'd come in very late last night, stumbling inside the room, and Dorie had thought it best not to say a thing. Both of them needed sleep more than they needed an argument.

Shane didn't look as if he'd rouse soon.

She'd let him sleep off the whiskey while she dressed and cleaned up a bit, then she'd wake him.

Ten minutes later, after she'd given herself a quick wash and pinned up her hair, she opened her trunk, pulling out the gown she'd fashioned just for this occasion. The material had cost her a pretty penny, eating into her profits, but it was necessary in her estimation. Dorie had to appear well established in society with no monetary concerns; the gown, not too different in style from the one she wore last night, would create that impression. The pretty shade of soft pink would complement her complexion, and the bodice, cut a bit higher on the chest with a lovely heart-shaped neckline, was the latest in fashion. Dorie lifted the gown over her head to settle nicely over her chemise and petticoats. She struggled with the buttons, fastening them from behind as best she could.

"Having trouble?"

Dorie whirled around to find Shane's lazy, liquor-shaded eyes upon her. He lifted the bottle to his lips and took a drink while eyeing her from head to toe. His leisurely perusal reminded her of last night, when he'd nearly made love to her. He had the same look in his eyes now.

"I'll manage."

"Good," he said, gazing at her with those narrowed green eyes. He sipped again from the bottle.

Dorie raised her brows. She walked over to him and took the bottle out of his hands. When she glared at him, he smiled.

"Are you drunk?"

"I hope so."

Dorie breathed in deeply. She counted to three just

like Mrs. Whitaker told her to do when she wanted to scream. She spoke slowly, with as much patience as she could manage. "We have to meet the Parkers at the stagecoach depot at ten o'clock. Henry is bringing Jeremiah there to meet up with us."

"What time is it now?"

"Eight-thirty."

"I'll be there. Give me some time."

"Shane, about last night—"

"I'm trying to forget last night." Shane closed his eyes and rested his head on the back of the chair. "You got any more secrets I should know about?"

Dorie hesitated.

Shane opened his eyes. "Well?"

"Well, uh, it's not a secret or anything. But I've got to find some way to get the gowns to Mrs. Miniver's House."

Shane looked her up and down again as if puzzling something out. "How'd you do it the other times?"

"They'd, uh, send someone to meet me at a location. I'd give them the trunk, and wait. If all went well, then they'd return the trunk to me with my payment."

"Where would you meet?"

"It doesn't matter."

Shane leaned forward, bracing his elbows on his knees. He looked up at her. "Another secret, Dorie?"

"It's not as bad as it sounds. I'd meet him at a clearing behind the Episcopal Church. There's a bench. I'd wait there."

Shane let out a derisive chuckle. "The irony."

"You don't have to get involved in this," she defended. She'd managed all these years without benefit of help from Shane and she'd do it again if need be. She considered herself lucky that she's stumbled upon this livelihood just before her mama had passed. Her mama had taken the one and only fancy gown Dorie had sewn to Virginia City to place in her friend's dress shop, hoping to earn some extra cash. Mrs. Miniver had seen the gown and purchased it on the spot, expressing her admiration for such style and quality workmanship. Dorie's mother had given full credit for the sale to Dorie and from then on she'd taken orders for all the ladies Mrs. Miniver employed. Dorie figured her mama knew her days weren't long for this earth, otherwise she'd never had agreed to such an arrangement. "This isn't your problem."

"Right. Tell me, if all doesn't go well, then what happens?"

"Well, it only happened one time. One of the gowns didn't fit the, uh, lady. She'd put on weight. I had to make alterations."

"How'd you do that?"

"I had to go into the brothel."

Shane slapped his hand on his knee then fell back against the chair. "Damn it, Dorie!"

"It only happened once and they snuck me in through the back door, early in the morning. It wasn't too bad."

Shane shook his head and eyed the bottle in her hand. If he wanted another drink he would have to wrestle her for it. She couldn't have him showing up to meet the Parkers tipsy.

"This time, they don't know you're here?"

"I didn't know for sure I'd be coming and then, well, I didn't get a letter off in time. But, Shane, I don't want to worry about that now. I'll figure something out."

Shane rose then and approached her, those green eyes locking onto hers. He smiled, snatched the bottle from her hands and, before she could protest, he took a long drink. "Last one."

He set down the bottle and came up behind her. His warm whiskey breath caressed her hair as he fastened her last three buttons on her gown rather briskly. "You will not go to that whorehouse alone, got that? We'll figure out something later."

He spun her around to look her dead in the eyes. "I need to sober up. You go down and have breakfast. I'll be ready when you get back."

"Shane, you need a meal, too."

"I'm not hungry, Dorie. Now go on."

Dorie stared into Shane's eyes, debating.

"When you come back, I'll be the perfect pretend husband," he reassured her.

"It's only for two days, Shane. You know how important this is to me…and to Jeremiah."

Shane nodded and, as she approached the door, ready to leave, he came up behind her. He spoke quietly, but firmly. "Stay out of trouble, Dorie."

Dorie promised, but she figured she was already in big enough trouble. She wanted Shane as her real-life husband.

No other man would do.

But he wasn't free to want her back.

Chapter Twelve

Shane stood at the depot alongside Dorie and Jeremiah, waiting for the stagecoach to arrive. There wasn't enough seating in the crowded station as people milled about and chattered loudly. Virginia City was as remote as a town could be, set high in the hills of Nevada; but that didn't curtail the population growth as prospectors and business people alike sought wealth and prosperity in the Comstock.

Shane glanced at Dorie standing tall and proud, holding on to Jeremiah as if her life depended on it. Even through his anger and stunned surprise last night, he couldn't help but feel admiration for her now, a young girl who had done everything in her power to keep food on the table and raise her brother right. She looked elegant in that soft pink dress, a reticule in her hand, wearing a hat of black velvet decorated with pink flowers and one delicate feather. He'd never seen her wear such a hat, and he wondered if she'd fashioned that, too, or had she dipped into her savings to purchase it for the occasion.

Shane had almost claimed her innocence last night, too eager and lusty to really hear what Dorie had tried to tell him. He'd jumped to the wrong conclusion and had immediately felt the need for retribution. But he wondered if it had been more than that. Had he simply wanted to find a way—any way—to claim her as his and ease the desire that had grown too powerful to control? Had he wanted so badly to think he could have her that he'd deliberately mistook her meaning?

Shane had known Dorie for a long time. She'd always been inexperienced and innocent. He should have controlled his anger and his lust until he fully understood the situation.

That she was eager to comply, to give him her body and her heart, made it all the more difficult to turn her away. She'd been generous and giving, responding to him with more willingness and desire than any other female he had known. Once he'd discovered the truth, he'd cursed himself to high heaven. He'd taken solace in a bottle of whiskey, tempted to ease his lust in the brothel down the street, but in the end he'd returned to his hotel room and to Dorie.

As the stagecoach approached Shane took his place beside her, winding his arm around her waist, the three of them creating the illusion of the perfect loving family. Shane glanced her way, noting her beauty, her stately elegance as she stood ramrod straight, her expression unable to mask her unease. "You look beautiful," he said, hoping to ease her tension. "And we'll do fine. All of us."

"You think so?" she asked with trepidation, her eyes searching his for truth.

"I really do. We look like a happy family."

Dorie's gaze lingered a little too long and he began wishing for things that would never happen.

"We'll be fine, Dorie," Jeremiah reassured her.

Dorie released a breath and nodded, looking from him to Jeremiah and back. "Thank you," she said softly. "I hope you're right."

The minute the passengers began to step down from the stagecoach there was no mistaking the Parkers. Two sweet-faced elderly people descended with anxious looks in their eyes. Once they spotted Jeremiah, their faces brightened with joy.

As they approached, Shane noted the gray-haired lady with blue eyes wearing a black silk traveling dress appeared younger close up and the gentleman with the bowler hat had a spring in his step. These were not people with one foot in the grave but rather two very vital human beings.

The woman stepped up, smiling at Jeremiah with certainty that she had the right boy. "Are you Jeremiah? Are you my grandson?"

Jeremiah nodded. "Yes, ma'am."

"Oh," she said, clasping his hands in hers, restraining herself from hugging and kissing him. "I'm your grandmother. I'm Helene Parker."

"Nice to meet you, ma'am."

"And I'm your grandfather," the man announced in a booming voice. "I'm Oliver Parker."

Jeremiah looked up at the tall man and shook his hand. "Nice to meet you, sir."

The two barely managed to tear their gazes away from him, but once they had, introductions went full circle. "I'm Shane Graham and this is my wife, Dorie. She's Jeremiah's sister, as you know."

"Yes, yes. We know. It's so nice to meet you all," Helene said, taking Dorie's hand while Shane shook Oliver's.

Their gaze swept over to Jeremiah again and, with tears in her eyes, Helene said, "He looks so much like Steven."

"I don't likely remember my father," Jeremiah admitted.

"We know, dear," Helene said with regret. "I'm so glad we found you, Jeremiah. We have so much to discuss."

Jeremiah glanced at Dorie.

Dorie barely smiled.

"Well," Shane said, "Let's get you settled into the hotel. Jeremiah, grab your grandparents' valises. I'll get the trunk."

"There's more than one, Shane," Oliver said with a big grin. "My wife doesn't travel lightly."

Oliver lifted one trunk while Shane took the other, and they loaded everything up in the back of the buckboard. Shane helped Dorie up in the front, while Oliver helped his wife into the backseat. Jeremiah took a place between them. Once all were settled, he urged the horses toward the center of town.

"The hotel is quite nice, from what I hear," Helene said as they drove on.

"Yes, it's lovely," Dorie said. "Isn't it, sweetheart?"

Shane took his cue. "Can't complain. Though our room is bigger on the ranch."

Dorie smiled. "Yes, that's true. We're fortunate to have a very big ranch. I'm so proud of Shane for all he's accomplished."

Shane cleared his throat.

"How many head of cattle do you have?" Oliver asked.

"Uh, well, at last count around…three, uh, thousand." More like three hundred, but Shane couldn't divulge the truth to him.

"Impressive," Oliver said. "And Jeremiah, do you work alongside of Shane? Do you know something about raising cattle?"

Jeremiah nodded. "Yes, um, I do, sir. Some. Mostly I help muck out the stable stalls and feed and groom the horses."

"Shane's going to teach Jeremiah all about raising cattle, soon as Jeremiah's schooling is finished," Dorie added quickly.

"Jeremiah is fast to learn," Shane said with honesty. "Whatever I teach him, sticks. He's a bright boy."

"Oh, do you enjoy going to school, Jeremiah?" Helene asked.

Jeremiah hesitated with his answer. Dorie nibbled on her lip. Shane quickly responded with a chuckle, "What thirteen-year-old likes school? But the boy holds his own. Does his work and gets good grades."

Dorie's stricken face relaxed some. "We're very proud of him."

"I like to read," Jeremiah said. "Don't always have time with all the chores."

"Your father loved to read, too. He was always picking up a book or periodical to look at. Sometimes, he'd read dime novels, but mostly he liked to read books. I brought along some of his favorites for you. I hope you'll enjoy them."

"You did?" Jeremiah seemed genuinely pleased.

"Yes, and we brought you a few he never had the

chance to read. Oliver, open the valise in back if you can. I want to show Jeremiah what we brought."

"All right, woman. You can't wait to spoil this young man, can you?"

"I'm not spoiling him. Just making up for lost time, dear."

Oliver struggled with the valise, coming up with two books. He handed them to Helene and she, in turn, took great pleasure in offering Jeremiah the books. "This one is *Moby Dick* by Herman Melville and this one is a first edition. I do so hope you enjoy it."

Jeremiah read the title aloud. "*Twenty Thousand Leagues Under the Sea,* by Jules Verne."

Shane turned around in time to see Jeremiah smile with gratitude. "Thank you. I'll read them as soon as I can."

"They are yours to keep, Jeremiah."

Jeremiah swallowed and Shane turned around to find Dorie's face flaming. He shook his head at her in silent warning. The Parkers had given Jeremiah a gift, nothing more. They weren't trying to buy his love, but by all estimations Dorie didn't seem to understand that fact.

Shane feared what she might say, but she surprised him. "That's very kind of you. I'm sure he'll think of you when he's reading them."

"Oh, I hope so, dear." Helene couldn't take her eyes off her newfound grandson.

"Well, we're here." Shane stopped the buckboard in front of the hotel, helped Dorie down and began unloading. Once done, he drove to the livery, leaving Dorie and Jeremiah alone with the Parkers.

The deception had begun. And Shane couldn't help feeling guilty about duping such obviously nice people.

* * *

Two hours later, after the Parkers had settled into their hotel room, they all met in the hotel dining room for the noon meal. Dorie noted Helene looking refreshed with obvious joy on her face as the woman could not stop staring at Jeremiah. Once they'd been seated at a table, Helene had made sure to sit directly across from him, taking in every movement, every expression that Jeremiah made.

Dorie noted how much the Parkers seemed to be accustomed to the finery surrounding them, while Dorie sat in the dining room truly awestruck by the ornate draperies, bone china settings, the silver vases on each table embossed with one beautifully sculpted rose. Dorie glanced down at the silverware, summoning her teachings from Mrs. Whitaker. While her mentor had faith in Dorie's ability to learn, she'd also said, when in doubt, wait until someone else picks up a utensil from the table and repeat what they'd done.

Dorie watched Helene Parker with steely eyes, noting how she sat with such grace at the table. She'd already changed from her black silk traveling suit to a more colorful taffeta print. Oliver Parker looked dapper as well, wearing a three-piece suit with gray pinstripe trousers.

"Aren't you hungry, dear?" Helene asked, smiling at Jeremiah.

Jeremiah glanced down at the layering of utensils beside his plate. "Yes, it's just that, I'm not sure—"

"If we should say grace," Dorie finished for him. He'd obviously been confused as to which fork to pick up to begin his meal. Dorie couldn't blame him, wondering if he shouldn't have been included more in Mrs. Whitaker's teachings.

"I don't mind if I do," Oliver said with his booming voice. His soft brown eyes belied a voice that would make an army general proud. "If you please."

Shane nodded. "Please do."

Dorie smiled, noting Shane's obvious relief.

Shane took hold of Dorie's hand, Dorie took hold of Jeremiah's and Helene reached over to grasp his other hand while Oliver held hers. They made a complete circle and bent their heads. Oliver began in a quiet revered voice, "Dear Lord, we thank you for this bountiful meal before us. We thank you for all the blessings bestowed upon our family. We keep our son Steven in our prayers every day and thank you from the depths of our hearts to have found our grandson Jeremiah after all these years. We thank you for his wonderful sister, Dorie, as well, and for Mr. Shane Graham, who has protected and loved them both. Lord, our hearts are heavy with gratitude. We thank you for all these blessings. Amen."

"Amen," they chorused softly.

"Now we eat!" Oliver's voice once again boomed.

Dorie glanced at Jeremiah, who had obviously been just as affected by Oliver's prayer. She breathed in deeply, praying for guidance. She'd noted the proprietary look in Helene's eyes while watching her brother, and she'd been annoyed that the woman couldn't wait to gift Jeremiah with books even before they'd exited the wagon earlier. But those feelings waned some, after hearing Oliver's heartfelt prayer. Dorie recognized the fact that Jeremiah was the only grandchild they would ever have. She realized their obvious love. But she couldn't and wouldn't give up her brother. She'd rather die than lose Jeremiah.

Shane laid his hand on her thigh from under the table and, when she gazed into his eyes, he smiled and winked, reminding her to stay the course. She must have appeared stricken after Oliver's endearing speech provided by way of a prayer.

"Has Dorie told you folks how it is that we met?" Shane asked.

Dorie sat in stunned surprise as she regarded her pretend husband.

"No," Helene responded immediately. "Do tell. We're eager to learn as much as we can about you all. So, Dorie, dear, how did you meet this fine man?"

Dorie searched Shane's eyes, realizing he'd done this for her benefit. He'd given her a way out of her dire musings. "It…it was love at first sight."

"Yes, it was," Shane said, covering his hand over hers. "Tell them, sweetheart."

And Dorie plowed into her storybook tale of how Shane had fallen deeply in love with her, hopelessly embellishing the story and wishing by all accounts that even a small morsel of what she relayed would have been true.

"Oh, how lovely," Helene offered once Dorie had finished her tale. "You two appear to be very happy."

Dorie forced a smile.

Shane bent over to place a kiss on her cheek. "We are. Very happy."

Dorie nodded and stole a glance at Jeremiah, who had kept his head down the entire time she'd been speaking.

Oliver leaned in and spoke with quiet regard this time. "We feel very fortunate that you have taken such good care of Jeremiah. When we found out we had a grandson, well…Helene and I were astonished at first. We'd thought we'd lost our Steven for good, but it seemed that we hadn't. Jeremiah is a part of Steven. And a part of us now. Naturally, we'd been concerned about the boy's welfare. We had to come here to meet him. We simply couldn't let another day go by. And it seems that he's a fine healthy boy."

"Actually, what Oliver is trying to say is that…well we would so much like to get to know Jeremiah better," Helene said. "We have a lovely home, far too big for just the two of us. We thought that Jeremiah might want to come stay with us in New York, for a time."

Heat flamed Dorie's face and anger curled her stomach. She opened her mouth to protest, but then she clamped it shut, counting to three. She remembered her manners and thought best to formulate her thoughts first.

"I think Jeremiah would like to get to know you both better, as well," Shane said. Dorie kicked his leg from under the table. The darn man didn't flinch. He went on, "That's why we're here, isn't it? Why don't you take some time now, spend the day with Jeremiah. The boy doesn't know you at all. I think it best for the three of you to get acquainted. My wife and I will meet up with you later this evening."

Dorie burned Shane a look.

"Well, if it's all right with you, I think that's a fine idea," Helene said.

Oliver nodded. "I can't agree more. But it's up to you, Jeremiah. Would you like to spend some time with your grandparents?"

He hesitated, making his point clear. "I don't want to leave Silver Hills."

"Oh, no. We'd never force you to leave your home. But we...we had hoped you would spend time with us now. Today. We can see some of Virginia City together. Would you like that?"

Jeremiah smiled at his grandmother. She had a soothing voice and seemed so...sweet. Dorie hadn't planned on being separated from him. What if he forgot himself? What if they plied him with questions he couldn't answer?

The entire table waited for Jeremiah's reply. He hadn't so much as granted her a look so she could signal him that it wasn't a good idea. In his hesitation, Helene laid her hand over his and squeezed. Jeremiah smiled at the woman, giving her the answer Dorie had feared. "Yes, I'd like that."

Oliver spoke with his commanding voice again. "Great, then! Let's order dessert while Dorie and Shane give us an idea of the sights we need to see in Virginia City."

"Shane, how could you send Jeremiah off alone with them?" Dorie paced the hotel room rug, her hands on her hips, her face red as a tomato.

"It couldn't be helped, Dorie. They came here to spend time with their grandson."

"But they're gonna try to convince him to live with them in New York. They're gonna fill his head with notions of a better life. They'll entice him, that's what they'll do. They'll have his head spinning by the time he returns."

Shane figured this the best option. The Parkers

wanted to get acquainted with their grandson. He'd
judged them to be fair-minded people. He didn't for a
second believe that they'd try to entice Jeremiah away
from his home. He shook his head, disagreeing. "I don't
think so, Dorie. The Parkers won't want to tear Jeremiah
away from…uh, us. They can see that he's had a good
life here."

Dorie stopped her pacing, her expression thoughtful.
"Do you really think so?"

"Yes," Shane said. "I do. I think you've done a
great job so far. They believe us. And Jeremiah is a
smart boy. He won't slip up. Didn't you see his expression when Helene took his hand? Jeremiah
deserves some time with his grandparents, you must
admit. He's not being disloyal to you. He just found
a part of his father in his grandparents. Naturally, he'd
want to get to know them, too. I thought it best for Jeremiah's sake."

"Well, I'm not putting a thing past them. We'll still
have to keep up the ruse. Keeping Jeremiah with me is
too important to let down our guard now."

Shane walked over to her. He lifted her chin and planted
a soft chaste kiss to her lips. "We won't. I promise."

Dorie's blue eyes softened on him and Shane immediately stepped back, away from the tempting woman
who had created chaos in his life.

"I'll hold you to that, Shane," Dorie said softly.

"Do that. Besides, we have another worry. We need
to get this trunk over to the…uh, house on C Street."

Dorie took a look at the leather trunk filled with the
gowns she'd sewn. "I know."

"Well, we only have the afternoon. I figure I'll load

up the trunk in the buckboard and drive it over myself. You stay here, where it's safe."

Dorie began shaking her head immediately. "No, that won't work. I have to go, too."

"No." Shane didn't want Dorie anywhere near the brothel. "There's no need for you to go."

"I *have* to go. If there's a problem with any of the gowns, I'll have to make the adjustments. You said it yourself that we don't have much time. A few hours at best. I have all the sewing supplies I might need in the trunk. It's the only way, Shane. I need that money."

Shane raised his brow and realized he'd been backed in to a corner; Dorie had a good point. There wasn't time enough to make several trips back and forth if they indeed needed Dorie's expertise. "I hate when you're right."

Dorie grinned.

"Okay, I'll get the buckboard and we'll get on over there now."

"We can't go marching up to their front door."

"We'll use the back door. It's a slow time now. They won't be overly busy."

Dorie's head snapped up. "How do you know that?"

Shane didn't answer. That was one foxhole he wasn't willing to jump into with her.

Twenty minutes later, Dorie knocked on the back door of Mrs. Miniver's House. Shane hated to see Dorie anywhere near the brothel but, as she'd pointed out, she really needed to be here with him. He set the trunk on the steps and waited behind her.

A young woman wearing a silk wrapper answered the door, her eyes going bright when she recognized

Dorie. "You're here with the gowns! I remember you from the last time. Oh, we've been waiting for these."

"Yes, they're all ready," Dorie said, raising her chin a notch. "I've got a trunk full of new gowns for you."

The woman peeked behind Dorie and Shane winced when she'd recognized him. "Hi there, Shane. Long time, honey."

Dorie whipped her head around, stunned. With accusation in her eyes he felt her immediate silent condemnation.

"Ginny."

The woman ran a hand down her long dark hair and studied them. "You two together now?"

"No!" Dorie blurted ungraciously, forgetting all of Mrs. Whitaker's teachings in that one moment.

Shane raised a brow and smiled. "Dorie is my wife. We're newly married."

Ginny appeared confounded, eyeing them with curiosity. "Oh…that is sweet."

Shane lifted the trunk and ignored Dorie's heated glare. "Where should I put this?" he asked.

"Both of you come inside. Cook's just fixing us some afternoon dessert. Have a seat. I'll get the girls."

"No, uh, let me bring the trunk on up," Shane said with a smile. "The girls can try on the gowns and let us know what they think."

Dorie gasped.

Ginny glanced Dorie's way first, then stared at Shane. "You want to bring it up?"

Shane nodded, then turned to Dorie. "I'll set it upstairs and come back down to wait…with my *wife*."

Ginny chuckled. "Yeah, I suppose it would have to

be that way, honey. Okay, follow me. Don't you worry," she spoke directly to Dorie now, "I'll be sure to send him down right away."

Dorie smiled sweetly, but he was certain he'd heard her grumble something about not worrying at all. He could stay as long as he liked.

Shane had to smile at that.

His heart shouldn't be flipping over itself that she was jealous.

But it was.

If that didn't beat all.

The two molasses cookies Dorie nibbled while waiting for Shane to return went down like sawdust, but the cook insisted and she had to do something to keep busy. Where was he? Dorie half believed him when he said he'd be right down. The thought of Shane upstairs with those women didn't set right. When the cook turned her back to stir soup for the evening meal, Dorie peeked out the kitchen door. Upon hearing voices, she stepped into the parlor meant to entertain the gentlemen callers. From there, she heard females chuckling and the sound of one deep familiar male voice at the top of the stairs.

Dorie's skin prickled. She moved quietly to the base of the stairs and looked up. Surrounded by prostitutes, Shane wore a smile wider than a fat cow's behind.

"Are you really married to our little seamstress?" one lady asked.

"Too bad, Shane, honey," another lady purred, touching Shane's sleeve.

"Doesn't mean you can't stop by to see us now and again."

"That's if our little Dorie isn't enough woman for you."

"Maybe I will," Shane said, grinning. "I'll stop by again sometime soon."

Dorie watched the scene play out, her heart beating hard, her eyes misting up. When she'd seen enough, she stomped out the front door, unmindful to the noise and calamity she caused. Anger and injury fueled her desire to get out of that house, before she heard another word.

Shane was married to her!

Or at least, he pretended to be.

For all the times he'd denied them both, pushing her away until she questioned her own femininity, he'd readily agreed to visit the prostitutes.

Our little Dorie isn't woman enough for you.

Dorie marched down C Street wiping her eyes, ignoring the curious glances of miners and businessmen alike entering into the whorehouses.

"Hey!" Shane ran up beside her, grabbing at her arm to halt her movement. "What's gotten into you?"

Dorie yanked her arm free of him. "Don't touch me, Shane Graham!"

Shane's eyes widened with surprise. "Don't *touch* you? I've been trying not to for the past two weeks, in case you haven't noticed."

Dorie spit back. "Oh, I've noticed. But it doesn't seem to bother you that you'd break your marriage vow to have…your way with those prostitutes." Dorie pointed her finger at Mrs. Miniver's house. "Go back there, if that's what you want!"

Shane suppressed a smile, angering Dorie all the more. "Don't you laugh at me, Shane!"

"You overheard that conversation, didn't you? You little eavesdropper."

"Yes, I heard. And if you want one of those women, don't let me stop—"

Shane covered her mouth with his hand. "Shhh. You're making a spectacle of yourself. And you shouldn't be seen on C Street. Let's get out of here. Keep your voice down now and I'll let up my hand. Agreed?"

Dorie hesitated, burning her gaze into Shane's, the only way to convey her hurt and anger at the moment.

"Agreed?" he asked again.

Dorie couldn't stand in the middle of the street all day, so she nodded her head.

"Fine, then. Let's get out of here. I'll explain later."

"Hah! What explanation is that? That you find me so lacking as a woman that you agreed to come back here for—"

"Keep your voice down. I'm warning you," Shane said through gritted teeth. He grabbed her hand. "Let's get to the wagon. We're through here."

"Jeremiah, isn't that your sister, Dorie, with Shane?"

Shane and Dorie instantly froze, turning slowly to the sound of Helene's voice.

Before Dorie could form a rational thought, Helene, Oliver and Jeremiah marched up the street to face them.

"Oh, dear heavens, what an awful place," Helene said. "We took a wrong turn looking for the theatre. I swear we've been in the heat too long." She fanned herself.

Oliver seemed more astute as to what kind of neighborhood they'd accidentally ventured into. He glanced at the sign above Mrs. Miniver's house, just yards away, and arched thick white brows in acknowledgment.

Jeremiah simply studied the ground.

"Seems you two got lost, as well," Oliver said suspiciously. "Or did you come down here for a purpose?"

"Oh, uh," Dorie hesitated.

Shane wrapped his arm around Dorie's waist. "Tell him why we're here, sweetheart."

Dorie's heart raced as fast as her mind. She couldn't lie quickly enough and no useful thoughts entered her head. She hadn't expected to get caught in the center of the Barbary Coast of Virginia City.

"It's okay. Tell them why we were visiting the cemetery," Shane said quietly.

"Yes, uh, that's right." Dorie remembered about the cemetery at the far end of town. It was a good excuse. "We always visit the cemetery when we come here."

"Oh, dear," Helene said. "Is this where your mother is buried?"

"No!" Jeremiah blurted. "Our mother is buried at home, in Silver Hills."

Dorie looked at Jeremiah, aching for him. She wouldn't have lied about that. She wouldn't have brought her dear deceased mother's memory into her deception. "Yes, that's right. Mama is buried close to home. Jeremiah and I put wildflowers on her grave every Sunday."

Oliver continued glancing around, realizing that this was indeed a most sordid part of town. Dorie had to come up with something in a hurry. "It's where Shane's first wife is buried."

Shane took a quick breath, loud enough for Dorie to hear. Then he lowered his head. She'd shocked him. She'd probably shocked them all. Jeremiah's expression changed to utter disbelief, while Oliver and Helene cast Shane sympathetic looks.

"We don't come here often and, well, Shane doesn't like talking about it. But I know it's important to him. And heavens, I got so tired of walking in this heat that we decided to take the shortcut home. Otherwise, we'd have never come into this part of town."

"Oh, dear. Yes, this is an ungodly place," Helene said, darting quick glances at the row of brothels along the street. "Maybe we should all walk home together and have some refreshment."

Shane finally raised his head and smiled softly. "No, that's not necessary. We'll be fine. We don't want to cut short your visit with Jeremiah. Go on. Dorie and I will head back to the hotel and meet with you for dinner, just as planned."

"If you're certain, then we'll find our way to the theatre," Helene said. "There's an afternoon show with dancing dogs. Jeremiah is curious, aren't you, dear?"

Jeremiah smiled at his grandmother. "I've never seen a dog dance, before. I've seen 'em sit and lay down and howl at the moon, but I've never once seen a dog dance."

Dorie plastered a smile on her face. "Well, then you'd best all hurry up. The theatre is up three streets, then two more to your left. Keep walking until you see a life-sized hourglass outside. That'd be the Hourglass Theatre."

"Fine then. Off we go. See you folks later." Oliver nodded to Shane, then added. "Better get Dorie off this street as soon as you can."

"I will. We're heading back right now." Shane snuggled Dorie close and kissed her cheek, the quick brush of his lips making her knees buckle, but she hadn't forgotten his betrayal at the brothel. Her heart wasn't up to much more of this.

"Enjoy the show!" she called out, waving to all three of them.

With that, she turned on her heels and strode quickly toward the buckboard wagon, leaving Shane in the dust.

Chapter Thirteen

"**Y**ou'd better get out of your mood, Dorie. The Parkers will be here any minute with Jeremiah." Shane pulled out a chair for Dorie in the hotel dining room, watching her take her seat gracefully but for the ramrod stiff set of her spine.

"My mood will be just fine when the Parkers get here." She placed her hands in her lap and hoisted her chin in a haughty manner. Shane almost wished for the old Dorie, the one he sort of knew how to figure out. "I don't have a thing to say to you right now, so let me be."

Shane took his seat beside her on a velvet-trimmed chair. "You're still angry even though I explained what happened up there at the—" he lowered his voice "—brothel."

Dorie lifted her napkin and fanned herself, turning away from him. "I know what you said."

"You don't believe me?" he asked incredulously.

Dorie turned to him with eyes sparking blue flames. "You humiliated me."

"We're not really married," he said through tight lips.

"Even so, you told them we were, then you stayed up there with the 'ladies' letting them *touch* you."

Shane huffed out a breath. "I told you. Mrs. Miniver told me to wait so that she could give me the payment for the gowns. She told the ladies to entertain me while I waited."

"You liked being *entertained*."

"No. I didn't. Why would I want anyone of them when I had a pretty new wife waiting for me downstairs?"

"I'm not your wife."

Shane rubbed his forehead. "Hell, woman. Are you trying to confuse me?"

"You said you'd go back there, even though they think we're married."

"I was willing to agree to anything to get out of there."

"They all seemed to know you."

"I haven't seen the inside of that place for a long time. I have no plans of going back there, Dorie."

"Ever?"

"*Ever* is a long time." Then he thought about it. He had enough problems right now without riling Dorie anymore. "No. Not ever." And he meant it. He'd been younger back then and women had been scarce in the territory. Shane had become much more selective. And the more he looked at Dorie, the more he hated admitting that she'd become the object of his desire. "They all loved the gowns."

Dorie's expression softened for a second, before she eyed him with suspicion. "How do you know, did they show you?"

"Not that any of this matters, but they didn't. I waited in the hallway. You're just going to have to believe me.

You're talented and they said you're the best seamstress they'd ever had."

"Thank you," she said finally, releasing a breath. "And it does matter…to me."

Shane smiled but wouldn't say that it mattered to him, too. His fate was sealed already, no sense wishing for the impossible. Shane took her hand and squeezed it gently, hoping she didn't witness the regret in his eyes.

"I like your hair that way," he said. "It's pretty."

Dorie touched a few strands of hair as if recalling how it was different. She wore a ribbon that matched her silk gown, allowing the tresses to flow down onto her bare shoulders making a perfect picture of delicate femininity. Unable to resist the sweet expression on her face, he bent his head and kissed her lips softly, their eyes meeting for a brief instant, before Oliver's booming voice interrupted.

"There you two lovebirds are! You made it downstairs before us."

Dorie glanced at Oliver then gazed into Shane's eyes with question. Shane tried to silently assure her the kiss had been real, instead of a ploy for the Parkers' sake, but he doubted he'd succeeded in convincing her. Dorie's expression turned cold for a minute and then she smiled graciously at the Parkers and her brother as they sat down for dinner.

"Jeremiah, where did you get that hat?" Dorie asked with puzzlement. Jeremiah wore a new John B. with silver braided trim.

"It was a gift from…Grandmother Helene and Grandfather Oliver."

"I'm afraid I insisted," Helene said softly. "I saw Jeremiah admiring it at Miller's Mercantile."

"Looks good on the boy," Oliver said.

"He's such a dear. He didn't want us to spend any money on him. We're making up for lost time. I've tried to explain that it brings us joy to indulge him a little," Helene said.

"It's very…handsome," Dorie said, her voice tight. "I'm sure he thanked you properly."

"He did," Oliver said, "about a dozen times. There's no need for that. We're family now. We can pamper our family."

"Speaking of that," Helene said with a big smile. "I've brought a little something for you and Shane, as well." Helene reached deep into her reticule, coming up with a plush blue velvet box. "This is for you, Dorie, dear."

Dorie stared at the box handed to her.

"And for Shane," Helene said, reaching deep into her bag again. "I hope this is something you might use."

Shane took the offered wrapped gift and waited for Dorie to open hers first. "Dorie?"

She cast him a small smile, then glanced at the Parkers. "This is so…unexpected."

Shane recalled Dorie's reaction when he'd brought her the dress from the general store. She'd been deeply moved. She wasn't a woman accustomed to receiving gifts. Now, well, he was certain guilt played a part in her staring at the box with trepidation.

"Please open it," Helene urged.

Dorie lifted the lid. Stunned surprise registered on her face instantly. "Oh, my."

"Jeremiah thought you might like it," Helene added.

"It's…lovely," Dorie breathed out. Shane took a look

at a necklace of tiny pearls with a drop cameo. "It's just like the one my mama had…once."

Oliver cleared his throat. "That's what Jeremiah said. It reminded him of the necklace your mama had to sell. Helene and I, well, we wanted you to have it."

"Not that it's a replacement for the one your mother had," Helene added delicately, "but maybe one day you'll be able to hand it down to your own child, when you and Shane start a family."

"A family," Dorie repeated wistfully, fingering the small pearls then gazing up at him.

Shane made the mistake of returning Dorie's gaze. Her eyes, gleaming bright blue with promise and hope, spoke to him without benefit of words. Shane took a swallow, his emotions jumbled up. It was one thing faking a pregnancy to fool the Parkers, but quite another to actually be thinking of having children someday with Dorie. Much to Shane's surprise, he didn't dismiss the idea. In truth, he couldn't imagine having a child with anyone else.

"Are you planning on a family?" Oliver asked pointedly.

Shane smiled at Dorie, then answered, "Maybe, someday."

Then Shane realized the foolishness of that statement. He and Dorie weren't ever going to have a family. No, his family was ready-made with a pregnant Marilee, who might likely be waiting for him back in Silver Hills.

"I'd like a family," Dorie said on a whisper, and Shane noticed that when she spoke the light vanished from her eyes. She turned her attention back to the Parkers. "I don't know what to say. It's most generous of you."

"Enjoy it in good health, dear. Shane, why don't you open yours?" Helene gestured toward the unopened package he'd laid on the table.

"Sure," he said, "but this wasn't at all necessary." Shane felt a measure of guilt as well, accepting gifts from the Parkers under false pretenses. He untied the string and spread apart the paper to find a belt buckle with a silver stamping of a cowboy breaking a bucking horse. "This is very nice."

"Sort of looks like you, Shane, when you're breaking a wild mustang." Jeremiah kept his eyes trained on the buckle.

"Yeah, though I haven't done that for a while. The Boyd brothers take those honors lately."

"Who are the Boyd brothers?" Helene asked.

"Oh, they are two young boys who work for me. School chums of Jeremiah."

"How nice of you to offer them work," Helene said.

Shane let that comment go. He was lucky to have the boys on a part-time basis, not the other way around. They worked for whatever Shane could afford to pay them without complaint.

"Dorie, why not put on the necklace," Jeremiah said, changing the subject. The boy was sharp as a whip. It was a damn shame that his father had run out on him. The boy deserved better.

"Oh," Dorie said, glimpsing the necklace with longing. "Should I?"

"Here, let me, sweetheart," Shane said, lifting the necklace from its box and undoing the fastener.

Dorie lifted her hair and turned while Shane set the necklace in place and fastened it in back. She smelled so good, like a fresh spring morning and, as his fingers caressed her throat, she reacted to his touch with a little shudder that only Shane could notice.

He looked his fill, unmindful of the Parkers. Being "married" to this new graceful Dorie, tied his stomach in knots. "You look beautiful," he said, "not that you didn't before. But the necklace looks perfect on you."

Dorie's smile was only for him.

"I like it," Jeremiah said and the compliments flowed forth from around the table.

The waiter appeared and the focus shifted to what specials were on tonight's menu.

Grateful for the interruption, Shane gathered his thoughts. He was starting to feel too much like a real husband, married to a spirited young woman with more backbone and tenacity than ten women combined. And he was beginning to feel comfortable in the role—too comfortable for his liking.

As the evening wound down, Shane wondered how on earth he'd manage to sleep in the same room with Dorie tonight. As fate would have it, two glasses of wine during her evening meal solved his problem. After saying good-night to the Parkers, Shane drove Jeremiah up to Henry's house while Dorie made ready for bed. When he entered their hotel room, his pretend wife had fallen fast asleep tucked safely under the sheets on the bed.

Shane undressed in the dark room and found what little comfort he could in the wing chair.

He closed his eyes and wouldn't think of the tempting picture Dorie made, her coppery tresses spilling onto the pillow, her shoulders bare but for the straps of her chemise.

Nope, Shane shut his eyes and kept them shut until sleep claimed him, as well.

Dorie sat in Virginia City's Church of Christ next to Shane, with the Parkers and Jeremiah one pew in front. They practically hadn't let Jeremiah out of their sight from the moment they'd met him and they took every opportunity to keep him near. She couldn't blame them entirely. Her younger brother was a fine boy most of the time, when he wasn't sassing off to her. He did his work, complaining about it at times, like any other thirteen-year-old boy; but he loved Dorie and she loved him back...with all her heart.

Dorie half listened to the preacher's sermon on the evils of deception. She'd heard enough to make her certain that the lies she told today would send her straight to hell. But the deception had worked. She'd minded everything Mrs. Whitaker had taught her, and she'd become a real lady—on the surface anyway. She still had frustration, times when she wanted to scream out in anger and times when she wished she could spit out the truth. She wished she'd been good enough an example to the Parkers on her own. That they would see how very hard she'd tried to supply Jeremiah with everything a boy could need. But she couldn't chance it. The Parkers were born and bred in wealth. Why, Oliver Parker owned three large freight houses in the east and was leaving tomorrow to purchase a possible fourth in San Francisco. Secretly, she prayed for the deal not to occur. Having the Parkers nearby, if only for business, would cause her more anxiety. They'd have reason to travel west on occasion. She couldn't worry about that at the moment. She'd have to concentrate on today's subterfuge in order to send them on their way tomorrow.

"Lies told, will come back in evil ways to haunt your days!" the young, exuberant preacher lectured to the crowded congregation. "Only truth will set you free."

The "truth" wouldn't set Dorie free. The truth could only ruin her. Why, if the word got out how she made her living, sewing gowns for prostitutes, and sneaking into the back doors of brothels, she'd lose the only freedom she'd known. The money she earned provided for Jeremiah and kept up the homestead.

She'd often dreamed of setting up her own shop, sewing gowns for respectable ladies, letting the whole world see her talent. How proud she would be to see her dresses worn around town, to see her creations fitted to women, young and old alike. Dorie had always wanted to sew children's clothes, as well. She'd made all of Jeremiah's shirts and trousers, but they were plain work clothes, made without much style. With a shop of her own, Dorie would have the freedom to design new styles and fashions. But her dream was just that. No amount of wishing would ever make her fanciful notions come true.

"I think we've convinced them," Shane said later, as they walked out of church several yards behind the Parkers. "They haven't asked to take Jeremiah with them since yesterday when we first met."

"The day's not over yet," Dorie replied sourly.

"Did you get anything out of the preacher's sermon?"

"Yes, I did. I'm surely going to burn in hell for what I've done."

"Then I'll be right along with you, Dorie."

Dorie stopped walking, taking a quick look around

the churchyard making sure the Parkers were well enough away. "No, not you, Shane. You've only helped me. If we have convinced the Parkers of anything, it's because of you."

"I've lied, too."

"You hate lying, don't you?" Dorie asked.

"Yep."

"I don't much like it either, Shane. But in this case, it's necessary."

"Was is necessary to dream me up a first wife—a dead first wife at that?"

Dorie drew in her lower lip. "It, uh, couldn't be helped. I had to think up a reason to explain why we were walking in the worst part of town."

"And you killed off my first wife, without blinking an eye?"

Dorie glanced around the church grounds. Lowering her voice, she reminded him, "You don't have a first wife."

"Or any wife, for that matter," Shane said with a shake of his head. "The truth is, you astonished me with that lie."

Dorie opened her mouth to defend her actions, but Shane spoke again quickly. "I must admit it was a damn good one."

Surprised, Dorie met his gaze.

"You think on your feet, Dorie. You're a survivor."

"A survivor that'll probably see the fires of hell."

"Like I said, you and me both."

"But it's a noble thing you're doing. You're helping me keep Jeremiah."

"The truth might have worked. Anyone who meets you would instantly see what a determined woman you are. When you want something bad enough, you find a way. You've raised Jeremiah without complaint. Nobody could love that boy more than you."

Dorie closed her eyes, absorbing Shane's words. It was kind of him to speak plainly, but she couldn't trust what he said. The Parkers didn't know her at all. They would only see a run-down homestead with meager supplies of food and clothing and how hard life had been for the two of them. "If only that were true and I had faith enough they would believe in me. But can you understand why I couldn't chance it?"

Shane stared in her eyes, his green gaze studying her. His answer was important to her. She needed to know that he believed in what she was doing. If she hadn't been so desperate, she wouldn't have involved him in this. Of course, that would mean he'd be married to Marilee right now and Dorie just couldn't abide that.

"I believe that you believe it, Dorie." When Dorie frowned, dejected by his answer, he added, "And that's good enough for me. Try to relax. We only have a few more hours and it will all be over. We can get back to our own lives. Come on," he said, grasping her hand and leading her toward the Parkers. "Let's finish this."

Getting back to their own lives meant that Shane would eventually marry. Dorie placed a hand on her suddenly queasy stomach. She ached so much inside that she had trouble keeping pace. Tomorrow would bring great relief seeing the Parkers leave town, but tremendous sorrow as well.

At the next sunrise, Dorie would lose Shane forever.

Dorie and Shane spent the next hours with the Parkers and Jeremiah. They were treated to a musical revue at the opera house, enjoyed a buggy ride that toured the town and then dined in extravagant style once again at the hotel. She relished the time she spent with Shane, enjoying the pretense of their marriage. Shane had played his part well, with gentle caresses to her shoulders, soft deliberate touches to her waist and brief kisses that left her wanting more. She longed for it never to end, but it would…tonight. They would say goodbye to the Parkers and she would lose Shane by morning's light.

Yet, she worried as well about the Parkers. They seemed to be taking parting with Jeremiah very well. Dorie couldn't help but worry that they had an ace or two up their sleeves. She'd given them two days with her brother, but had that been enough? Had she convinced them that Jeremiah was in good hands, wanting for nothing?

Guilt weaved its way into her heart. She knew Jeremiah would have a wonderful, full life in New York if she would agree to let him go. He'd have the best of everything, new clothes, proper schooling, security and all the love the Parkers had to give, but Dorie couldn't face life without him. She wasn't that unselfish. Besides, she told herself that Jeremiah wouldn't want to live in the east. He wouldn't leave Silver Hills. And that brought her some measure of comfort.

"It's been a quick two days," Helene said with tears in her eyes as they approached the hotel staircase. "I can't believe we're going to leave you wonderful people tomorrow."

Oliver placed an arm around her shoulder, his face no longer bright and cheerful, his voice no longer booming with vitality. "Jeremiah is a reflection of both of you. He's more than we hoped."

"Thank you," Dorie said quietly, her emotions tied up in knots.

Oliver smiled sadly then glanced at his grandson. "You have a place with us anytime you'd like, son. We'd love to have you for a visit, to live for a time, anything you wish. But for now, we realize you've got a good home here with Dorie and Shane. We understand, but remember that you're our only living heir. One day, should you venture to the east, it might suit you to learn about the freight business. There's no doubt," he said with deep sincerity, "it'll all be yours one day anyway."

Jeremiah's eyes widened with surprise. Dorie hadn't given the Parkers' passing any thought, though both were getting on in age. But it had become instantly clear to her brother that one day these two people, true blood relations to him, would pass on. His expression saddened, as well.

Shane hugged Dorie close, the snugness of his arms lending her great comfort. "I'm sure Jeremiah will visit you one day in the future." Dorie stiffened. Shane wouldn't allow her to step out of his arms. "He's still a boy and we need him here with us for now."

Dorie relaxed then, realizing Shane only had her best interests at heart.

"I'm sure you'd like to visit your grandparents sometime, wouldn't you, Jeremiah?"

Jeremiah didn't hesitate. His eyes filled with tears. "Yes," he said softly, "I would like that."

"Promise?" a hopeful Helene asked.

"I promise, Grandmother."

"You're a good boy," Oliver said, grabbing Jeremiah and wrapping him in his big burly embrace and

Jeremiah hugged him back. When the embrace ended, both sets of eyes held tears.

"Oh, this is so hard," Helene said. "We don't mean to make you both uncomfortable."

"It's okay," Dorie said. "We understand."

"I only wish we had more time with you, but Oliver has this appointment in San Francisco and we must leave first thing in the morning."

"I can always wire ahead and change the date of our arrival," Oliver said to Helene.

Dorie glanced up at Shane with pleading eyes.

"I'm afraid we're heading out tomorrow," Shane said quickly. "We have…an appointment of our own to keep. We must leave in the morning, as well."

Jeremiah studied the ground once again and Dorie wondered if she'd made a big mistake by including him in this deception. She hadn't seen any other way at the time, but poor Jeremiah. He was caught between his loyalty to her and the newfound affection he had for his grandparents. Dorie hadn't expected this. She hadn't expected the Parkers to be so kind and loving. She'd thought the worst of them and they'd proven her wrong.

"Jeremiah, dear boy, promise me you'll write us every month."

"I will, Grandmother," he said, forcing a smile before he entered her embrace. Dorie had to look away. She couldn't bear to watch the sad scene. She tamped down the jealousy she felt seeing Jeremiah's obvious love for Helene. She could afford them this moment, since her plan had worked. She wouldn't have to worry about losing Jeremiah ever again.

Helene pulled away from Jeremiah long enough to

look into his eyes one last time. "We'll be leaving on the first stage to San Francisco. We'll spend a few days there, then we'll take the railroad home." She handed him a piece of paper. "If you need anything, anything at all, here's where we'll be staying. Wire us." Then she turned her attention to Shane and Dorie. "If any of you ever need anything, please let us know. We're family now."

Oliver nodded in agreement. "We know Jeremiah is in good hands now. That was our main concern, but we're always here to help."

Shane shook Oliver's hand. "We appreciate that."

Helene came forward to hug Dorie. "You're a dear girl. We hope to see you one day again."

"Yes, I would like that," she said, remarkably meaning every word. Helene's unabashed kindness and genuine nature reminded Dorie of her own mother.

"We'll say so long for now. Not goodbye." Oliver placed his hand on Helene's back, urging her up the stairs to their room.

The three stood at the foot of the staircase waving. When the Parkers were no longer in sight, Dorie rushed to Jeremiah's side and wrapped him into her arms. "I'm sorry."

Jeremiah put his head down to hide his tears. "It's okay…they…are nice."

"They are," Shane said, placing his hand on Jeremiah's shoulder. "Very nice. And you will see them again."

Dorie agreed. "When you're older, Jeremiah. You'll visit them, I promise."

He nodded. "I…will."

"Do you want to stay with us tonight?" Shane asked.

Jeremiah shook his head, wiping the tears from his

cheeks. "No thanks. I want to see Henry one last time before we go home."

"Okay, I'll get the wagon and drive you out there. Dorie, want to come?"

Shaken by the events of the day, Dorie declined. "No thanks. I'll go up, if you don't mind."

Shane nodded. "Okay, let's go, Jeremiah."

"Good night, Jeremiah," Dorie said, relieved that the ordeal was over. She couldn't help but feel sorry for the Parkers, though she rejoiced that her worst fears wouldn't be realized. They'd be on the stage tomorrow and she and Jeremiah would return to their homestead.

Dorie's thoughts turned to Shane.

They had one night left together.

As she climbed the stairs to their hotel room, she knew in her heart what she had to do.

She only prayed Shane wouldn't deny her.

Chapter Fourteen

"**Y**ou know Dorie only did what she thought best for you," Shane explained to Jeremiah, as they traveled the road to Henry's house.

Jeremiah shrugged. He'd been quiet since saying goodbye to his grandparents earlier. "I suppose."

"If you wanted to leave Silver Hills to live with them, I think she'd understand."

"I don't. I mean, maybe one day I'd like to visit them. It's just…all the lying."

Shane smiled. "None of us liked deceiving such good people."

"Dorie didn't seem to mind."

"She did. Your sister puts on a good front, but I know she felt as guilty as the both of us. She's been both mother and sister to you since your mama died. She feels it her duty to protect you."

"From my grandparents?" Jeremiah seemed truly puzzled. He stared straight ahead, watching Smart and Sassy amble down the dirt path.

"She didn't know what kind of people they were. She

thought they'd take advantage of her situation to persuade you to leave with them. She loves you, Jeremiah. And having Dorie's love, well, it's like thunder and lightning rolled up into one. She's a force all her own. When you get older, you'll understand better."

"I suppose," he said with a twist of his mouth, then he turned to face Shane. "So how do you reckon with her force?"

"Me?"

"Yeah."

Shane stopped the wagon a few yards from the turnoff to Henry's house. "What do you mean?"

Jeremiah didn't hesitate. "I mean…my sister's got a hankering for you, Shane. All that stuff you said about thunder and lightning, I was thinking, most of that's for you."

"Are you saying…" Shane stopped that train of thought. He had no business thinking about Dorie, not when he'd be heading home tomorrow and probably facing Tobias Barkley and impending nuptials. "Never mind. Doesn't matter. We'll get our lives back tomorrow. And we won't ever have to think this hard again."

Jeremiah smiled. "Yeah, it was hard thinking and saying the right things all the time."

"Well, now you don't have to worry over that anymore."

Shane urged the horses forward and reached Henry's house in a matter of minutes. Jeremiah jumped down, clutching his new hat to his head. "I'm not gonna forget my grandparents. I promised to write and I will."

Shane nodded. "They'll appreciate that."

"One day, I'll visit them."

"When you do, you can tell them the truth. That should ease your mind some."

Jeremiah thought on that a second, then grinned. "Yep. I'll tell them everything."

"See you in the morning, son." Shane winked and turned the horses around heading back to Virginia City. Shane left Jeremiah feeling a great sense of pride in the boy.

Half an hour later, Shane arrived back at the hotel, ready for sleep. He hoped Dorie would be fast asleep herself. He'd fulfilled his part of the bargain to her and starting tomorrow he'd have another bargain to carry out, to Tobias Barkley. It'd just make things a whole lot easier if he didn't have to deal with Dorie tonight.

He opened the door slowly, hoping his boots wouldn't creak on the floorboards under the plush carpeting. Dim lantern light cast shadows on the walls, then as he stepped inside he found Dorie set in silhouette, standing by the window, staring out.

"I thought you'd be asleep by now," he said quietly.

"I waited for you," she said, turning to face him, her eyes glittering fine specks of blue fire. "I thought we could celebrate."

Shane glanced down at the small table by the chair. Light reflected off two crystal glasses and a bottle of whiskey. "You want to celebrate?" Shane swallowed. He didn't like the look in Dorie's eyes. Thunder and lightning came to mind.

"I do."

She poured the amber liquid into both glasses, three fingers high. Shane raised his brows, recalling how the wine last night had affected her. "You don't drink."

"I'll just have one," she said softly. Pink taffeta ruffled as she approached with the drinks. She'd worn the same damn pretty dress as yesterday, the hue creating rosy tones on her face and making her skin look creamy soft. The pearl necklace she wore dipped down in the generous hollow of her bosom. Seeing her dressed this way in the light of day was one thing, but seeing her now as a gentle glow of light surrounded her was another thing entirely.

Shane took a step back. His heart pounding, his brain muddled, and he knew if he took a drink with Dorie there'd be hell to pay. "No, thanks."

Dorie smiled and continued her approach, until she faced him squarely, looking up at him. "Are you afraid to have a drink with me?"

Hell, yes. "No, damn it." He grabbed the glass from her hand and gulped the whiskey. "There. I had a drink with you."

Dorie took a delicate sip of her drink, her expression thoughtful for a moment as she contemplated. "I think I prefer wine." Then she gulped down the whiskey, a triple shot of liquor vanishing in a matter of seconds.

"Hey, be careful with that!"

"I'm tired of being careful, Shane." Her eyes studied his and she smiled so prettily, his groin tightened instantly.

"I think it's time for bed."

"Not before I thank you for all you've done. The Parkers would have never believed me if you hadn't been here. Without your help, I would've lost my brother."

"It's over now, Dorie. No more thanks necessary."

"Shane, the money I was paid from Mrs. Miniver—"

"Oh, right," he said, grateful for the change of

subject. He dug into his trousers. "Here it is. I forgot to give it to you."

Dorie glanced at the wad of money in his hand. "I want you to keep it. To pay off your debt to Mr. Barkley. You've earned it."

Shane glanced at the cash Dorie shoved back at him. "I can't take your money, Dorie. You *earned* it. It'll see you through the winter, but I appreciate the thought."

"But if you pay off Mr. Barkley, you won't owe him anything, anymore."

Shane marveled at her innocence, and he admired her genuine generosity. But if the Almighty came down to earth, urging him to accept Dorie's money, Shane would still refuse. "It's more than money, sweetheart. I've given my word. Besides, I owe him three times that amount."

"Oh," Dorie said, reaching again for the bottle of whiskey. She poured another three fingers worth into her glass.

Shane set her money down on the armoire, hoping she'd soon tire and go to bed. Instead, she walked over to him and refilled his glass.

"Go easy on that stuff," he said. "Or you'll wake up with a humdinger of a headache."

Dorie sipped the liquor again. "I'm getting used to the taste."

Shane watched the delicate workings of her throat and took another big swallow of whiskey. "Let's get some sleep now."

"Okay," Dorie said with a little coy smile. "You get the bed tonight."

"No. I won't have you sleeping in that cramped wing chair."

"I wasn't planning on sleeping in the wing chair, Shane."

"But then—"

Dorie halted his words when she reached up to brush her mouth over his in a kiss that stole all of his breath. He kept his hands at his sides, fighting for willpower, but his manhood rose and pressed against the juncture of her legs; even through layers of material there wasn't any way Shane could deny his need for her. His body had grown instantly hard, straining for her, his heart wanting her, his mind...his mind fighting a losing battle.

Shane tasted the heady aroma of whiskey on Dorie's breath, and when she opened for him, he kissed her fully, their tongues colliding in a ritual that had both their bodies swaying in lusty unison. Shane grabbed her, wrapping his arms around her, bringing her body even closer. Shane was beside himself to stop the onslaught of the desire burning in his belly. Dorie gave him everything he wanted, her body pressed to his, their lips mating, their tongues dancing.

Moments later, when the kiss ended, Dorie pulled back just enough to look him square in the eyes. "I want to know what it'd be like to be your wife for real, Shane."

"No, Dorie. We can't. It wouldn't be fair to you," Shane said, holding on to the shred of hope that Dorie would come to her senses.

"It wouldn't be fair to me not to, Shane," she said with quiet determination. "You're the only man for me. Ever." She spoke in a whisper now and Shane heard the heartbreak in her voice. "All we have left is tonight."

He felt the exact same way. He'd wanted Dorie for so long he couldn't reason it away anymore.

"You want me," she breathed out. "I know you do."

"Can't deny it, sweetheart."

Dorie pulled the pins from her hair, letting the silky coppery tresses fall loosely over her shoulders. She turned to expose her back to him. "Undress me, Shane."

Shane wrapped his arms around her, pulling her in, crushing his body to hers, his fingers finding the soft supple spot just under her breasts. He kissed her throat and whispered from behind, "I can't offer you anything but one night, sweetheart. Is that enough?"

Dorie put her head down and beseeched him. "You could take the money I offered, pay Mr. Barkley back some. We'll figure a way to pay off the rest. You won't have to marry his daughter."

Shane had to make things clear to her. She had to know that tonight would truly be all that they could hope to have. She had to know that there wasn't a way out of this for either of them. He spoke with regret. "You know I can't do that."

Dorie turned in his arms, the rosy glow on her face marred by sadness and regret, yet she smiled bravely. "Then tonight will have to be enough."

Shane closed his eyes briefly, wondering when Dorie had grown up. She'd become a woman right before his eyes and he'd fought the realization. Fought it hard. But he'd lost the battle. She was the woman he wanted. He couldn't deny her any longer. He wouldn't think of how it had come to this, or all the reasons he should walk straight out of this room. Instead, he'd make love to her tonight and they would have to part tomorrow as soon as the new dawn rose on the horizon.

"I'll make it right for you, Dorie." Shane placed

both hands on her shoulders and spun her around. She lifted her hair up so that he could unfasten the buttons on her gown. He kissed the back of her neck as he slid the gown down her arms. She wiggled out of her garment, petticoats and all, then undid the corset that confined her breasts. Shane watched as she dropped the tight-fitting undergarment onto the floor. And when she turned to him, fully unclothed, Shane was completely intoxicated—not by whiskey, but by the exquisite vision she presented. "You are an amazing... *woman,* Dorie McCabe."

"Oh, Shane," she whispered in the dimly light room.

Shane picked her up and carried her to the bed. Setting her down gently he gazed at her, feeling a deep measure of pride, seeing her exposed to him with such trust and acceptance. Her skin glowed smooth and creamy under the lantern light, her long wild curls spread out across the pillow and her blue eyes beckoned with a sweet loving smile.

Shane sat on the bed, tossing off his boots, and when Dorie reached up for him, he took her into his arms and came down onto the bed, kissing her with overpowering need. His nerves raw, he told himself to go slowly, to make this night memorable for her. He'd tried to be her protector, tried to help her in ways he might never have imagined, and now, he would claim her innocence. Shane struggled with the notion, while his heart and body rejoiced. Between deep lingering kisses, he spoke tenderly, "I never meant for this to happen."

"I prayed that it would," she whispered back.

Shane's heart soared. "I don't want to hurt you in any way," he said plainly.

"You won't, Shane. I want this. There won't be any regrets, I promise."

Shane smiled down at her, knowing that her naive perception wouldn't hold up. Oh, there'd be regrets, but he was defenseless to refuse her any longer. Only she could stop what they'd begun here tonight.

"Is this how it is?" she asked. "All this...*talking?*"

Shane chuckled. Dorie, innocent as she was, had registered a complaint. He wouldn't allow another one. Lying beside her, he cupped her breast in his hand and bent his head to kiss her lips. "No more talking," he said, gently moving his hand on her, his thumb sliding over the crest, flicking the nub until it rose to a peak.

"Oh!" Dorie gasped through his kisses. Her pleasured moans as he continued stroking her ripe full breasts created havoc below his waist. Shane struggled to control the fire in his groin, to take this night slow and take her even slower. But Dorie's unabashed reaction to his touch stirred something deep in his heart as well as his body.

He vowed not to hurt her in any way, so he fought for control. It wasn't an easy task. Dorie lying on the bed, bared to him in all ways, crying out in pleasure, created the prettiest of pictures. One he never dreamed he would see.

"I never thought anything could feel so good," she breathed out.

Shane bent his head and drew her into his mouth, his tongue flicking over her tight hard nipple. She whimpered and arched up, her body reacting with heightened pleasure. He moistened each globe again and again then lifted up to crush a kiss to Dorie's sweet mouth.

"I'm tingling clear down to my belly," she said with wonderment. "Are you, Shane? Is that how it is for you, too?"

Shane nodded. "Clear down to my belly, honey."

Dorie smiled, her eyes gleaming in the low lantern light. "Oh, Shane."

Shane stroked her shoulders, absorbed the feel of her creamy porcelain skin, while he continued to kiss her. Her arms wound around his neck and he deepened the kiss, his tongue probing hers. They kissed for long moments this way, until Dorie pushed him off slightly.

He looked down at her with question, but when she unbuttoned his shirt and tugged at the material, Shane helped her remove it entirely. Her hands went flat on his chest and the heat of her palms coursed a hot path straight down to his groin. When she moved her hands, caressing his skin, then rising to plant tiny kisses on his chest, Shane lay back, resting his head on the pillow, relishing the moment and allowing Dorie to explore his body.

Dorie's tentative hands became bolder and she stroked him with confidence, her fingers flicking over his flattened discs with a look of delight in her eyes. "You're so hard," she whispered in awe.

Shane groaned. His manhood strained the confines of his trousers. Soon she would see the true extent of her statement.

Dorie lowered her hand down his torso caressing the area just below his waist. She stopped short when Shane drew a sharp breath, then smiled and reached for his belt buckle.

Shane stilled her hands. "Not yet," he said, though the notion of what she was about to do dizzied his mind.

Dorie feigned a pout, the look so adorable that Shane took hold of her and raised her up so she lay atop him. "You need to get used to me first, sweetheart."

Dorie clearly got his meaning. Her eyes widened with surprise when his arousal pulsed beneath her through his clothes. Shane cupped her derriere and nearly died with pleasure seeing Dorie's eyes change from surprise to heavy-lidded desire. He stroked her bottom and she swayed, moving against his gliding hands, causing unbearable heady friction. Her breasts crushed his chest and, with her pretty face inches from his, Shane found her lips and kissed her hard on the mouth, his own undeniable desire mounting.

He continued to slide his hands up and down, gliding from her sweet behind up to her back and shoulders then down again. They moved together causing heat and passion, rubbing their bodies, learning and exploring. Enjoying.

Dorie uttered tiny gasps now, her breaths labored and short. The mere sound of her sighs brought Shane immeasurable satisfaction. He was ready for her, all of her, but she wasn't quite ready for him.

He rolled her onto her back and he immediately missed the feel of her breasts on his skin, her thighs pressed to him. Soon, he told himself. Soon, he would satisfy both of their needs.

Dorie looked up at him, her expression filled with aching need. Shane wasted no time. He brought his mouth to hers while his fingers found the juncture of her thighs. He touched her there and she opened for him, her body seeming to know what he wanted. His fingers found her core, the soft petals of flesh that would soon welcome him. He touched her gently there, and she was jolted by the sensation.

"Oh, Shane," she breathed out on a plea.

"Dorie, honey, just lie back. Won't be long now." He kissed her again, quick and hard. Then he cupped her, his palm open, his rough skin rubbing the soft petals of her womanhood. She arched up and whimpered, her body reacting immediately to his touch. She moved with him, her body undulating as he stroked her tenderly.

Shane had little willpower left. Her soft cries as he readied her for him made him ache, his manhood growing harder with each passing moment. He kissed her again, gliding one hand over her body, caressing her skin, brushing over her breasts again and again, while the other hand moved with her rhythm. Her breaths became as labored as his, her soft cries even more pronounced, and Shane knew it was time.

He rose up from the bed and worked at removing his belt. He was surprised when Dorie reached up to pull the belt completely off. He grinned at her impatience, then tugged his pants and undergarments off. Before rejoining her on the bed, he took in her stunned expression as she viewed his naked body. "I won't hurt you," he reassured her.

"I know you won't. It's just that, oh, Shane…you are an amazing…*man.*" She took a big swallow and lay back on the bed, her eyes focused below his waist.

Ridiculous pride swelled his chest at Dorie's obvious admiration. When she opened her arms to him, Shane put aside all of his misgivings. He lowered himself onto the bed and rose above her, gently spreading her legs for his entry.

Dorie closed her eyes with a sweet giving expression on her face. Shane touched the tip of her womanhood, teasing her with his full length. She opened more for him and he entered her with one slow but forceful thrust. He felt the exact moment when he claimed her innocence, the resistance that broke from his pressure. Dorie's slight grip on his shoulders tightened. Before he could ask, she whispered, "It didn't hurt, Shane."

Shane released his breath, relieved at Dorie's undeniable courage and tenacity. He gazed down at her, the beautiful woman with a generous soul and giving heart was joined together now with him and Shane realized that he'd never felt anything better in his whole life. He relished the moment, looking into Dorie's eyes, and he moved slowly, thrusting into her with slight measured movements. His manhood strained the tight confines of her body, yet she accepted him fully and moved with him, finding a pace that fit them perfectly.

Shane had had sex with women before, but he'd never made love like this. He'd never been so touched, so honored and so involved. He wanted Dorie to feel everything, enjoy it all, to make their night together something they'd never forget.

Shane had already achieved that for himself. And as he moved with her, plunging deeper into her, he knew he'd never in his life feel anything so fulfilling. He'd never want a woman the way he wanted Dorie.

Shane touched her skin, caressed her breasts, slid his hands over her belly, then cupped her face and kissed her deeply on the lips. She made little noises, her breaths labored, her body reaching up to his. They rocked in unison now, Shane driving his manhood deep, absorbing all of her.

She cried out. "Shane!"

He rose up and plunged as deep and as hard as he could, his body burning up. She met each thrust and they reached the fiery mountain together, climbing to the very top as flames erupted and Shane felt her spasms of release. She cried out again as if in stunned surprise spurring Shane's own potent sharp release.

Once their bodies relaxed some, they gazed at each other in wonder. Dorie blinked, her throat worked, but she spoke no words.

Shane wrapped his arms around her then rolled to his side, taking her with him. He kissed her forehead and spoke softly. "Your heart will slow down soon, sweetheart. Take some deep breaths."

Dorie looked into his eyes. "I don't think my heart will ever slow down, Shane. I don't think I've ever felt anything so wonderful or so…powerful."

Shane smiled above her head, relieved that she hadn't been disappointed in any way. "Are you all right?"

Dorie chuckled. "I think I'm stunned."

"Yeah, me too."

Dorie stayed cradled in his arms for a time before she asked, "Why, Shane?"

"Why, what?"

He'd begun to relax, his breaths almost back to normal again.

"Why were you…stunned? Was it me? Did I surprise you?"

Shane stroked her shoulders and toyed with her breast, then decided that diversion would only muddle his mind further. He held her loosely and admitted, "You always surprise me, Dorie."

"In a bad way?" she asked, with uncertainty.

"Not in a bad way, honey. I was stunned…in the best way." He kissed away her doubts and brought her close. "Let's get some sleep now."

Shane closed his eyes, but his mind wouldn't settle. Images of Dorie just moments ago flashed in his head. He'd never forget making love to her. He tightened his grip and nudged her even closer, needing her near, absorbing her warmth, for this one last night.

Mrs. Whitaker once told Dorie that the one you love can make you angry and frustrated and crazy all at the same time, but even so, you can't imagine your life without that person. She said to love meant to open your heart and give all you had to that one person, and know that they'd return the kindness without a second's hesitation. She said that loving meant joy and heartache. It meant happiness and sorrow. Loving meant putting that special someone's needs above your own.

If that were all true—and she believed it to be—then she had truly fallen deeply and completely in love with Shane Graham. She gazed at his sleeping form beside her and realized that she loved him with her whole heart. She'd probably loved Shane since the first time he'd kissed her more than a year ago. And to love him genuinely meant to let him go.

She shook off the sheet and rose, taking one warm coverlet with her to wrap around her body. Still reeling from their profound lovemaking, Dorie's sated body ached from the loss that would surely follow. The wound she feared would only increase as time went on. Dorie had only this one night with Shane.

She loved him.

It was different from the love she felt for Jeremiah, but it was the same, too, because she couldn't imagine living her life without him.

Dorie tiptoed to the window and, parting the curtain slightly, she peered out at the empty night for a moment. Bereft as the starless sky and vacant as the deserted streets below, Dorie knew sleep would elude her. She found solace in a finger high tumbler of whiskey. She sipped carefully, trying not to make a sound, but when she turned from the window, Shane's eyes were upon her. "Trouble sleeping?"

She shook her head. "I...don't want to."

Shane stared into her eyes, his grass-green eyes holding her hostage. "What do you want, honey?"

"You," she said honestly, noting the enticing picture he made laying lazily across the bed. "I thought we'd have the whole night together."

Shane shook his head. "It's your first time—"

"My *only* time," she corrected. And she meant it. She didn't want to bed any other man but Shane. She would go her entire lifetime recalling this one special night with the only man she would ever love.

"I thought you'd be...thought you'd need...I didn't want to..." And as Shane searched for the exact right words, Dorie let the coverlet that warmed her body drop unceremoniously to the floor. She stood naked before him, her eyes meeting his without shame.

Shane visibly gulped. His eyes gleamed, roaming over her from head to toe, his direct perusal heating her like a slow simmering fire. He slid to the other side of the bed, making room. "Come back to bed. And bring the bottle," he ordered.

Dorie turned to do his bidding, grabbing up the whiskey bottle and making her way back to bed. She tripped on her shoes that jutted out from under the bed and toppled onto him, spilling liquor all over his body. "Whoops, sorry."

Shane laid back, stretched out and welcomed her with a grin. "Now you have to clean me up."

Dorie nodded, feeling like a clumsy fool, and spun around to get a cloth. Instantly, Shane grabbed her wrist and she turned to him in question. "Not with a cloth, honey," he whispered, his tone quite mischievous. "Use that wild imagination of yours."

Dorie nibbled her lower lip, contemplating, until she figured out what Shane had in mind. Heat rushed to her cheeks and she prayed Shane wouldn't notice how his enticing invitation had affected her.

Dorie stretched out her body fully atop Shane, no longer unfamiliar with his form. His heat became her heat, their bodies meshing together like puzzle pieces, each part connecting to the other. She rose slightly to look him in the eyes, then dipped her head and kissed away the whiskey on his throat, his shoulders and, shimmying down a bit, she kissed his chest. Whiskey wet her lips and she licked at them, tasting the heady elixir. Becoming bolder even still, she dipped down once again and licked the liquor from his skin this time, eliciting pleasured moans from him. Dorie continued to kiss and drink up the whiskey with her tongue, sipping from his chest like a road-weary thirsty traveler.

Shane reached for her, bringing her face to his. "I want to taste you." He kissed her fully on the mouth, his tongue making sweeping swirls gathering up the moistness still on her lips. Then with one fluid, graceful movement, he rolled her over, so that she rested her back against the bed.

Their eyes met.

Dorie witnessed the passion burning deep in Shane's hungry gaze. And she jerked slightly when he dripped whiskey onto her body, slowly, deliberately, pouring the liquor from her chest to her navel.

Shane bent his head and sipped from her skin in much the same fashion as she had. His lips wiped up the liquor with small urgent kisses and his tongue licked at her with long sweeping motions. He suckled the moistness from her breasts making her cry out and, when he dipped his head further down, drinking from her navel, hot hungry sensations pulsed through her body.

His hand found the folds of her tender skin then and she arched up, the pleasure almost pure agony. He stroked her again and again, and when she thought surely he'd drive his sleek manhood into her body, he rolled onto his back. Dorie followed his movements until she sat upon him, straddling his thighs. He showed her the way, guiding her atop him and, once positioned over his hard length, he helped ease her down.

Rapid all-consuming heat engulfed her instantly, her body burning up from the heady sensation. She took him in slowly, by increments, until finally he filled her. She moved up and down, his hands on her hips guiding her, his eyes intent, filled with passion.

Dorie moved more fluidly now, adjusting to his size,

finding a distinct rhythm. She tossed back her head, her hair as wild and loose as she felt right now, relishing the tight flaming friction she created. Moaning softly, she met Shane's own soft cries of passion. They moved and rocked and jerked, Shane letting go, allowing her to find her own way now.

"So beautiful," he uttered. He thrust up and she slid down time and again until friction and heat built to an earth-shattering climax. Dorie's body convulsed uncontrollably. She called out, "Shane!" and he responded with a cry of his own.

She floated back to earth as if on a cloud. Shane embraced her and she folded herself into him, the scent of whiskey and love surrounding her.

"Mmmm," she breathed out.

Shane kissed her cheek and sighed. "I bet you could sleep now."

Dorie smiled and searched his eyes. "I don't think I want to."

Shane cursed vividly but smiled back. "I'm afraid to ask. What do you want now?"

"I want to know it all, Shane. I want you to teach me. There's more, isn't there?"

Shane grunted. "Yeah, but—"

"There are different ways, aren't there? And things we haven't done?"

Shane nodded, albeit with reluctance. "We've done quite a lot, honey."

"So you don't want to make love again?"

Shane let out a deep-throated groan. "I didn't say that."

"So you do?" she asked eagerly. If this was her only real night with Shane, she had to know him in every way. She had to make this night last as long as possible. For Dorie, no other man would measure up. But she wondered if she were less than he had expected. "Unless you're tired of me already. Is that it, Shane?"

Shane tightened his embrace. "I don't think I'd ever tire of you, Dorie."

Dorie's heart soared with that declaration. "I'd never tire of you either, Shane. So, will you show me?"

Shane kissed her lips and nodded. "Give me a few minutes. A man needs time…to perform again."

Dorie nodded in understanding, relating it to chopping wood. Sometimes after splitting a log, you needed to rest up some before picking up that axe again.

Shane had done a wonderful job chopping wood so far, having no trouble raising that axe. And one thing was for certain, splitting logs was a whole lot more appealing than sawing logs.

Dorie didn't plan on doing much of the latter tonight, just as long as Shane could continue to lift his axe.

Chapter Fifteen

Shane pulled Smart and Sassy to a stop in front of the McCabe homestead, the mood in the wagon on the trip home mighty grim. Jeremiah hadn't much to say since leaving his grandparents yesterday and Dorie, well, she'd been deep in thought, glancing his way more times than not. Shane had all he could do to keep from staring into her pretty blue eyes, recalling the night they spent making love in all sorts of ways.

Dorie had been an eager lover, surprising him at every turn. She'd given him a night he'd never forget, his body still humming from their encounter.

But Shane hadn't a good thing to say about himself. Guilt plagued him, weighing him down heavily for taking Dorie's virginity. She'd wanted it so, but Shane should have resisted the temptation. He'd tried his damnedest and had succeeded for the past two weeks to put aside his yearnings for her. But last night, after Dorie made him realize they'd only have one chance together before both of their lives would change so drastically, Shane's willpower had crumbled. He'd always been an honorable man, a man who knew to do the right thing, and last night had been wrong. Painfully wrong.

And the best night of his life.

"We're here," he said unnecessarily. Jeremiah had already jumped down from the wagon.

Shane did the same, coming around to Dorie's side to help her down. He reached for her waist and lifted her. Once her feet hit the ground, he meant to release her, but he couldn't quite manage it. He'd held her all through the night, becoming familiar with her body, and had a hard time reckoning the fact that this would be the very last time he might ever touch her. He held her tight and she wrapped her arms around his neck, setting her head on his shoulder.

"Jeremiah, grab Dorie's things and bring them in the house," he said. "I want to speak with your sister."

"Sure, Shane." Too wrapped up in his own thoughts, the boy hadn't even noticed their embrace.

Once Jeremiah entered the house, Shane took hold of Dorie's arms and lowered them down to hold her hands. "There's nothing I can say to make this easier, honey. I'll never forget last night, but I'm afraid everything has changed."

Tears misted in her eyes and she nodded. "I know."

"I think it best not to see each other anymore."

Dorie bit down on her lower lip and stared into his eyes. When he thought she'd argue, instead she nodded in agreement. "If that's what you want."

"It'd be easier for us both that way," he said firmly, trying to convince himself, as well as her.

Again, she nodded without qualm.

Shane released her hands and stepped away. He

removed his hat and ran his hand through his hair several times. "Hell, it's not what I want. But I have no choice. We both know that."

"What *do* you want, Shane?" Dorie asked quietly, her voice a mere whisper.

You, he wanted to say. He wanted her. If he had a choice in the matter, he'd marry her and become a father to Jeremiah. And he knew he'd never live a moment of regret. That the crazy notion hadn't shocked him down to his socks *did* surprise him. He'd been falling in love with Dorie these past two weeks, without even realizing it. After last night, he figured he'd never want any other woman but her. But Shane wasn't getting what he wanted any more than Dorie was.

"I want this to be over," he said regretfully.

"Then you'll make Marilee your wife?" she asked, though both knew the answer. He'd never lied to Dorie about that. He had to marry Barkley's daughter. He'd given her his word. Honor and blackmail tied his hands.

Shane nodded then a thought struck and he spoke aloud what he should have kept to himself. "Maybe old man Barkley won't find her."

Hope registered in her eyes. "I've been praying for that, Shane."

Shane looked at Dorie and smiled sadly with regret. He shouldn't have blurted out that notion. Barkley always got what he wanted. He'd find his daughter, if he hadn't already. The look of hope on Dorie's face right now was another crime he'd committed on her behalf. Shane couldn't bear to hurt her any longer.

He stepped closer, took her into his arms and kissed her hard on the mouth. "I have to go."

Dorie clung to him a moment, then let go. "Good-bye, Shane."

"If you ever need me…"

Dorie smiled bravely and with a shake of her head, she said, "Jeremiah and I will be just fine."

Shane climbed into the wagon, looking at Dorie one last time as wrenching pain seared through his heart.

Dorie wasn't just fine. She was miserable. So miserable that she'd spent two sleepless nights, tossing and turning, trying to forget Shane and the incredible night they'd spent together. She'd been so sure she could make things right. She'd been certain she could help him find a way out of his dilemma. She'd been so sure the feelings they shared would be enough.

She'd been wrong.

On all accounts.

Her heart had broken into tiny pieces the other day watching Shane ride off her property. She'd been grateful to him. Jeremiah would remain with her because of his help. She should feel satisfied, but instead, she wanted more. She wanted Shane.

Dorie sat slumped in her kitchen chair, wearing her old baggy work clothes again, slowly mixing batter for her biscuits. She'd gone about her chores these past few days without any joy in her heart. All she knew now was a powerful ache that refused to go away. She kept thinking of what Mrs. Whitaker had said about true love.

"If you truly love someone then you put their needs above your own. I did that, Shane. I let you go."

Dorie churned the batter again with languid move-ments. "But I never planned on it hurting so much."

Dorie closed her eyes for a moment, allowing herself thoughts of her time in Virginia City. She'd had a few days of pretending that Shane had been her husband. She'd always remember his soft touches, his sweet kisses on the cheek and the times he'd called her "sweetheart." She'd remember their one night together, pressing those memories of making love with him into her memory for all eternity.

"You have to beat that dough harder if you want it to blend."

Dorie looked up. Mrs. Whitaker stood beside her holding a basket in her arms. "Jeremiah let me in. I hope I'm not disturbing you."

Dorie straightened in her seat. "Oh, no. Not at all. I meant to visit you when I returned. But I just…"

Mrs. Whitaker waved off her explanation. "It's all right." She sat down and set the basket on the table. "I made you and Jeremiah supper for tonight. There's chicken and potatoes and cornbread pudding."

Dorie smiled. "Thank you. That's very kind. And I did mean to come by to thank you for your help. I think our plan worked. I…I didn't mess up…much. The Parkers left Virginia City without knowing the truth. And, well, as you can see, Jeremiah is still with me."

"Yes, yes. That's all wonderful news. So why do you look so sad, dear?"

Dorie shrugged, holding back tears. "No reason."

"I see."

"How is Mr. Whitaker?" Dorie asked to be polite.

"Fine. As ornery as ever. Some days I don't know why I married that man." Then she grinned. "Of course, I love him more than my next breath."

Dorie glanced up to peer into Mrs. Whitaker's eyes. They were soft, with the light of love shining through. Dorie didn't think she'd ever have that look in her eyes. She loved Shane more than her next breath, too, but she wouldn't have the happy ending Mrs. Whitaker had. "You're lucky, Mrs. Whitaker."

She appeared momentarily puzzled. "Why so?"

"You got to marry the ornery man you loved."

"Ah, I see. You know, Shane stopped by yesterday. He looked about as unhappy as you."

"He did?" she asked, unable not to inquire about him.

"Yes. He told me that the Parkers left Virginia City without worry about Jeremiah."

Dorie nodded. "Did he say anything else?"

"Just that he was proud of the way you handled yourself with the Parkers. He said you were a woman to be admired."

Tears she couldn't hold back trickled down her cheek. She pursed her trembling lips and wiped them away.

"Dorie, what's wrong? Did Shane do something to upset you?"

She shook her head adamantly. "He was…he was perfect. The perfect husband. Only now, I'm in love with him. For real."

Mrs. Whitaker nodded her head in understanding. "I do see. Has he expressed his feelings for you?"

"No, but, oh it was wonderful being with him. And we…we…got closer than ever."

Mrs. Whitaker sighed deeply. She remained silent a moment, her eyes softening with understanding. "He must care a great deal for you, Dorie."

"He thinks it best that we don't see each other anymore."

"That might be wise," she said carefully, "but not easy for either of you."

"I keep recalling what you said about wanting what's best for the one you love. I let Shane go so he wouldn't lose his ranch to Mr. Barkley. But it just doesn't *feel* like what's best, Mrs. Whitaker. I miss him so much."

"Dear girl, judging by the way Shane appeared yesterday, I'd say he misses you just as much. He seems to have no options in the matter. If he could change things, I'm sure he would."

"Really?"

"Really." She smiled giving Dorie a measure of hope. "It's been my experience that things seem darkest just before the light. I'll be praying for you, dear." She patted her hand gently. "I know you're a strong enough woman to endure whatever trials come your way. And I'll be here, if ever you need me."

Dorie cast her a small smile, though she wasn't convinced she could endure losing Shane forever. "Thank you."

Mrs. Whitaker rose and hugged Dorie's shoulders, then bent to kiss her forehead. "Shane was right," she said softly. "You are a woman to be admired."

Dorie tossed and turned once again that night. Instead of lying in bed hoping to sleep for the third night in a row, she rose to do some late night mending in the parlor. She made sure to keep the lantern light low, so not to wake Jeremiah. Although usually her brother slept soundly, she'd sensed his own restlessness lately and didn't want to disturb his sleep. Tonight, it seemed all was quiet.

She worked for several hours, until her eyes hurt and she'd exhausted her mind. She fell into bed well past midnight and when she awoke the next morning it was as if she hadn't slept at all. She rose from the bed, dressed quickly, unmindful of the shabby clothes she'd donned, and ventured into the kitchen.

Dawning light broke, filtering early rays of sunshine through her window. Dorie squinted against the brightness and her grouchy mood worsened. She looked around her home with critical eyes, seeing all its shortcomings. Dorie had been too busy raising Jeremiah before to care about the appearance of her homestead, meager as it was.

Now, she did care.

She wanted better for Jeremiah. And for herself. And now that she had some ready cash from the sale of those gowns, she decided it was high time they worked on fixing up their home. She needed to keep busy, to distract herself and work so hard that she'd fall asleep the minute her head hit the pillow at night. Mostly, she had to try to forget about Shane.

When Jeremiah sat down at the kitchen table ten minutes later, she barked orders. "After breakfast, you're going to fix the fences, Jeremiah. And after that, you're going to fix the planks on the porch, nail them down but good and we'll paint them. In fact, we're going to paint the entire house. You and me."

Jeremiah looked at her with baffled amazement. "We are?"

"Yes, it's time we make this house a more respectable home."

"It's respectable enough for me." He spooned up the oatmeal she'd set in front of him.

"Don't sass me."

Jeremiah thought better than to argue with her when she was in a mood, and she knew it. "While you're outside fixing things, I'll be out back ripping up weeds and tilling the soil. It's time we had a real garden. We'll grow corn and all sorts of other vegetables. And flowers. I always wanted a flower garden."

"Okay," Jeremiah said with no shred of enthusiasm.

Dorie had a plan to better their lives, but five hours later, with calluses on her hands and sweat beading on her forehead, she wondered if maybe her plan had been a bit too ambitious for the two of them. In truth, she wanted everything she'd never had and she wanted to accomplish it quickly. But the labor was difficult, not that she minded hard work. She'd worked hard the better part of her teen years, but it was tedious and exhausting and she still had all of her other chores to do.

Dorie wiped sweat from her forehead and headed into the house for a drink. She poured water into a glass and gulped down half of it immediately, the cool liquid helping to refresh her parched throat. She listened for any sound of Jeremiah working and when she was met with silence, she ventured to the front door, deciding to check on him.

She popped her head out and lifted the glass of water to her lips when she spotted her brother. Shock, dismay and dread jolted her system with terrifying force. The glass slipped from her fingers, crashing to the parlor floor. Dorie closed her eyes, wishing away the sight before her, but when she opened them again, her fears were confirmed.

Jeremiah stood in the shade of the oak tree by the barn with two other people.

Oliver and Helene Parker.

Chapter Sixteen

"I told them, Dorie. I told them everything," Jeremiah declared in earnest. "And I'm glad of it."

Dorie sat facing the Parkers in her parlor, her tattered horsehair sofa looking unsightly against Helene's taupe raw silk traveling gown and Oliver's fine light woolen russet suit. Dorie felt every bit as dreadful appearing before them in her most soiled work clothes. To their credit the Parkers didn't seem to judge her appearance, but she knew they couldn't be happy about her part in their deception.

"He did," Helene stated calmly. "Jeremiah told us everything."

Dorie faced them directly, fearful of their retaliation, but also ashamed of deceiving such nice people. "I suppose you hate me for lying to you."

"We don't hate you, child," Oliver said in voice devoid of anger.

"We're trying to understand," Helene added. "We only wanted to meet our grandson.

"You wanted to see if he was well cared for. Well, he

is. I've raised him the best I know how. We don't have a lot of money or fancy things, but we manage. And he's as well cared for and loved as any boy on this earth, I can assure you of that."

Helene glanced at her husband. Oliver pursed his lips.

"Dorie...takes good care of me," Jeremiah added. "Even if I got chores to do. Everybody I know has chores."

Dorie reached for Jeremiah. He stood beside her and she took hold of his hand.

The Parkers sat stonily quiet for a time, then Helene asked, "Who is Shane?"

"He's our neighbor," Dorie answered, wanting to say that he was so much more to her now.

"I understand he's got some troubles, yet he helped you out."

"He didn't like lying to you," Dorie said in his defense. "Once we saw what kind people you were, we were both sorry for the pretense."

"It wasn't necessary," Helene said sweetly.

"I didn't know that. I didn't know if you'd force me to give Jeremiah up. I can't lose Jeremiah. He's all I have."

"And this fellow, Shane," Oliver began. "Did you really drag him away from his wedding?"

Jeremiah averted his gaze when Dorie glared at him. Jeremiah really had told them everything. "I did. I didn't see any other way. Besides, Shane doesn't want to marry Mr. Barkley's daughter. He's being blackmailed."

"We know," Helene said. "We heard about it from Mr. Charles at the hotel and a Miss Caty Rumsford at the diner. Seems everyone knows the goings-on in this town."

"Why did you come here?" Dorie asked pointedly. "Didn't you believe our...our..."

"Oh, we believed you," Helene said. "You and Shane appeared the happiest of couples and Jeremiah couldn't have been any more kind and sweet. We left Virginia City feeling quite good about the place our grandson had in your lives. No, we came back, because, well, we missed him so, for one. We found a few more books he might like and…this."

Helene reached into her reticule and came up with a jeweled box. She handed it to Dorie. "I couldn't believe it when I saw it. Oliver and I wanted you to have it."

Stunned, Dorie looked down at the box in her hands. "What is it?"

"Open it," Oliver said kindly.

"Are you still sure you want to give this to me?"

"Of course, dear," Helene said with a smile. "We're not angry with you. But well, I think I can speak for Oliver, as well, we are disappointed in your behavior. You judged us before meeting us. I'll be honest, I don't know how we would have reacted if we'd come here and witnessed all this beforehand. But now, we do have a better understanding of just how very much love you have in your heart, Dorie. I'm not agreeing with what you did. It was wrong. But well, you're family now. And we can forgive you."

Tears streamed down Dorie's face. "I don't believe I deserve this gift."

"You do," Helene said, handing her a handkerchief, "and more."

"That's right," Oliver said, in total agreement. "Now go on and open it."

Dorie wiped her tears, her heart wrenching from their kindness. She felt smaller than small for hurting and deceiving them. With trembling fingers, Dorie fumbled with the box, until finally she managed to lift the lid to find a dainty pearl bracelet. "It matches the necklace...the one like my mother's. There's even a tiny cameo."

Helene leaned back with a satisfied expression on her face. "We thought you'd be pleased."

Dorie's eyes watered up again. "It's the kindest...the kindest gift I've ever received. I...truly, I don't know what to say."

"Promise us no more lies and we'll call it even," Oliver said without reproach.

"I do. I promise."

"Is there anything more you want to tell us?"

Dorie blinked her eyes and decided that these people should know the whole truth. "I'm in love with Shane Graham. He's destined to marry a woman he doesn't want. There's no hope for it. And I'm only telling you this in case you had it in your mind that one day Shane and I might truly marry. It's my fondest wish, but it'll never be."

"I'm so sorry, Dorie," Helene said. "It was plain to see the love you two had for each other."

She wasn't certain if Shane loved her, but she sure as anything had enough love in her heart for the both of them.

Helene took hold of Oliver's hand and glancing at him first, she turned to her. "So, in that case, would you and Jeremiah consider moving to New York? Would you consider living with us? We have plenty of room. There's a school only minutes from our home. And Oliver could teach him the freight business. You and Jeremiah would have whatever you needed. We'd be a real family, Dorie."

A cold shiver ran down her spine. This was what she

feared—that the Parkers would force Jeremiah to move away from Silver Hills. Then she realized that they had included her as well. They wouldn't break up her small family but only add to their own.

"It's a good life, Dorie," Oliver stated. "And I understand you have quite a talent. We could open a shop for those gowns you create. You wouldn't have to sell them to brothels. You'd have your own shop."

"Jeremiah, you told them that!"

"I...I," Jeremiah stammered with a look of fear in his eyes as if he'd just nailed her coffin shut.

"It's okay, Dorie. I'm glad it's all out in the open," Helene said. "You did what you had to do to survive. We admire that."

"Indeed," Oliver said. "Our grandson says that you're very talented. I'm sure you'd like to see decent folks wearing your creations."

"It's been a dream of mine," she admitted, once she'd settled down. She didn't know if she could leave Silver Hills, and Shane, behind. Still, somewhere in the back of her mind, she'd held one tiny iota of hope that he'd return to her.

"Will you think about it?" Oliver asked.

Yes, she could do that. She could think of a better life for Jeremiah and herself—of owning her own dress shop and not struggling for every dollar she earned. "Yes, I'll give it some thought."

"Fine, then." Oliver rose from his seat and helped his wife up. They stood facing her without recrimination and Dorie knew that they would truly welcome her into their home if she decided to leave Silver Hills. "We'll be staying at the hotel in town for a day or two. We'd like to see Jeremiah during that time, if that's all right."

Dorie glanced at her brother and when he eagerly nodded, she smiled. "That would be wonderful."

Helene took hold her hand and squeezed. "You give it some real good thought, dear. We'll abide by your decision, whatever it may be."

"Thank you," she said. "For everything."

"You're entirely welcome."

With that, they left her homestead leaving Dorie with some serious thinking to do.

Shane had been hard pressed to allow his herd to graze on Barkley's land. The coldhearted threats Barkley had issued, as well as the unkind, callous words he'd spoken about Dorie, hadn't set right with him. He hated that he needed Barkley's money and grazing land, but he did.

For now though, he made due with making his small herd stay within his own property lines, not wanting to give Barkley the satisfaction. He'd informed the Boyd brothers to keep the herd contained on the Bar G only, for the time being.

Shane brought Sassy up to a trot as he rode back in after a long day on the range. He'd been working long hours, keeping his mind busy and his body exhausted, trying to forget about Dorie, but it hadn't been easy.

Thoughts of her filtered in at the oddest of times. Seemed he couldn't look at the newest baby calf on his property without thinking of a mud-stained Dorie, working alongside of him, helping him pull the baby from its mama. Or every time he cooked beef stew, or ate a biscuit, he'd think of her. Lord, Dorie and her stone biscuits! Or every time he smelled a flower, or saw a wildflower growing in his yard, he'd remember her light flowery scent.

And at night when he closed his eyes, her image appeared and he wished he would turn to find her there, beside him in bed.

Shane shoved those thoughts away time and again. But they kept returning with powerful force. He'd even sent up a prayer to the Almighty to help him recover from the feelings that kept him from true peace.

He reined his horse in and after bedding her down with a good rubdown and brushing, he brushed himself off as well, removing range dust and earth from his pants before entering his house. The walls screamed of loneliness and he'd begun to hate the quiet that surrounded him.

He splashed water on his face, ate a quick meal of cold chicken and vegetables then headed outside to sit on a chair on his front porch. Stretching out, he lit a cheroot, a rare ritual that he seldom indulged in any more. Taking a puff, he leaned back in his seat and watched the late afternoon sun descend.

When a rider approached, Shane straightened and squinted his eyes to get a better look. With the setting sun's glare obstructing his vision, it wasn't until the rider had entered his front gate before he recognized him.

Tobias Barkley.

Shane reached for his gun then dropped his hand. He'd taken it off inside the house.

"What do you want?" he called out, before the heavy-set man dismounted from his horse.

"That's no way to speak to your future kin, boy."

"I'll speak to you any way I want," he said, drawing from his cheroot, "as long as you're on my land."

Barkley barreled over to stand just beyond the steps of his house. "You'll be happy to know that you'll be debt-free soon. This land you call *yours* will be just that."

Shane narrowed his eyes. Barkley was being just a little bit too amiable. "Yeah, and why's that?"

Barkley grinned from ear to ear. "Marilee has come home."

Shane tossed the cheroot to the ground. He stood and stomped out the flame, all the while watching Barkley's smug face. "You mean you dragged her back home?"

He shrugged. "No sense quibbling over words. She's home now. She's not running away again. I'll make sure of it this time. And you're to be married day after tomorrow."

Shane braced his hands on the porch railing and looked past Barkley, toward the setting sun. "I'll need to speak with her first."

"You come by anytime you want. She'll see you. Oh, and don't even try to take her off my land. She's to stay home until the nuptials."

"You're holding your own daughter hostage?"

Barkley removed his hat and scratched his bald head. "Now I don't see it that way. The girl's been through enough. She needs her rest. In a few days, she'll be your headache. Oh, and don't you try any funny business or I'll call in those loans and put up fences faster than you can blink your eyes."

Shane spoke through tight lips. "Tell Marilee I'll come

by tomorrow morning to speak with her. She still has to agree to this marriage. I won't force her into anything."

Barkley nodded. "She'll agree. Get your wedding suit ready, boy." He strode over to his horse and mounted, then tipped his hat. "Day after tomorrow, we'll be family. Don't you forget that."

Shane swore an oath the minute the man turned his horse around. He watched him leave then kicked the porch rail so hard his toes felt the jolt clear through his boot.

An hour later the barkeep at the Silver Shadows Saloon asked, "What'll it be?"

Shane leaned against the bar. "A bottle of your best." He needed a drink and the drops left in his own liquor stash at home meant for "medicinal" purposes just wouldn't do. Barkley's appearance on his ranch today had galled him, but nothing was worse than the desperate pain shooting through his gut right now, thinking of his upcoming marriage. For some odd reason he hadn't thought this day would ever really come. He knew that it would, but in his heart he'd held out hope that he'd never have to go through with the marriage.

The barkeep set a bottle of whiskey in front of him. "My best."

Shane glanced at the amber liquor and his mind flashed an image of Dorie tripping onto the bed, spilling whiskey on him. He recalled her wide-eyed expression when he'd asked her in no uncertain terms to clean it up, and how she managed to knock him to his knees with her unabashed passion. They'd played whiskey games the rest of the night and, in turn, Shane had stolen her innocence, but he'd been the one truly robbed.

Dorie had stolen his heart.

And now he faced a marriage he couldn't abide to a nice enough woman whom he didn't love.

Shane shoved the bottle away. He wouldn't drink a drop of that whiskey. Dorie had ruined him from craving that particular alcohol again, not without her by his side. "I changed my mind. Bring me a beer."

The barkeep shot him a puzzled look but did his bidding. Half an hour later, Shane strode out the doors of the saloon and right smack into the Parkers.

At first Shane thought he was seeing things. Hell, he'd only had one tall beer, not enough to make him hallucinate.

"Mr. Graham," Oliver said, once each of them had recognized the other's presence. "It's good to see you again."

Shane's mind muddied up. He didn't know what to say. He'd never expected them to show up in Silver Hills. What were they doing here?

When Shane hesitated for long moments without responding, like a fox caught in the henhouse, Mrs. Parker intervened. "It's all right, Shane. We know the truth. We've already been to see Dorie and Jeremiah. Our grandson told us everything."

Shane swallowed hard. "Everything?"

"I think we know it all now," Oliver said clearly. "We've had a good talk with Dorie about it."

"Have you?"

"Yes, and we've come to an understanding."

"That's...good." Shane still wasn't sure what truths Jeremiah told, so he had to be careful with what he said.

His puzzled expression must have been obvious, so Helene clarified. She placed her hand on his arm. "We know you two aren't married. We know where Dorie lives and how she manages. We know you may have to marry another."

Shane put his head down. "Yeah, I guess you do know everything." And when he looked up again, he saw genuine sincerity in their eyes. "Listen, you're nice people. We didn't like lying. None of us did, but I suppose Dorie explained her reasons for it all."

"She did," Helene said.

"I hope you'll accept my apology."

Oliver glanced at his wife. "We've forgiven Dorie and Jeremiah. I think we can forgive you, too."

"You must care an awful lot about her to have gone along with her plan," Helene said. "Oliver and I know you're an honorable man, someone who has watched out for Dorie and Jeremiah since their mama died."

Shane sucked in a breath. "Dorie didn't always make it easy, but she's…a good woman."

"Yes," Helene said with expectant eyes, "she's worth the trouble."

Shane shot her a look and realized that the Parkers may know even more than they'd let on.

"You two appeared well suited," Helene continued, "like you were really in love."

"You certainly fooled us," Oliver added.

Shane rubbed his temples. "I'm destined to marry Marilee Barkley. If you know the circumstances, then you know that Barkley won't take no for an answer."

"Yes, but we understand that Marilee ran off."

Shane pursed his lips. "Yep, she did. But Barkley found her and she's back home. The marriage is set for day after tomorrow."

"Oh, dear," Helene gasped, her hand flying up to her mouth. "Does Dorie know?"

"No." Shane frowned. "I'm going over there tomorrow, just as soon as I speak with Marilee. I'll tell Dorie myself."

Helene glanced at Oliver. The Parkers' expressions fell at the same time. "Be careful with her, Shane. The news is bound to hurt her."

Shane nodded and spoke from the heart. "I never meant to hurt her. I lo...never mind," he said, heaving a sigh. "It's too late now to change things."

There wasn't anything more to say. Shane shook Oliver's hand and the older man patted him on the back with true affection. Helene hugged him tight and Shane felt he didn't deserve any of their kindness.

He rode off, heading back to the Bar G, with only one thought in his head.

Dorie.

"It appears that you are stuck with me," Marilee said to Shane. "Father won't have it any other way. I'm to be married to you tomorrow."

She handed him a glass of lemonade as he sat facing her in the Barkleys' elegantly furnished parlor. A carved walnut clock chimed the hour in one corner, while in the other, a pianoforte angled out. Fresh flowers filled the room in abundance with too strong a fragrance for Shane's liking.

In truth, he'd rather be anywhere but here at the moment, but it wasn't Marilee's fault. He couldn't blame her for any of this. No, this was all her father's doing.

Shane smiled with regret. "I'm afraid you're the one

stuck…with me. Why did you run away? Was it because you thought I'd backed out of the wedding?"

Marilee took her time in answering. Her eyes closed briefly and then she looked away. "No. Father thinks I was humiliated, but I wasn't. I saw it as a chance for me to leave town." She laid a hand on her stomach and lifted her lips with a sad expression. "I was to meet up with the real father of my child. Father made it impossible for him to stay on at the ranch so we had a plan to meet south of here in a small town called Angel Springs. He has family living there. But, as you know, father caught up with me and now, here I am."

"Your father's got a man guarding the house, doesn't he?"

Marilee pursed her lips and spoke with scorn. "Men, Shane. I've noticed at least three of them. I'm not allowed off the property until the wedding."

"Can't you reason with your father?" Shane asked, yet he knew Barkley to be a tough businessman. He'd only hoped the man would go easier on his only daughter.

"I've tried, Shane. Father has a plan in mind for me. And now that I'm carrying the heir to the ranch, he won't hear of me going off with whom he believes is a drifter. He wants me here, married to you, so that he can keep an eye on things. I know he loves me in his own way, but he doesn't think I know what I'm doing. Oh, Shane, I'm really sorry to put you through this. I'm sure you'd rather not marry me. If I can take a guess, I'd say you're in love with someone else, too."

Shane lifted his brows. "Why would you say that?"

Marilee smiled quickly. "Father tends to rant a great deal. I've heard Dorie McCabe's name associated with yours on a number of occasions. And she did drag you away from the church the first time."

Shane studied his boots. He pursed his lips. And when he spoke, he chose his words carefully. Though it pained him terribly, he kept his emotions at bay. "Dorie has nothing to do with us. If you'll still have me, we'll marry tomorrow. I'll be a faithful husband and a good father to your child. But…it has to be what you want, Marilee."

"What I want doesn't seem to matter, Shane. Sorry if this is hurtful. It's just that Father has made some veiled threats…and I'm afraid of what he might do to Johnny if I don't marry you. With his wealth and power he can ruin a man if he sets his mind to it. And I know father is holding something over your head, as well. I can't abide any of that. So, yes, we'll marry tomorrow."

Shane rose then and helped Marilee from her seat. They stood facing each other, her eyes pitifully sad. "Thank you, Shane. I'll try to be a good wife."

Shane nodded, the realization setting in. Tomorrow, he would marry and take a wife. And the hardest part in all this was that he'd have to ride over to the McCabe homestead and tell Dorie.

"Any chance the baby's father will come back?" Shane had to ask, the thought niggling him all morning. He couldn't imagine a man abandoning the woman who carried his child.

Marilee shook her head. "I made him promise not to. If he sets foot on my father's land again…there'd be no telling what would happen. I'm afraid when I didn't show up to meet him this time that he lost all hope."

Shane understood. A man's pride was at stake. So now, his fate was sealed. He'd be a married man by this time tomorrow. Shane tried to smile warmly, but didn't know if he succeeded. "Then I'll see you in church tomorrow, Marilee."

She rose up to kiss his cheek. "Thank you," she said.

And Shane rode off thinking there was something entirely wrong with a woman who would kiss a man on the cheek in gratitude for marrying her.

Chapter Seventeen

Dorie dug her fingers into the earth and pulled up a giant-sized weed. She tossed it into a bucket along with the others she'd yanked up and wiped her brow. She'd been at it all morning, clearing the dry soil readying it for her garden. With a straw hat on her head protecting her from late morning sun she looked about her homestead with honest eyes.

It wasn't much.

But it was hers...and Jeremiah's.

She'd managed all these years with little help. She and Jeremiah had food enough and clothes and a roof that didn't leak...too badly. They'd been happy in Silver Hills for the most part, but Dorie couldn't help wondering what life would be like for her brother living in New York with the Parkers. He'd have so much more than they had now. They wouldn't have to worry about an especially bad winter or whether Mrs. Miniver's ladies would tire of her creations.

Jeremiah had years to go before he'd be able to make a decent living working a ranch or lumberyard. And just maybe, he'd want better for himself. Just maybe, he would love to be schooled in other things. He could become a doctor or an attorney, or go into some other fine profession.

But as Dorie gazed down at the soil she'd just tended and smoothed readying for planting, she realized she wanted to see the garden grow. She wanted to anticipate the carrots coming up and the corn lifting to the sun. She wanted to witness her flowers blooming in spring. She wanted to make her life here. And Jeremiah did, too. She'd already spoken to him about it.

She'd told the Parkers she would think about their kind offer, so she had…all night long. Yet, she couldn't imagine leaving the only town she'd ever known or the man she loved so desperately that her heart ached to see him once again.

Dorie planted her seedlings, covering them carefully and when she heard footsteps coming around from the front of the house, she said with newfound hope, "Jeremiah, lookee here, we're going have vegetables in a few months."

"It's not Jeremiah."

Dorie snapped her head up and her heart warmed immediately. "Shane!" She rose up and lost all rational thought, seeing him looking so handsome, just a few yards away. She ran into his arms, her hat flying off her head. He welcomed her, wrapping his arms around her, tucking her head under his chin. "I knew you'd come back. I knew it, Shane. Oh, it's so good to see you. I've missed you something terrible."

She lifted her head and pressed a kiss to his mouth.

He resisted for a moment which caused her a measure of uncertainty, but then he kissed her back passionately, his lips locked to hers with dire yearning.

He pulled away all too quickly. "Dorie," he spoke quietly, his hands coming to her face, his thumbs wiping soil from her cheeks. He held her that way, his eyes searching hers. "I came with news."

"I know the news, Shane. I know the Parkers are in town. They came for a visit. We spoke for a time and we've come to an understanding. I think...I think they've forgiven me."

"That's good, honey."

"Oh, Shane. It's so good to see you."

"It's good to see you, too," he said, his tone serious.

"I must look a mess." She wiped soil from her apron, ran a hand down her hair, trying to tidy up a bit.

Shane took both of her hands in his. "No, you don't look a mess. You're the prettiest thing I've ever seen, Dorie."

Dorie smiled wide, her insides melting. "Thank you."

"Let's talk." He led her over to the shade of the barn, his hand holding hers tightly.

It felt so good, so right being with him. She couldn't think past that. She hadn't known if she'd ever see him again, and here he was just four days later seemingly unable to stay away. Oh, she'd prayed for this.

Shane braced his back against the wall of the barn. Dorie faced him still holding his hand. Unable to contain her joy, she simply grinned.

Shane put his head down. He wouldn't look at her. "Shane?"

"This isn't easy, Dorie."

"What's not easy?" she asked, puzzled.

He looked into her eyes finally. "Coming here, saying what I have to say."

"You can say anything to me, Shane. Fact is, you pretty much have in the past."

Shane winced, then on a heavy breath, he announced, "I'm getting married tomorrow."

"Married?" She dropped his hand and blinked her eyes. The joy she'd felt just a second ago vanished.

"Marilee is home. Barkley found her. He set the wedding for tomorrow."

"No, Shane. No." She shook her head fiercely then turned away from him as overwhelming grief struck her system. She didn't even try to hold back tears.

Shane braced her shoulders from behind. "I'm sorry. I didn't want to hurt you, Dorie. I didn't want any of this."

"I…didn't think this would ever truly…happen."

"I know, but I never lied to you, honey. This is how it has to be."

She spun around to face him, wiping at her tears. "But *tomorrow,* Shane? It's so soon. And what of Marilee?"

"She's resigned to the marriage. Her father has given her no choice."

Dorie closed her eyes. She halted her tears, realizing she had to face facts. Shane hadn't lied to her about this. She'd known he was destined to marry another, but the ache of losing him sliced through her like a mortal wound. "Will you sleep with her?"

Stunned by the question, Shane snapped his head back. "She's with child, Dorie. I won't touch her."

"And what about after…when she has the baby you're intent on raising?"

"She'll be my wife," he said quietly.

"And you'll be honor bound to do your husbandly duty?"

Shane's patience seemed at an end. He flung his arms up. "Hell, I don't know. I've haven't given it a thought."

"Well, I have! I can't abide the thought, Shane. I can't."

Shane paced the small distance of the barn length with his hands on his hips. "Damn it, Dorie. Don't think I want this. I don't want to marry Marilee. I never did." He turned to her then, his green eyes cast in shade and shadows looking dark as midnight. "I want *you*. I want you so bad I can't sleep at night. I can't eat a meal or take a drink without it burning in my gut."

Dorie's heart fluttered at his pronouncement. His words warmed her enough to thaw out the bitter cold consuming her. "Shane, there has to be a way."

His face flamed with anger for a moment. She saw his frustration and pain and knew it matched her own. "Tell me, Dorie? I'm listening."

"We could run off?"

Even she didn't believe that would work, but she was desperate to find a way out of this situation.

"We can't and you know it. And what's worse is that I'll be married to someone else and worrying over you, all the time."

Dorie stood strong now, her self-respect taking a direct blow. She didn't want Shane's friendship any longer…or his protection. She wanted his love. She wanted to live her life with him by her side. If she couldn't have that, then she wouldn't have him living down the road from her, married to another woman, worrying about her. She folded her arms around her middle and lifted her chin. "You won't have to worry about me. If you marry Marilee, I'll leave town."

Shane's frustrated expression changed to bafflement. "What do you mean? You can't leave town. Where will you go?"

"New York."

Shane narrowed his eyes. "New York?"

She nodded and picked her pride up from the gutter. "The Parkers offered Jeremiah and me their home. They want us both, Shane. And they'd even set me up with my own dress shop. So you see, you won't have one care about me, not one."

"That's where you're wrong. I'll always care for you. But it's a good offer, Dorie. I'll understand if you take them up on it."

"You want me to go?" She couldn't help raising her voice.

Shane ran his hand down his face before gazing into her eyes. He stepped close to her, near enough for her to see the flecks of gold sparking from his green eyes. Taking her hands in his once again, he spoke gently, "Dorie, you know what I truly want. It's not to be. But moving to New York would be good for you and Jeremiah. You'd want for nothing and—"

"Nothing, but you," she interrupted.

He continued on a sigh. "And you'd have a dress shop all your own. You could do what you love to do."

"It's always been my dream, Shane."

"Then do it, Dorie."

To love someone means to want what's best for them. She recalled Mrs. Whitaker's words. But she'd never told Dorie that doing what's best could break your heart.

Finally, she'd come to understand that there was no hope left for her and Shane. She'd had faith enough to spare, but it had all withered away the moment Shane stepped onto her land a minute ago with news of Marilee's return.

Her mind made up, she nodded. "Guess I have no choice, either. I can't stay here, knowing you're...living with another woman. I can't, Shane."

Shane stared at her then in stony silence. He put his head down and spoke with regret. "I can't imagine my life without you, sweetheart."

Dorie couldn't either. She'd expected life would have offered her better than this. In her heart she knew she'd never love another man again. She also knew that she couldn't fathom seeing Shane and his new wife on the streets of Silver Hills with a new baby in tow. She couldn't fathom seeing him smile at her or hold the child that should have been theirs. She couldn't fathom aching for another woman's husband every night in bed.

It had suddenly become clear in her mind that she had to leave the only home she had ever known. She'd regret never seeing her new garden bloom or the house painted up pretty again, but Dorie couldn't stew on that any longer.

With sadness, she offered Shane a smile.

They stared at each other for a long moment.

And when Shane took her into his arms, she entered his embrace freely, knowing this was the last time she would ever feel his warmth. She let it seep into her, absorbing all the comfort she could.

He tipped her chin and kissed her soundly, a final

farewell that lingered for more moments than was wise, Shane clinging to her this time, refusing to break the bond.

And when he did finally, his eyes softened to hers in a way they never had before. "Have a good life, Dorie."

She swallowed, watching him turn from her and walk away.

When he was halfway through the yard, she called out, "I love you, Shane Graham!"

Shane stopped. He put his head down. She witnessed his chest heave. He didn't look back but continued to walk away and out of her life.

She whispered quietly into the noontime air, "And I always will."

Dorie spent the next few hours lying on her bed, sobbing. The thought of losing Shane forever was almost too much for her to bear. She loved him so. Tomorrow, he would marry another.

The past two weeks had led her down a path that she couldn't have ever imagined. She'd kidnapped Shane, taken him hostage, implored him for help and then she'd fallen deeply in love.

Her life hadn't been her own for so long. After losing her mother, she'd had the responsibility of raising Jeremiah. She'd struggled. They both had to keep what was theirs. She'd tried to make sense of what the Almighty had planned for them. She'd told herself that life would somehow get easier. She'd prayed for the day when she'd have some stability in her life.

Now, she had that. The Parkers had offered her a way out of the hard life she'd known. Little did she know that the very prayer that had been sent up every night for the past three years would solve her problems, yet make her the most miserable.

Dorie felt that she had no other choice. She'd been dreadfully honest when she told Shane she couldn't live in this town knowing he was married to Marilee. Imagining him bedding her at night, putting his hands on her, making love to her, would surely destroy her. Dorie couldn't stay in Silver Hills once Shane had married. The Parkers' offer had come at the most opportune time. She would take them up on it.

Dorie rose from her bed. She poured water into a bowl and splashed her face with the cool liquid. Taking deep breaths she steadied her nerves. She needed to speak with her brother, to make him understand. When she heard the door slam and footsteps entering the house, she knew now was the time. "Jeremiah," she called from her bedroom door. "Come in here."

Within moments, Jeremiah popped his head inside her door. He took one look at her face and immediately asked, "What's wrong?"

Dorie mustered a small smile. Her younger brother had become a blessing in her life. She noted the telltale signs of stubble developing on his otherwise baby face and realized that one day soon he'd be all grown up. "Come and sit down. I have something to tell you."

Twenty minutes later, after explaining to Jeremiah what she felt in her heart and all the reasons the move to New York would be good for them, Dorie took his hands in hers. He'd met her with resistance at first, not understanding why they had to leave, but in the end he'd finally agreed reluctantly. "I don't want to go," he said.

"I know. I don't want to either. But we must, and I

bet once we're there we might be glad of it. Trust me, Jeremiah. We'll always be together. That won't change."

He slumped his shoulders and nodded. "If you think it's best."

"I do. It's the only way for us now."

"Okay," he said quietly.

Dorie's heart broke again seeing the trepidation and confusion on his face. She rose and helped him up, hugging him to her chest. "It'll work out, Jeremiah," she reassured bravely keeping doubt from her own voice. "Go into town and fetch your grandparents. Invite them to supper. They'll be glad to see you, I'm sure. We'll tell them together tonight."

Once Jeremiah took off for town, Dorie set about making the meal for the Parkers. Though her heart wasn't in it, she fussed in her kitchen, dusted the furniture and straightened out the house the best she could. Wishing she had flowers to set on her table, her thoughts turned to the garden she would never see flourish. She held back tears, refusing to cry anymore. She'd shed enough tears to fill a wishing well.

Dorie washed up then donned the blue cotton dress Shane had given her. Wearing it made her feel feminine and brought back tender memories that she kept close to her heart. She fastened the necklace the Parkers had given her around her throat and its new mate dangled prettily from her wrist. Next, she pinned up her hair partway, keeping it out of her eyes and allowing her curls to fall to her shoulders.

When Jeremiah returned riding in the Parkers' rented buggy, she was ready. Standing outside the front door, she welcomed them graciously with the full realization that her life was about to change drastically in the next few hours.

"Hello," Helene said, coming up the steps. She always wore the finest clothes, tonight a beautiful sunny yellow taffeta gown and a matching hat that relayed her position of great wealth, yet her smile was genuine and her face was lit with joy. Dorie had liked her from the moment they'd met, though she'd feared what both Helene and Oliver represented—a means to take Jeremiah away from her. But now, Dorie looked upon both of them differently. If truth be told, they had become surprisingly like surrogate parents to her.

"It's good of you to come," Dorie said graciously.

"Why wouldn't we come?" Oliver boomed in that big voice of his. "We'd love any chance to see both of you again." When he winked her way, Dorie's nerves settled down.

"Come in," she offered, "please. Supper is heating on the cookstove."

They both entered while Jeremiah saw to the buggy and horse. "Please have a seat." Dorie wished her sofa was in better repair, but it couldn't be helped. She wasn't ashamed of their home but she wondered what the Parkers' had thought about the meager surroundings.

Helene and Oliver took a seat on the sofa.

Dorie asked, "Would you care for something to drink?"

"Not unless you've got a cold beer in there," Oliver said with a grin.

Helene jabbed his arm. "Honestly, Oliver. Must you always tease?"

Dorie chuckled, releasing the tension she felt moments ago. The two seemed hopelessly devoted to each other, even through their silly bantering. "Sorry, I have no beer. But I have iced tea and lemonade."

"No, dear. We're just fine. Mmmm," Helene said lifting her nose slightly. "Something smells very good."

"It's nothing fancy. Beef stew, vegetables and biscuits."

"Oh, how lovely. Is there anything I can do to help?"

"No, not at all. I thought while supper is cooking we could take time to talk." Dorie swallowed the lump in her throat. "Jeremiah and I have come to a decision about your kind offer. We, uh, would very much like—"

Loud knocking on the front door startled her from her next thoughts. Had Jeremiah been locked out? She didn't think so. She hadn't put the latch on the door that she could recall. "Excuse me. I can't imagine who that would be," she said, rising and walking to the door.

When she opened the door, the last person on earth she thought she'd ever see on her doorstep stood ramrod still, beseeching her with marked desperation in her eyes. "Hello, Dorie."

"Marilee?"

"I'm sorry to disturb you, I must speak with you. May I come in?" She darted her gaze behind her to the path, the gate and the road beyond that. "Father doesn't know I'm out. I have to get back home quickly."

Dorie had never liked Marilee with her prim and proper, I'm-better-than-you ways, but she realized that most of her disdain had stemmed from Shane's involvement with her. In truth, she didn't know Marilee all too well. The woman standing before her now didn't appear prim and proper at all. No, she looked frightened, determined and distressed. Seemed the roles had reversed.

Dorie stood there appearing the prim one now. "Come inside," she offered, stepping out of the way to allow Marilee entrance.

Relief registered quickly on her face the moment Marilee stepped inside. "I don't have much time."

"What's wrong?" Dorie didn't have an ounce of pity for the woman about to marry Shane Graham. What she wouldn't do to be in her shoes. "Why are you here?"

Dorie realized that the Parkers were privy to the conversation but she didn't feel it appropriate to make introductions. Marilee hadn't much noticed them anyway. "I couldn't marry Shane tomorrow without speaking with you first."

Anger bubbled up. Had Marilee come for her approval? Well, she wouldn't get it, or her blessing. "I know about the wedding. Shane rode over this morning to tell me." She let go a labored sigh. "You're getting a good man, Marilee."

"I know, but that's just the point." Marilee looked Dorie directly in the eyes. "There's no way to ask this politely. Do you love Shane?"

"With my whole heart," she answered without hesitation. "Not that it's any of your business."

"It is my business. And yours, too, if you'll hear me out."

Dorie didn't want to see Marilee gloat over her admission of love for the man she would marry. Marilee and her devious father had won the battle. Dorie had lost Shane. There weren't enough words in the world to make things right now. Dorie opened the front door for Marilee as cool evening air wafted inside. "I think I've heard enough. What more is there possibly to say?"

But Marilee persisted refusing to use the door Dorie had opened to see her out. "So much more, if you truly love Shane."

Shane stood in a small room behind the altar, adjusting his string tie and waiting for the ceremony to begin. Only a few weeks had passed since he'd done this very same thing, yet so much had changed in his life since then. He'd fallen in love with a young impetuous woman who had proven to be more than a match for him. He'd always admired Dorie's courage and gumption, but now that he truly knew her spirit, he believed no other woman would ever compare to her.

No one was more surprised than Shane that his feelings ran so deep. He hated hurting her and couldn't imagine any joy in his life without her.

He stood in that room like a man going to his own execution. When Tobias Barkley walked in dressed in a three-piece suit in true father-of-the-bride fashion, Shane's day went from bad to worse. "What the hell?"

"You're in the Lord's house, boy. Be careful what you say."

"You're a fine one to speak about the Lord, Barkley. Last time I noted, the Lord didn't hold much for blackmail."

"Not blackmail, just incentive. As soon as you are properly married to my daughter, those notes I'm holding on your ranch will be burned. And as a wedding present to you and Marilee, I'll be adding to your herd with one thousand head. A man's got to be able to feed his wife and child properly."

"I can provide for my...family." Shane had trouble

getting the words out. Lately, he'd come to think of Dorie and Jeremiah as his family.

"I insist. The heir to my fortune won't want for anything. I'm just making sure of that in advance."

"Forgive me if I don't thank you."

"Now, now." Barkley slapped him on the back. "I hope we can put all this unpleasantness behind us, Shane. Soon, you'll be married into the family, raising my grandchild."

Barkley poked his head out the door and nodded. "Yep, soon. The church pews are all but filled. Won't be long now. I'll leave you. Oh, and I made sure there won't be a repeat of what happened last time. I have men watching out for that McCabe woman. She won't get within fifty feet of the church."

"I don't think you need to worry about Dorie anymore," Shane said, "but isn't it funny how one little woman's got you putting up guards around the church?"

Barkley grunted and didn't respond. When the organ music began, he said, "I'd better get to my place in church. Marilee is being stubborn. I won't be walking her down the aisle this time, but I'll be in the front row."

Shane watched him leave then drew a big breath. This was his cue to walk to the altar and wait for his bride. With forced steps he made his way inside the church and stood on one side of the altar. All eyes seemed to focus on him.

He took a deep breath.

When the music stopped, heads turned toward the back of the church. Marilee stood there wearing veiled white, holding a bouquet of yellow roses.

The organist began playing again.

Marilee took a step toward him.

Shane looked at her, without really seeing. He wanted to be anywhere but here.

She took another step then another moving slowly, as if she too were walking toward her own execution.

Shane's gut clenched.

Marilee continued on, only steps away from the altar.

Shane silently prayed for strength.

Marilee finally made her way to stand beside him.

Shane knew that this time no one would dare stop the wedding.

Marilee turned toward him, her full lacy wedding gown rustling softly in the stonily silent church.

"Shall we begin?" Reverend O'Malley asked.

Slowly, Shane nodded.

Marilee lifted her veil.

And smiled.

Shane's heart thumped hard in his chest. He looked straight into the beautiful blue eyes of Dorie McCabe.

"Are you okay with this?" she whispered urgently.

Shane didn't know how she managed it, but he'd never been happier in his life. "More than okay. I've dreamed of this."

"Oh, Shane. So have I, but this isn't a dream."

By then the entire congregation had caught on. Their shocked mumblings were immediately outdone by Tobias Barkley's boisterous outrage. "Wait a minute! What have you done with my daughter! Where is Marilee?"

Dorie spoke softly to Shane, unmindful of Barkley's rantings. "She's with her beau. They are probably married by now. She needed this time to get away."

"Married? Where?" Barkley's face nearly exploded with fury. "This is unacceptable. Graham, we had a deal!"

Shane ignored him and stared into Dorie's eyes. "The deal's off."

"I'll ruin you! You won't have a dime to your name when I get through with you! You *owe* me!"

"No, he doesn't, Barkley," a voice boomed with clarity. "He doesn't owe you a dime."

Shane and Dorie turned to see Oliver Parker standing in the back of the church. He looked at Shane squarely. "My wife and I are paying off his debts as a wedding present. And we've bought the Whitaker place. Seems they'd like to spend some time with their grandkids back east. Jeremiah will be your partner, Shane, if you desire. He'll help you run both ranches as one. You won't need Barkley's grazing land or anything else he's held over your head."

Barkley's eyes bugged out then he narrowed them on Oliver Parker. "Who are you?"

"I'm Dorie's kin and there'll be no more threats to her or Shane from now on. Kindly leave the church. The preacher has a wedding to perform."

Barkley darted his gaze around the church. He opened his mouth to speak then clamped it shut. He'd been defeated and he knew it. Everyone watched as he strode out of the church with purposeful steps.

Once he was gone, Shane turned back to his love. "Dorie McCabe, let's make it real this time. I love you deeply and I'm asking you before God and all these fine people, to be my wife."

Dorie beamed him a beautiful smile. "Yes, Shane. I'll be your wife."

Shane smiled also then kissed his bride-to-be. Reverend O'Malley cleared his throat and Shane apologized. "Sorry, but it's an engagement kiss."

"Shall we proceed with the wedding?" the minister asked.

Shane and Dorie turned to the Parkers. They were seated with Jeremiah in the back of the church, smiling.

Dorie and Shane smiled back. Then they turned to the Reverend, and Shane said, "Please, go on. I've been waiting all my life for this woman." He turned to Dorie. "And I don't want to wait another second."

Holding Dorie's hand in his they spoke vows from the heart ensuring that she'd never need a temporary husband again.

Dorie stood beside Shane at the front desk of the Silver Rose Hotel as he registered for their room. "Mr. and Mrs. Shane Graham."

"It's nice to have you and the Mrs. back, Mr. Graham," the desk clerk said.

"It's nice to be back," Shane replied.

"Will you be needing anything?"

Shane shook his head then peered into Dorie's eyes. "No, I have everything I need now."

Dorie's heart rippled with joy. They walked up the stairs together with smiles on their faces and once they reached the door to their room, Shane lifted her up into his arms. He carried her over the threshold and set her down gently, placing a kiss on her lips. "It's for real now, sweetheart."

"I'm truly your wife," she said breathlessly.

"Finally." Shane took her into his arms.

"Marilee came up with the perfect plan. I slept inside the church last night and when she arrived two hours before the wedding, we switched clothes in the bride's room. It was all terribly easy."

"My thanks go to Marilee." Shane removed his hat.

"And what about Helene and Oliver coming to our aid just when we needed it. I surely misjudged them."

"Uh-huh." He loosened his string tie.

"Did you see how happy Jeremiah was? I've never seen him grin so much in his life."

"Yep." Shane unfastened his belt.

"And what of the Whitakers? I'd never have guessed they'd want to sell their ranch. I suppose Alberta wanted to spend her days with her children. But Iggy? I wonder if he'll be happy—"

"Dorie?"

"What?"

"Get naked."

"Oh!" Dorie gasped at her husband's blunt command. Then she giggled and turned around, her gown swishing between them. "Undress me, Shane."

"Gladly."

An hour later, Dorie stood above the man she loved with her whole heart, admiring his form, the sated peaceful look on his face as he lay across the bed. She'd never tire of looking at him, of appreciating his strength and dignity.

He opened his eyes and stretched lazily. "I'm a lucky man."

Dorie bit her lip. She still had doubts, not of his love, but at the way they'd entered into this marriage. "Are you sure about that?"

"Absolutely."

"Because, well, most men don't get, uh…"

Puzzled, he lifted his head and looked up. "What, honey? What don't most men get?"

Dorie hesitated a moment wondering if she should speak her mind. After all, Shane had married her. He'd spoken vows and made incredible love to her just minutes ago, yet she still needed a measure of reassurance. "They don't get *shanghaied*, Shane. Not just once, but twice."

Shane sighed then with undeniable pleasure. "I know, sweetheart. As I said, I'm a lucky man. Now, come over here. There's something else we have to do twice and it has nothing to do with the butt end of your gun, and everything to do with making me dizzy."

Dorie smiled and lowered herself down on the bed.

She had an understanding husband after all.

She'd shanghaied her groom.

And he'd stolen her heart.

* * * * *

*Set in darkness beyond the ordinary world.
Passionate tales of life and death.
With characters' lives ruled by laws the everyday
world can't begin to imagine.*

*Introducing NOCTURNE, a spine-tingling new line
from Silhouette Books.*

*The thrills and chills begin with UNFORGIVEN by
Lindsay McKenna*

Plucked from the depths of hell, former military sharp-shooter Reno Manchahi was hired by the government to kill a thief, but he had a mission of his own. Descended from a family of shape-shifters, Reno vowed to get the revenge he'd thirsted for all these years. But his mission went awry when his target turned out to be a powerful seductress, Magdalena Calen Hernandez, who risked everything to battle a potent evil. Suddenly, Reno had to transform himself into a true hero and fight the enemy that threatened them all. He had to become a Warrior for the Light....

*Turn the page for a sneak preview of UNFORGIVEN
by Lindsay McKenna.
On sale September 26,
wherever books are sold.*

Chapter 1

One shot...one kill.

The sixteen-pound sledgehammer came down with such fierce power that the granite boulder shattered instantly. A spray of glittering mica exploded into the air and sparkled momentarily around the man who wielded the tool as if it were a weapon. Sweat ran in rivulets down Reno Manchahi's drawn, intense face. Naked from the waist up, the hot July sun beating down on his back, he hefted the sledgehammer skyward once more. Muscles in his thick forearms leaped and biceps bulged. Even his breath was focused on the boulder. In his mind's eye, he pictured Army General Robert Hampton's fleshy, arrogant fifty-year-old features on the rock's surface. Air exploded from between his lips as he brought the avenging hammer down. The boulder pulverized beneath his funneled hatred.

One shot...one kill...

Nostrils flaring, he inhaled the dank, humid heat and drew it deep into his massive lungs. Revenge allowed Reno to endure his imprisonment at a U.S. Navy brig near San Diego, California. Drops of sweat were flung in all directions as the crack of his sledgehammer

claimed a third stone victim. Mouth taut, Reno moved
to the next boulder.

The other prisoners in the stone yard gave him a
wide berth. They always did. They instinctively felt his
simmering hatred, the palpable revenge in his cinna-
mon-colored eyes, was more than skin-deep.

And they whispered he was different.

Reno enjoyed being a loner for good reason. He came
from a medicine family of shape-shifters. But even this
secret power had not protected him—or his family. His
wife, Ilona, and his three-year-old daughter, Sarah, were
dead. Murdered by Army General Hampton in their
former home on USMC base in Camp Pendleton, California. Bitterness thrummed through Reno as he
savagely pushed the toe of his scarred leather boot
against several smaller pieces of gray granite that were
in his way.

The sun beat down upon Manchahi's naked shoulders, grown dark red over time, shouting his half-
Apache heritage. With his straight black hair grazing his
thick shoulders, copper skin and broad face with high
cheekbones, everyone knew he was Indian. When he'd
first arrived at the brig, some of the prisoners taunted
him and called him Geronimo. Something strange
happened to Reno during his fight with the name-call-
ing prisoners. Leaning down after he'd won the scuffle,
he'd snarled into each of their bloodied faces that if
they were going to call him anything, they would call
him *gan,* which was the Apache word for *devil*.

His attackers had been shocked by the wounds on
their faces, the deep claw marks. Reno recalled doubling
his fist as they'd attacked him en masse. In that split

second, he'd gone into an altered state of consciousness. In times of danger, he transformed into a jaguar. A deep, growling sound had emitted from his throat as he defended himself in the three-against-one fracas. It all happened so fast that he thought he had imagined it. He'd seen his hands morph into a forearm and paw, claws extended. The slashes left on the three men's faces after the fight told him he'd begun to shape-shift. A fist made bruises and swelling; not four perfect, deep claw marks. Stunned and anxious, he hid the knowledge of what else he was from these prisoners. Reno's only defense was to make all the prisoners so damned scared of him and remain a loner.

Alone. Yeah, he was alone, all right. The steel hammer swept downward with hellish ferocity. As the granite groaned in protest, Reno shut his eyes for just a moment. Sweat dripped off his nose and square chin.

Straightening, he wiped his furrowed, wet brow and looked into the pale blue sky. What got his attention was the startling cry of a red-tailed hawk as it flew over the brig yard. Squinting, he watched the bird. Reno could make out the rust-colored tail on the hawk. As a kid growing up on the Apache reservation in Arizona, Reno knew that all animals that appeared before him were messengers.

Brother, what message do you bring me? Reno knew one had to ask in order to receive. Allowing the sledge-hammer to drop to his side, he concentrated on the hawk who wheeled in tightening circles above him.

Freedom! the hawk cried in return.

Reno shook his head, his black hair moving against his broad, thickset shoulders. *Freedom? No way, Brother.*

No way. Figuring that he was making up the hawk's shrill message, Reno turned away. Back to his rocks. Back to picturing Hampton's smug face.

Freedom!

* * * * *

Look for UNFORGIVEN by Lindsay McKenna,
the spine-tingling launch title from
Silhouette Nocturne™

Available September 26,
wherever books are sold.

Silhouette
Desire

**Introducing an exciting appearance
by legendary**
New York Times **bestselling author**

DIANA PALMER
HEARTBREAKER

He's the ultimate bachelor...
but he may have just met
the one woman to change his ways!

Join the drama in the story of a confirmed
bachelor, an amnesiac beauty and their
unexpected passionate romance.

"Diana Palmer is a mesmerizing storyteller
who captures the essence of what
a romance should be."—*Affaire de Coeur*

Heartbreaker *is available from Silhouette Desire*
in September 2006.

nocturne™

Save $1·⁰⁰ off

your purchase of any
Silhouette® Nocturne™ novel.

Receive $1.00 off

any Silhouette® Nocturne™ novel.

Available wherever books are sold, including most bookstores, supermarkets, drugstores and discount stores.

Coupon expires December 1, 2006. Redeemable at participating retail outlets in the U.S. only. Limit one coupon per customer.

5 65373 00076 2   (8100)0 11265

SNCOUPUS

nocturne™

Save $1·⁰⁰ off

your purchase of any
Silhouette® Nocturne™ novel.

Receive $1.00 off
any Silhouette® Nocturne™ novel.

**Available wherever books are sold, including most
bookstores, supermarkets, drugstores and discount stores.**

Coupon expires December 1, 2006. Redeemable at participating
retail outlets in Canada only. Limit one coupon per customer.

52607136

SNCOUPCDN

Introducing...

nocturne

a spine-tingling new line from Silhouette Books.

These paranormal romances will seduce you with dark, passionate tales that stretch the boundaries of conflict, desire, and life and death, weaving a tapestry of sensual thrills and chills!

Don't miss the first book...

UNFORGIVEN

by *USA TODAY* bestselling author

LINDSAY McKENNA

Launching October 2006, wherever books are sold.